Lunatic
Villas

Marian Engel

Lunatic Villas

McCLELLAND AND STEWART

The Canadian Publishers
McClelland and Stewart Limited
25 Hollinger Road, Toronto M4B 3G2

CANADIAN CATALOGUING IN PUBLICATION DATA

Engel, Marian, 1933-
  Lunatic villas

ISBN 0-7710-3077-0

I. Title.

PS8559.N44L86   C813'.54   C81-094088-4
PR9199.3.E5L86

This is a work of fiction. Any resemblance to
persons living or dead is purely coincidental.

Printed in the United States of America

For my mother, Mary Passmore,
who once put four sticks in the
flower bed and said, "Give them
all names and you'll have someone
to play with."

Prologue

In 1967, to celebrate Canada's hundredth birthday and to give the woman something to do, a broker named Morgan Wickwire bought his wife a street in Toronto.

In terms of the streets other people were buying, it was not a very large one. In terms of the neighbourhoods others were choosing, he did not choose well. His "charming cul-de-sac," as it was subsequently called in real-estate advertisements, consisted of a dozen houses facing each other in two rows like broken teeth, bounded on the south by a hydro substation, on the west by a mattress factory, and on the north by a neighbourhood where no one has spoken English since 1926. Still, Morgan and Wilma Wickwire thought, for a while, that they had a bargain, as indeed they would have had the wind of development blown west instead of east; and Rathbone Place did, in the end, achieve some of Morgan's aims: it kept Wilma busy, provided Morgan with a larger tax loss than he had dreamed of, and survived to be christened Ratsbane Place by Mick and Melanie Ross, thus escaping mediocrity forever.

Two of the owners refused to sell, but permission was obtained from one, the lady who ran the Finnish rooming house, to sandblast her house and remove her front porch. The other, the owner of the hardware store on the corner, was adamant about remaining faithful to dirty brick, but since he had his shop attached to his house so that it faced politely to the east, it was easy to detach him from the development. Three of the houses, already condemned, seemed beyond repair. Two—one on each side of the street—were removed to give owners access to the hovels' back yards by means of a narrow right-of-way that condemned them eternally to Volkswagens. This left Wilma Wickwire six houses and a wreck to play with, and soon enough she was supervising crews of groggy-eyed dew-worm pickers as they heaved rotten window frames and rusted sash weights into bulk loaders. She had decorated many houses in the past, but never had the satisfaction of starting quite so close to the beginning. It was like unravelling knitting. She began with buoyancy and quickly learned the vocabulary of Rathbone Place.

Like much of the "near west" of the city, as she liked to call it, the street had been thrown up in a hurry during some kind of real-estate boom that preceded the First World War. The wiring dated from 1913; so did the plumbing, except for the extra toilets and kitchen sinks that had been installed in every available room in the immigrant fifties. None of the owners, who had, after all, been overtaken by war, Depression, and more war when their houses still smelt of new pine, had seen fit to make any changes other than converting their furnaces from coal to gas. There were fading Sicilian marriage wreaths over some of the doors, and mezuzah marks in archways; alas, the pine had never been good, and the fireplaces were of a period ten years ahead of Wilma Wickwire's time: the art-deco revival was too late to help her.

But, as everyone said, you could say a lot about Wilma—she landscaped Number 8 before she brought the bulk loader in to sit on the new turf—but you couldn't say she wasn't a worker. Although she did not fail to notice that the mattress factory was attractive to rats, she did succeed in getting ivy started up its ugly walls. She bossed and stripped and shivered and plunged; by Christmas she had worked so hard and learned so much about heating, plumbing and electricians that she collapsed in her ski lodge at Collingwood and raved for some time about party walls and by-law restrictions. It was a month before she was on her feet again, shivering in the house she kept for an office, staring at blueprints and samples of wallpaper. Her designer was complaining about the houses.

"They're just not interesting," he said.

"Don't give up on me, Hal."

"If you'd bought in the east end you'd have got some space. How do you expect me to work with fourteen feet wide by sixty feet long and no stained glass?"

"Stain some, darling. Everything is possible. You were the first one to say it."

"The soil is all coal dust; you'll have to do stone sets instead of grass."

Wilma, who had been idly calculating the cost of four new furnaces and four rewirings if they all cost as much as Number 6's, merely muttered, "Brilliant, darling," and went back to her scribbling. She wasn't paying Hal: Hal was paying off innumerable cocktail parties.

Wilma looked back at the figures and knew that, however well brokers are paid, the only thing to do now was cheat. She spent the next two weeks at bankruptcy warehouses and insurance brokers' outlets. She went to wholesale houses and bought enough velvet and braid to please Scarlett O'Hara. She reminded her brother-in-law that he owed her some money and could pay it off in plumbing. She ordered appliances on her Eaton's credit card, dug from her basement chiffoniers, escritoires, washstands, dry sinks, breakfronts and kitchen tables, chipped speckled pottery, fern stands, wicker chairs, violin cases, butler's tables, brass hooks, half-broken Tiffany shades, stone crocks, pots, and innumerable porcelain doorknobs – the kinds of things she found irresistible at country auctions. She looked over the collection and knew at last what her husband really thought of her.

But she was made of strong stuff: she did not give up. Her

9

children complained that she smelled of turpentine and her husband complained of the food: she was flushed with the effort of turning defeat into victory. With the aid of Hal's plans, striped wallpaper, and all the gilt rope she could lay her hands on, Number 11 became a Regency bijou. Number 8, which had been lived in, unpainted and unannealed, by the same old woman between 1913 and 1966, when she died there, was dusted, sanded, vacuumed (and there is an enormous feeling of satisfaction, Wilma found, in running an industrial vacuum over a coal bin), and lit so brilliantly that the workmen could not complain about their fear of rats. While they were knocking holes in walls for wiring, she was painting with buttermilk paint and applying a homemade stencil to the kitchen. While they groaned and wrenched at drains, she ran wild over wicker with aerosol cans of white paint and sewed cushions. Number 8 got mottled brown doorknobs, except on the insides of closets. Hal, meanwhile, supervised the conversion of the remaining condemned house into a dream of skylights, catwalks and cathedral ceilings, reducing a six-room house to the size of a very smart bachelor apartment. It needed no doorknobs at all; it had very little in the way of doors.

At the end of March, just before her note with the trust company regarding the purchase of the houses fell due, she called a friend, victim or heroine also of a thousand cocktail parties, editor of a women's magazine, and asked her around for a drink. Without covering up her mistakes (she had papered one room before the electricians worked on it; she had begun to remove all the verandahs before she realized that Number 4's was attached to Number 6's), she stuck to her principal guns and played—not even faintheartedly, but knowing that although she would never make a profit she must keep Morgan Wickwire at all costs—the role of victorious woman.

"I don't know how the hell you're going to sell them, Willy. The back bedrooms are just too small."

"Nurseries, darling," not confessing that the heat hardly reached the back at all.

"Have you put them on the market?"

"There's an ad going in on the weekend."

The editor frowned. "I never do a straight promo, you know."

Wilma made a moue to indicate that she thought such things were shocking.

"But I'm kind of interested in all this activity. Let's see through your Old Ontario house again. You've done a fair job on that. The one with the cathedral ceiling's too small, you'll never get rid of it. I wish you could have laid hands on some bigger ones, like the ones Doug Swan's been working on on St. Nicholas Street. Still, that's out of your class. These were tacky little houses to begin with, weren't they? But there's the hardware store, and the Italian place up there doesn't look bad for bread and veg: you might do it. What are you asking?"

"Thirty," Wilma said firmly.

"If I was a real bitch I'd ask for a cost-accounting on that. Still, you tore down two, didn't you? At twenty-two you might do something."

They went over Old Ontario again. The editor shuddered at the long, narrow bathroom, which wasn't quite modernized by a long sink full of ferns.

"Saunas are going well these days, but I suppose these places would fall apart in the steam. Tell you what: I've got a staff member who's come into some money and is looking for a place. She's been living in some god-awful studio on Spadina, a place so arty the Children's Aid nearly took the kids away. I don't know how she's going to squeeze four kids into those three rooms but I'll send her around. She knows a lot of people, too: might come up with someone else. Give her a break, though, eh? I don't pay her that much. She's called Harriet Ross, and I'll tell you her story some time."

Which is how Harriet Ross, and Sim, Melanie, Ainslie and

Tom's Mick came to christen the Wickwires' expensive toy Ratsbane Place. It didn't come to be Lunatic Villas, however, until it had met Vinnie and Winnie and Sylvia and Roger, Michael Littlemore and the twins, Madge and Adge, Elaine and Pen, and Marshallene, Bob the Painter and his friend Fred, the people from Saskatchewan and oh ... all the others.

It took some time for the street to reach this height; first Sylvia had to buy Number 7 in order to install her wheelchair ramp and her aviary; and meet and marry Vinnie at the Bird Fanciers' Association; and even before that, the trust company fell into receivership so that two houses were sold for the price of one to Harriet, who, to avoid the embarrassment of having two front doors, made a two-storey flat out of Number 8, which she rented then and still does, to cover taxes and utilities, to her friend Marshallene. And Adge had to buy 9 and die, but not until her great orange tomcat, Rudolph, had ravaged the aviary; then, before Tom's Mick was even big enough to break a window, Harriet made the mistake of marrying Michael Littlemore and the twins appeared; Adge was mourned but Roger bought her house, adding another realist to the block. What the people from Saskatchewan had besides mystery was eventually tragedy, but who could then have known? The gaps remained, the hardware store remained, but the Finnish boarding house ended with the harsh life of its owner and was remodelled and sold and resold and resold. Bob the Painter bought the corner store when the Italian grocer retired, and kept the Salada tea letters but silvered the inside of the window, so he could paint unobserved, which was spiteful but not quite, because he was Bob Robbins whom they loved. Hal did what he could with the house beside Harriet, but that was resold and resold as well. The new people all seemed to want larger cars and a neighbourhood that summered up north instead of noisily under its grape arbours. And the neighbourhood lacked, in addition to a library, it is true, a non-ethnic

12

butcher, silence and a mailbox. Some of these difficulties Roger assuaged by getting them all involved in city politics. A city magazine wrote the place up as "trendy"; Roger said it could hardly be trendy when the twins went to the bathroom on his lawn. Harriet fired her housekeeper and spent the money she saved on a psychiatrist and a downstairs john. The people from Saskatchewan remained silent and Bob Robbins scratched a very small hole in the silvering on his window so Mick could stand and watch him paint.

By 1979 the houses had settled as far as they were going to for a while, and the owners had settled down. Harriet's tribe was no longer a band of fiendish infants, Vinnie and Sylvia had given up sleeping together and were concentrating on breeding chattering lories and macaws, and Roger had given up a number of committees, though not the effort to procure a library, and become curiously domestic. Marshallene gave up her second marriage and returned permanently to the street with a case of Scotch, and two quiet young couples who were devoted to their children and needed Harriet's to baby-sit them had moved into the ever-changing houses. The place no longer looked new and trendy. It looked comfortable, and more or less was: in short, it was ready for Mrs. Saxe.

CHAPTER ONE

Harriet loves winter nights: the quiet of them. The street wrapped in snow, muffled; the way the white world never darkens under the lamp posts. On nights like this, she is particularly conscious that last winter she committed a *folie de grandeur* and bought and had installed on the front half of the house a complete Victorian gingerbread portico as Gothic as the gatehouse of the Necropolis Cemetery, as inappropriate and unreal as the fates we are handed out, and that the snow is looping it now with white lace, and it looks lovely. She knows this because every winter evening she puts on her galoshes and goes out to see. It reminds her satisfyingly of a story she was told as a child of a wicked family who were always in debt and inherited money: then they bought a grand piano. I wear my grand piano on my house, she thinks and laughs and cocks a snook at fate.

It's late, the house is quiet, the snow is so white it looks as if it ought to make slicing noises in the air but it falls mysteriously, quietly. Harriet, who has been comparing her cheque book with her bank statement and has found herself miraculously, once again, solvent, shoves the papers ahead of her on the desk, forgetting for once the article on abortion, the article on welfare wives, and the treatise on the children of divorce. The cat walks by like a grey cloud. She is suddenly happy as she puts her head down to doze.

ITEM CHARGED

ron: Kathleen Dawn Kenyon

e Date: 04/01/2006 09:00 PM

e: Lunatic villas / Marian Engel. --
hor: Engel, Marian, 1933-1985.
l Number: PS 8559 .N4 L86
meration:
onology:
y: 1
Barcode:

0 1 0 9 8 9 0 8

Upstairs, Simeon works in his aerie at the back under the halo of a student lamp. He is nineteen now, well-muscled, blonde, and ambitious. He has been strong-minded enough to resist the fashion for studying one's roots: he knows he has none; he knows he has only his mind to go on, and the fact that Tom once loved him and Harriet loved Tom.

He is doing his mathematics, clicking softly on a small calculator. It is sticky from the fingers of his roommate, restless little Peter P., who, even in his sleep, is running a Dinky toy rhythmically up and down the wall. Sim gets up and takes it away from him, covers him, smooths his forehead. Harriet isn't good enough to Peter P., he thinks, because he's so much like his father. He eases himself back into his calculus and scratches his head. If he wants to go on with this he's got to get a scholarship.

It is Harriet's vanity to supply the girls with little white batiste nightgowns. Melanie's is rucked up around her rump. She pulls it down angrily and goes back to her dream, which is not a good one. Sidonia, in the twin bed beside her, is laid out like the Lady of Shalott, counting money in her sleep. Under the carpet she has stashed half a dozen long-playing records shoplifted from the A&A, not yet added to her police record. Sim would notice it if she played them; Melanie would tell Harriet if she even saw the cellophane wrappers. Mick wouldn't.

Patsy grunts and digs her fat butt into the thin mattress she got because she was the last one to stop wetting her bed. No one can tell if Patsy thinks or dreams: she is like a root, she just is.

Mick's room is empty, black in the dark night. He has deserted it for an even blacker corner beside the furnace room, the part of the cellar they are always going to refinish and never do. It is his black year.

Ainslie has been away now for months, in California where the climate is good for her. She is the good-tempered one and the house dreams of her.

In Harriet's room, the bed is not made. None, in fact, of the beds is very often made. "If you won't do yours I won't do mine" has been a running argument for so long that they have all taken to comforters. Let them get thrown out of the army, Harriet thinks.

But she is downstairs now, and she shivers. The chill part of the night is setting in; it is good and late, and she wonders if she should warm herself up with a quiet pedal on her exercise bicycle. She despises gadgets but, having inherited the figure of her Scottish ancestors, short women who appeared to have been hit by pile drivers, she bought the bicycle to combat together a disappearing waist and the chill. One of the children removed the device that shows how far and how fast she can go, which is half the fun. It's not the night for exercise. Perhaps a hot bath and an early turn-in, anything to escape "Welfare Women: How the Other Quarter Lives" and trying to depict Linda L., who said, "I've had my nerves out, that's what it is, it's so bad around here what with the Pakis and those things they write in the elevator, I went in the hospital and he took my nerves out." How, Harriet wishes to cease wondering, do you transpose that for a magazine that promotes women's intelligence? Or pretends to.

She has no illusions any more about either *Maga* or *Household Words*, for which she writes a column signed "Depressed Housewife." For twenty years she has written about welfare and aprons, abortion and fitted sheets, hyperactivity and hyperacidity. But sometimes she wonders what to do with things like cockroaches and Linda L., the unmentionables of society, a sordidness less sanctionable than sex: the fact that dirty things have not gone away you cannot deal with in a glossy magazine. It has been put to her by Roger that perhaps it is immoral to earn a living in a world so unrealistic. She was angry at the time, but now she smiles; for she snarled at Roger with violence and told him to find her a world where you could support six kids and where there was no unreality; and he took it, on the whole, well, agreeing that

16

even professors and politicians have their unmentionables and that one has to do the best one can.

She looks across at Roger's house: the lights are out. Either he's taken to going to bed earlier than usual or he's out. He's been quiet lately, she thinks, something on his mind, something he won't talk about. Maybe he needs his nerves taken out.

The house ticks around her. Upstairs, she hears Sim shove his chair back and pad to the bathroom. Good idea, she thinks, Bedfordshire for me, too. Silly English expression I picked up from Adge. She begins to fold up the financial work and put the fragments of the welfare article in one place. Thank God the money is holding out, she thinks; if I can't finish it it won't be a disaster. Though she always does finish things.

The doorbell rings.

It shocks, astounds her. A moment ago she looked over to Roger's at a dead, white world and empty street. That something should have crept up and made a noise at her door . . . who? What? Roger locked out of his own house? Unthinkable. Vinnie? Marsh? She can hear Marshallene snoring through the party wall.

She gets up slowly and lumbers to the door, half unwilling, half curious. *Rat-tat-tat* with the knocker, now: someone impatient? Or just willing to try all the systems?

Even Harriet, who is not a tall woman, has to look down. It is a little old woman and the little old woman has dragged up on the Gothic porch a big black bicycle. She has a face like a boil and looks up pleadingly at Harriet.

"Oh, do please pardon me for coming so late at night, dear Mrs. Ross. I'm Mrs. Adeline Saxe."

Harriet opens the door farther in astonishment. Mrs. Adeline Saxe ducks under her armpit and begins to wheel the bicycle in.

"Oh," she says, and her voice is thick and deep and English, much younger than she is, "not a night for man or

17

beast. I set out quite early in the day. I was staying with my friend Mrs. Gartle in Bond Head. The traffic here is so difficult. Your name was given me by my cousin's niece, Fenella Fitzherbert-Clarke-Stephenson."

Dumbfounded, Harriet reaches for Mrs. Saxe's coat, an ancient black broadcloth; she receives also her hat, a declining woollen toque. In order to struggle out of her coat, Mrs. Saxe props the bicycle (an old black Raleigh: heaven for Mick, Harriet thinks) against the white hall wall. She hands Harriet the coat without ceremony and bends over to unstrap an assortment of saddlebags. Harriet turns obediently to hang up the coat and is suddenly in England listening to Fenella over the whine of a gaunt, white machine into which she is stuffing quantities of ox liver for her husband's hounds: "Well, I started off with two names," she is saying, "Saxe-Stewart, I was, before I took up with Peter. And I always think one ought to progress, don't you? Fitzherbert-Clarke-Stephenson's quite the monicker." Blood oozes as she turns the crank with both arms. "Damn, blast, oh, do lend a hand, will you? I've got to get this done before lunch and there are fourteen of us today. It's not me, it's Peter, he's related to half the Almanach de Gotha and he will ask them for the shoot."

Saxe-Stewart. Mrs. Saxe. Mrs. Adeline Saxe. I am a colonial paying for my shooting weekend. At midnight, she wheels her bicycle in: the mother country's revenge.

"You must be exhausted, Mrs. Saxe; come into the kitchen and I'll make you a cup of hot tea." I'll put her in Ainslie's room. "All the way from Bond Head? Where is that?"

"Highway 27 south of Cookstown."

"My God, and in this weather! Why on earth didn't you take the bus?"

"There is none."

"Are you hungry? Would you like something to eat?" Turning curiously and staring at the old woman, whose face is round and wreathed with decay: all that remains of her features is a small, aristocratic beak of a nose. "Shepherd's pie all right? Or there's some soup. I haven't seen Fen for years; I hope she's well."

"Well enough," Mrs. Saxe gargles from behind her tea. Then she shoves her cup forward. "More?"

"Oh, sure. Well, I must say, you're a surprise." What do you say to people who arrive from the moon? What are the conventions? "I'm afraid I don't have much time to act as a sight-seeing guide, but you're welcome to stay."

"Fenella is now a travel agent."

"That must be nice for you."

"Quite. More?" She shoves her plate forward. Her little fat hands hold the edges. Something there about paws, Harriet thinks, and what about towels, are the blue ones clean? Can't give her the thin yellow. . . .

"Oooorgh," Mrs. Saxe burps. "Delicious, thank you."

"It's late. Let me take you to your room."

Together they scoop up the bags from the bicycle, together they trudge up the stairs.

"This is my daughter Ainslie's room. She's in California with her grandfather at the moment."

Mrs. Saxe stands in the doorway, holding her reticule in her paws. She clucks, nods wisely, then moves to the centre and sits on the bed.

"I am most grateful, Mrs. Ross."

"The bathroom's down the hall, the one with the light on," says Harriet, crouching to sprint there first and pick up the towels and underpants from the floor. "Sleep well, Mrs. Saxe."

Sleep well, Mrs. Saxe! The words echo in her mind when she is in her own bed, huddled dead centre against the world. Mrs. Saxe indeed – me with an English houseguest. What do you do with English houseguests? Old ladies? Bicycles? Mumbled, warmed-over gossip: how Fenella's husband had met his end in a sports car with a girl who no longer looked

19

like Twiggy in the front seat, taking a wrong turn and barrelling into the castle wall: his brother inherited and Fen was a travel agent, not a duchess: an improvement. How Fen had located Harriet's address with difficulty, not now being able to remember whether her name was Somerville or Ross; how things were very different in England now, but how the war had taught us all to be amenable to change, hadn't it, and how good the tea is. . . .

But what will I do with her? Harriet thinks in an excitement that is too weary to be despair. She's a nice enough old thing but her generation stays for ages. What on earth can I do? If she pulls out that old British line that all Canadians are *wet* I'll run after her with an axe: I don't have any self-control any more, I don't want to look after people, I just want to stay in bed . . . a fat little pigeon of a woman, a walking pudding, by the Quangle-Wangle out of the Pobble Who Has No Toes. Little black pointed shoes slit for bunions: moleskin spats: heavens! Horehound eyes, yes, that's good, horehound eyes . . . the alarm? Set. I wish. . . .

Sleep takes over.

Mornings are precious new beginnings, every day a chance to exorcise yesterday's and before yesterday's sins: mostly. Harriet begins her day very carefully, without shaking it hard enough to break the thin film of semi-consciousness that keeps her close to her dreams. She scoots downstairs as soon as the alarm goes off, puts the kettle on, collects the paper: and this year, the first in fourteen, takes the coffee and the paper upstairs again with her, the better to protect herself from reality. They are really better off without her in the morning, the mob, and as long as there are milk and sugar and bowls and spoons and four kinds of cereal on the table they consider themselves looked after. Then, in bed, pretending to read the paper that is in fact reading her, she counts flushes, scrapes, shouts, clouts, hears Sim's gruff,

"Get on with it, you guys," before his great thumping exit and slam; Melanie's "Pervert" to Mick's "Slut" and the resulting clashing of spoons; piggish little snorts from the twins; Sidonia, late and serene, descending the stairs like a queen, "Good morning," which makes the others snigger. "Ma, where's my . . . ?" can be dealt with more easily from upstairs.

But this morning she remembers she has a guest and her heart fails her; she has to clutch the day around her with her housecoat, knowing that the white winter light, which was romantic in the evening, will show every broken piece of quarter-round, every chip, every broken bulb and badly painted drawer. Mrs. Saxe, a lady from England, children. Shall I make her bacon and eggs? Do we have any? No, bad precedent: she might stay forever, and the eggs all went in the lunches.

By the time the coffee is made she is in the middle of the mob wondering how she ever stood it before, the sound of their spoons is so loud, and suddenly Mrs. Saxe is down, too, joining their circle, unceremoniously pulling the kitchen stool to the end of the table and holding her hand out for a bowl.

"This is Mrs. Saxe, who's staying with us for a while," Harriet says, looking at their hopeless scruffiness; Melanie is the only one who has washed and she's all spotty, and Mick when he emerges from the cellar is filthy as Od in the Eddas, who lived in a heap of bones. "Mick, wash!"

"Gerah." His current language.

"Before you go. Really." To Mrs. Saxe, for no reason, "Mick's fifteen."

"Michael?" Mrs. Saxe asks.

"Mickle," he says. "For Mickle Cheese. My grandfather."

"Mickle," says Sidonia, who never looks as if she needs to wash but sometimes does, "would you be a darling and hand me the brown sugar?"

"Lay off, Sid," says Sim. "Gotta go, now. Bye all."

"What schools do you go to?" Mrs. Saxe mouths.

21

A concentration of the names of old heroes and city fathers ensues: Brant, Jarvis, Bloor, Aeneas Shaw. Mick tries and fails to tell about Central Tech. The fridge door takes a battering, lunches coming in and out.

"Mine. No, mine."

Goodbyes.

The Littlemore twins still spooning.

"Sidonia, it's Tuesday, go and see your social worker."

"Certainly, Aunt Harriet."

"Pat, Peter, the dentist, four-thirty, sharp, change at Bathurst."

"Jesus Christ, it's gym day."

"I'm baby-sitting."

After half an hour, Harriet has given in to the flow; she's actually sorry to hear the door slam the sixth time, although they'd look nicer, she thinks, if we had a maid and a nanny and they all did the English cold-bath routine in the morning.

"I don't make a hot breakfast," she says. "I'm only good at porridge with lumps."

"Bran flakes," Mrs. Saxe says. "Do you mind if I try?"

"No, of course not." Harriet begins to unload last night's dishes. Then she scrapes this morning's. The leftover milk adds up, but it isn't good for the cat. She dumps the assortment of soggy grains out of the sink strainer and begins to fold up packages. "There, they're gone. The day begins."

Mrs. Saxe looks at her like an expectant six-year-old.

"Usually," Harriet falters, "I start work right away. But I'm stuck. I write articles, and lately they haven't been turning out very well. I seem to have written them all eight or ten times before. So I guess I could take some time off. More coffee? Here. Well, I'll show you around the house and tell you who lives where on the street. That's funny, this morning nobody spilt the milk. Anyhow, if you know where you are you'll feel better. Aren't you tired after yesterday, coming all the way from Bond Head? Here's my office, it used to be the dining room. I sit in here like a spider in the middle of my

22

web. I know I've got too many typewriters, but they're always breaking down or I get fond of them. . . . I'm not really an exercise fanatic but the bicycle . . . my hands get so cold when I sit all day. . . ."

Mrs. Saxe moves coyly into the room, looks at the bookcases, sniffs. "Very nice, oh, very nice. Clever of you, earning their living by writing, not everyone could. What a lot of books. As my papa would say, you're a regular bluestocking. You have lovely children."

"They're not all mine."

"Eh?"

"Oh, I seem to acquire them, the way some people pick up furniture. Do you have children, Mrs. Saxe?"

Mrs. Saxe is ogling the exercise bicycle. Tenderly and affectionately she stretches a hand to the saddle. She looks up at Harriet, blinks, sucks her teeth. "Children? Oh, long ago, long ago . . . innumerable. The late Mr. Saxe . . . may I?" She puts one little foot tentatively on a pedal and hop, hop, swings the other limb (for it must be a limb, unless she is made of jointed and slotted wood like a Dutch doll) over, without so much as a flash of petticoat. "Oh, children, lovely. Gone now: grown. On the land, off the land: Australia, India, Cyprus, Egypt, Jo'burg. . . . Good thing, the Empire."

Harriet looks at her narrowly, and the old question flashes back that used to disturb her when she was the age of Melanie: why are one's elders betters?

"Come to the window," she says, "I'll tell you whom you can call on for a cup of tea. That house, directly across, belongs to my friend Roger, who used to live with the most beautiful English girl. He's out all the time: he teaches, and then there's his committee life. No social life there. To his left are Vinnie and Sylvia. You'd like Sylvia: she has an aviary. She's very blonde, and snappish because she was crippled in an accident about ten years ago – she was a figure skater. She makes costumes for other figure skaters for a living, so the house is up to its ears in braid and floss where it isn't feathered. You have to watch Sylvia when the spring comes and she starts using her mechanical wheelchair again: it's jet-propelled and she doesn't make way for anyone. Vinnie's a pet.

"Right next door to me here is Marshallene, an old friend of mine. You'll get on with her. On the other side, past the archway, there's a new young couple: not yet tried. They look all right. I don't know much about the two on the other side of them, either, but they are called Pen and Elaine; farther down, in the old store, is Bob Robbins, the painter: one doesn't call on him, ever. He doesn't like people, except for his friend Fred. Across from him is the hardware store. I don't go there because whenever I ask for anything Mr. Jatzmann argues with me, but he's good to everyone else. And then there's his house, you see, and the one we call Saskatchewan House: there was a terrible accident there once. I'll tell you about it some time. There are a new lot of new poor there, too, and I don't know them. Time was I knew everyone, but I seem now to be part of the Old Wave. Actually the Sask. House people are interior decorators and I like the look of them but time will tell."

Mrs. Saxe nods as if she has taken at least some of this in and trots happily back to the exercise bicycle. This time she hops on with an expression of joy and begins, very slowly, to try the pedals. Harriet looks at her gloomily: a houseguest this easily made happy may stay for a year.

"Haven't you any children in Canada?" she asks.

"A niece," says Mrs. Saxe, "who is supposed to live in this very city. But all efforts have failed. All."

"What does she do?"

"I believe she plays the violin."

"We could try the Conservatory of Music."

"That has been done; alas, there is no trace."

"We'll find her somehow." Harriet wonders about looking in the subway for her.

"Never mind, Mrs. Ross. Never mind. Tell me how you

acquired your lovely children. I'd be ever so much interested. First, where were you born?"

"Oh, here."

"Your parents?"

"Oh, my father was the owner of a cheese factory—you heard Mick mention it; my mother, I don't know. She died when I was very young. I think her relatives looked down on us because Father was in trade or something. They belonged to the old world of ladies and gentlemen, which is odd when you think of it, because, you know, well, Adam delved and Eve span."

"I do indeed. Although I must say, Mr. Saxe . . . "

"Yes?"

" . . . did not delve. He belonged to another time."

"I don't know how they put their time in."

Mrs. Saxe's eyes glazed. "Ho," she says, "it wasn't difficult. Continue."

"Oh, well, anyway, I grew up in quite a good neighbourhood, went to school and so on, but I thought my father was immensely old and I didn't get on with him and my sisters had married and gone away, so the first chance I got, I turned my summer job into a permanent one and moved away from home. I was a typist in a company that ran a lot of magazines; I've been in the magazine business ever since.

"Looking back, I don't know what I did with those years, but I remember that eventually I started taking night classes and then I took a couple of years off and finished at university; then my father and I made up and he sent me to England where I met your cousin and Fenella. But what else? Oh, I remember, and I don't like to, either: I did that awful thing girls with strong fathers do to themselves: I wasted about three years being mad smashed in love with a man who wouldn't leave his wife. And then I met Tom.

"I was working at *Maga* then, one of the assistant editors. They used to say they sent the nut cases to me, the people who wandered in and wanted to be written up. One day, long before it was fashionable to be a single parent, Tom wandered in with Sim in one hand and Melanie under his arm and Ainslie sort of staggering along behind and that was that: he plunked Melanie down, changed her on my desk, we decided to go out for coffee and then decided my place would be better and somehow we were together after that.

"Looking back, I can't even remember clearly what he looked like, but he was a lovely man, an American draft-dodger, tall and skinny and sweet, and somehow he'd acquired these three kids – he said the girls were his but Sim definitely wasn't – and they were living hand to mouth. I had a horrid moment when I wondered why he wanted me; I was so convenient, and then it struck me it probably wasn't bad to be convenient because I'd been alone for so long I could hardly even talk to anyone. It was the children who did it.

"He was the first house-husband anyone I knew had: I went to work in the morning, came home to them at night, and paid the bills. Soon after I got married I was pregnant with Mick, but I still went on working. We had a lovely time, lovely. It's all like a dream. He didn't dress the children well, he couldn't, so we looked like a rag-bag, but we had a marvellous time. I used to slam the lid on the typewriter and rush home at top speed for my macaroni and cheese.

"He was marvellous with the kids. When you were with Tom you had to be good-tempered. He took them seriously, you see, though I must say that's never worked with me, and he practically ran a little nursery school, though Sim went to a day-nursery later because he needed kids his own age. Anyway I, who had been conventionally brought up – my nanny stayed on and became my father's housekeeper – simply loved it. We lived in ropy old places and wore ropy old clothes except for my two outfits for work – and we loved each other: it was very good.

"And then he died.

"It was a hot Saturday in August, just after Mick was born. Oh, I feel like the Ancient Mariner telling it, there was a time

I had to tell it, I had to get it out of my system, though I feel now that as a story it has lost its shine, I've violated it by telling it too often, you know how you feel but . . . he died. That was it. Just . . . died. And I suppose it's still a story now, but I remember it mostly as little vignettes, bits out of a film: Melanie stubby and stubborn, fat as a baby bee: she turned to the crowd again and again, doing her set piece: 'Daddy fa' down,' she kept saying, 'Daddy fa' down,' as if it had been 'ring-a-rosy,' and she kept on for weeks, and every time, I cried: Mrs. Ross's automatic waterworks.''

And she remembers how at the morgue she said solemnly, ''Yes, it's his head,'' and fell into hysterics because the way the sheet or blanket or whatever the dark thing was that came up to his neck was arranged, all you could see was a head as disembodied as a picture on *Time* magazine's cover. The policemen, gentle, embarrassed, tried to explain that, um, they bruised him badly trying to revive him; though later Harriet found out that whoever was doing autopsies that mild and sunny day had started early, keen to know how, in a parade that was more of a shuffle, a man of only thirty-one, with one babe on his shoulder and a six-year-old wandering at his side, could have collapsed, died, at thirty-one in a trudge of draft-dodgers and flower children, not keeping step or exhausting himself, but casually, chewing gum, laughing with his friends and showing things to Sim, how he suddenly fell down and died.

And they explained to her gently, too, that she was not his next of kin, even though she was his wife. And she explained back that somewhere in Oregon, once, his mother had died; his father had remarried and died; his stepmother had remarried and died: there was no one. No one had treated him badly, but no one had stayed, only Harriet.

Because, she tells Mrs. Saxe, he was the kindest man I ever met.

''I didn't bother with his friends much,'' she says. ''They had a kind of network, like the Underground Railroad; you

27

had to take what came. I was a year older than Tom and I'd come home and the place would be full of people. I didn't mind, but I didn't have much energy for them, either. Some were just plain no good. And the others all said I didn't care enough about Vietnam, which was true. Vietnam seemed to me so crazy. After I left school I went back at night and got enough credits for university, then I took two years of French history, for some reason I was mad about French history, I read everything I could lay my hands on, took all the night courses. I knew Vietnam had been part of Indochina and that war broke out the year I was born; the French couldn't handle it and the Americans ... it made me mad that the Americans thought they could. I wanted them to stew in their own juice, those people thinking history is bunk and therefore condemned to relive it. I thought I had enough to worry about. Before I knew we were making napalm for them in Sarnia."

So, she goes on, she was living pretty much for Tom and the children, not seeing her own old friends, who were dispersed then also, most of them married, and Tom's death was not only the usual sort of shock: it left her in a vacuum. One young couple helped her with the funeral. They lent her money at the office for the funeral and gave her three months' leave to make arrangements for the children. And afterwards, when she didn't know what to do with the awful urn they sent home from the crematorium, the same two, Dennis and Sheila they were called, went with her to Centre Island, the urn in a knapsack they took turns carrying, heavy as lead; and they rented a rowboat and scattered the ashes in one of the lagoons and put the empty urn under a willow on one of the little islands, having of course scratched the label off, because she knew if Tom was on the mantelpiece she and the children would never get over it.

They have never got over missing him and they never will, she says. He was kind, he was good. But she has stopped thinking it is wrong to remember. She is glad, now, that the person they remember is kind and good, and did not live to be middle-aged and bitter.

The worst part was afterwards, she remembers, and *that* has not had its details effaced by time. There was no estate to worry about, and at first everything seemed straightforward and easy. At the inquest the coroner stated Tom's heart was, always had been, a mess. It was amazing that he had lived to thirty-one. Harriet testified that he had tired easily but avoided doctors. Perhaps he knew, perhaps he didn't. The magistrate had no comments, even on hippie parades. She reported his death to the Family Allowance people and the cheques began to come to her. She gave no thought to the provenance of Sim and the girls. The kids were Tom's and now he was dead so they were hers; she would love them and keep them, though she did not have Tom's skill, Tom's kindness for them. Besides, she was too busy with Mick, who was her own, but a dark-hearted squawly baby.

But in the background of her life someone was thinking otherwise. A week after Sim, in gray November, brought mumps home from the day-nursery, where he still went because he had no birth certificate and could not go to school – no, it couldn't have been a week, more like two weeks, because now they all had them, even Harriet – "and mumps is a disease of the connections between the ears and the nervous system, Mrs. Saxe, I was going crazy" – even the baby, who was very ill indeed, so ill the doctor broke his rule about visiting contagious diseases and drained poor Mick's ears – the Children's Aid sent a social worker to visit them.

"We were living in the studio then," Harriet says. "An artist's studio on Spadina Avenue. It was huge and, sure, unsuitable in a way – no yard, not enough wiring for a washer and dryer, a filthy little kitchen with a stove that didn't work much – but the rent was a song and the studio room was great for kids to play in; they ran their trikes all over it, had a wonderful time, and all Tom's friends were near and he shopped in the Kensington Market and Chinatown so our food was

29

always very good and very cheap. But the place oozed dirt. I think originally it had been a furrier's sweatshop, and that part of town was dirty and industrial anyway, so no matter how hard you worked – and I didn't – the windows were loose and the dirt flew in. The floor below us was a nightclub: the stairwell was foul. It didn't look like a suitable place for kids at all.

"One day we are all in various stages of mumps and I haven't dressed for days and the food is so low that I've had to send Sim out for four orders of scrambled eggs to go at a restaurant and I am trying to figure out whom to call for help, wondering if I've been nice enough to Tom's friends to ask them for something, and if I had any left of my own – which was ridiculous, I had lots, but I didn't feel that way, you know how they avoid you after a death, not knowing what to say – there is a tiny, nervous knock on the door I don't hear at first, and then I do and open the door and there is this young, smooth, neat girl from the Children's Aid with a form to fill out, saying that someone has said I wasn't managing too well.

"Well, we looked like hell. I was trying to train Melanie but she was afraid of the toilet – and the bathroom there was something to be afraid of, it was sordid no matter how I tried to cheer it up – and Ainslie had big, dark circles and was kind of yellow, the way they get after the mumps, and Sim was filthy as usual and Mick was howling. It was time to give him his medicine and he fought it and I had to whack him and hold him down: the doctor had said to. 'Excuse me,' I said, 'his ears hurt and he's fighting mad, but I have to do this.' She says as she karate-chops her kid. And I guess, out of sheer despair, the sloppiness of despair, I hadn't hung anything up for months. I mean, Tom did all that.

"And she's a social worker. From the Children's Aid. It's her first job. A nifty kid from Etobicoke or Don Mills, who's never seen any dirt before. I still remember her name: Susan Forbush. *Miss* Susan Forbush. I was going to make her a cup of tea but the teas we had were all suspect, Tom and his friends' funny, high-making things. At least the marijuana plants were drooping. So I made her some instant coffee. There wasn't any milk. She asked if we got milk delivered. Delivered! Left out on Spadina Avenue in the morning! Now I ask you. It would have been swiped in a minute.

"I, like a goose, had a beer. I had four bottles saved up, it was the only drink that didn't hurt my ears. Melanie, sensing tension, brought her pot close to us and sat on it and turned very red. Sim and Ainslie sat on the floor and rolled their eyes at her like idiots, and Mick just howled and howled. Finally, I asked her if she could go out and get us some milk and eggs.

"'Haven't you anyone to help you?' she asked. 'Haven't you a sister?'

"It was then that the penny began to drop. Babs and Harry were in Florida, I knew—you could ask my sister Babs for anything in those days, and she'd either give or not give, but she was straight—but there was my sister Madge sitting up in the empty mansion in Forest Hill, with all those dogs and a staff, brooding. 'Sister?' I said.

"'We understood,' she said, mincingly: if you can say something mincingly that girl did, 'that you have a sister.'

"'Oh,' I said, 'Madge. She came, she saw, she didn't like. She went away. I haven't seen her since.'

"'Perhaps she could help you now.'

"'Madge is saving her money to leave to the Home for the Purebred Canines of Distressed Gentlewomen.'

"While she was out getting bread, eggs, butter and milk and when I had finished deciding I would have to leave Sim in charge and go to the bank tomorrow even if he was only six and very busy taking Melanie's tricycle apart while she threw the bolts at him, I put the potty away, changed Mick and had a thought about Madge. She didn't come to Tom's funeral, but hardly anyone did, and funerals weren't Madge's style. Going to things wasn't Madge's style. Since the acci-

31

dent when her husband Stanley and the boys died, Madge had hardly been out of her house. But she did come one hot September afternoon, when the studio was oozing filth and I had taken the kids up to the little enclosure on the roof Tom had built, and filled the plastic tub with water, so they could laugh and sing and play their filthy summer game of picking roof stones out of the sticky tar and flinging them into the water and at each other. Madge had come, Madge in white sharkskin, dyed, marcelled, two-dimensional as an old hat-store window model; she had taken the one chair and had the children lovingly, one by one, press their tarry faces on her white sharkskin suit.

"The girl came back. I thanked her for her shopping. Accepted the change and forebore to look in the bag. Not the kind of girl who adds a packet of fags for Mum and some stickie bickies, but a useful sort of girl, one to be thanked, farewell.

"I was not surprised when the notice came that the Children's Aid wanted to see me. But the words 'custody hearing' drove me to rage, fury, and tears of fear.

"I never thought of it," she says. "They were his. They must, therefore, be mine. He brought Sim east because nobody wanted him; Melanie is his. Ainslie was his first wife's daughter, as far as I know. They were his assets, and I was his widow."

And she tells again how she met Tom, how Tom came to her office at the magazine, to ask if he can write an article about them, about how it's perfectly possible ... and he tosses Melanie, the baby, on her desk and changes her in a wink; and Ainslie clings to his trousers and stares soulfully at Harriet; and Sim sucks his thumb and fingers surreptitiously with the other hand at the typewriter: and Harriet is sold.

"They do not, of course, adore me as they adored him. But I have never been one of the admired, and don't expect to be, but I'm one of the competent. Tom and I were a fine combination.

"Mumpily, I stared at the Children's Aid letter. I wondered how many articles I'd written about the Children's Aid, about social workers, about social problems. I had always written about how well our social services worked, how good things were: but all I could see in this was sheer meanness. That day I wasn't Harriet Ross of *Maga*, I was just Mrs. Thing, and the Children's Aid wanted my kids. 'With reference to Ainslie and Melanie Ross and Simeon Semchuk' – well, three-quarters of my kids. Mick was wailing again. Damn you black, Mick, I thought, and started something bad.

"One of the police detectives had been through Tom's papers with me, looking for evidence of relatives. And a man from the US consulate had come, too. But all the papers Tom had were folded in tiny squares in his address book: a couple of draft notices with California addresses, and Ainslie's and Melanie's birth certificates. And all I really knew was that Sim's mother was a friend of Tom's Emily and left him with them in Berkeley and never came back; so when they went up the coast to British Columbia, where Emily had Ainslie by somebody else, and Tom had Melanie, too, by somebody else just to even things up, they took Sim, too. That's literally all I knew.

"I laid my mumps on the caved-in sofa once they were all in their Salvation Army beds and Mick in the cradle Tom made, the beautiful cradle that's down in his hidey-hole in the basement now. Then I got out the bottle of wine someone left me and I'd been saving, and then the Scotch someone left for Tom's wake that never happened, and I read the letter again and again and the problems grew.

"'Children don't belong to anybody, you have to earn them,' Tom used to say.

"It was obvious from the letter that the State did not agree. The State wanted the children. The State wanted children the way Babs used to want children, to make the State or Babs look good. That's it, I know it, they want *my* children. They

33

want me not to be anyone's mother because I wasn't anyone's daughter, that's it. No, I was Father's daughter. Mother died, or was put away. So I, because for some reason I caused her to be done away with, am to be de. . . .

"God, they're all howling again, would it matter?

"Yes, damn it. Yes, it matters.

"I'm not much good but, by God, I'm here. I stayed . . . I cared.

"The letter squashed me. The alcohol inflated and then deflated me. I saw the State standing over me in my father's Sunday suit, in high boots with a whip or a whiplash collar. I hate, I decided, the State. The people who ruined education. The people who helped Madge and my father to put my mother away. If they did. The people who wouldn't tell me if they did. The people who spied on Tom's parades.

"Tom was a landed immigrant. His papers were in order. Melanie and Ainslie were born in Canada. It was Simeon, Sim, dear Sim, who had no papers. Kitchener, on the recruiting poster, was pointing at Sim; his face faded and I saw Hitler again, and boots, high boots; whips, stern women, Senator McCarthy. The State wants Sim, I thought. No. I will stand and be martyred. I will hold him against my bosom as we stand against a wall. They–and the State was now embodied in my sister Madge–can shoot us both, all: he won't go to that . . . concentration camp. I won't. . . .

"I was ready to burn the place down to save them when mumps and mercy took over and I fell asleep.

"In the morning, I was bitter and ashamed. The State did not, I knew in the clear light of day, particularly want little kids. The State merely wanted their existence properly written down. So they could collect pensions without a lot of trouble. Once I got them all potted and wiped and sent to the day care, and Mick was fed and medicined, I phoned a lawyer who specialized in family law. I had once written an article about him, too.

"He had had a great deal of experience with this kind of

case. He calmed me and controlled me. After he phoned my doctor to ease his male queasiness about the mumps, he appeared and went through Tom's pitiful stack of papers. He shook his head once or twice, spoke soothingly.

"At the Children's Aid hearing, the social worker testified that she had found the house sordid and the children ill-cared-for. There was dust on the window sills, smeared faeces on the walls. Gently, the lawyer probed her experience of the world. She had not, she stated, ever had the mumps. Nor had she had children. Nor had she lived closer to the city centre than darkest Etobicoke. Yes, she had a degree in social work, a Master's, which was six months old.

"Her supervisor agreed that she was inexperienced; nevertheless. . . .

"I had put on my best navy-blue dress. Sim, like a shining, blonde angel, sat humbly but beautifully costumed beside me. The others I left with a baby-sitter the lawyer found, a fierce, clean woman who couldn't read. Yes, I testified, I was, indeed, at the time they had the mumps after Tom died, disorganized. The judge was surprised when I announced that Tom was the one who looked after the children while I worked. Yes, periods of adjustment are necessary, I agreed, but difficult to undergo when everyone has the mumps.

"A letter from the doctor was read: Harriet and Tom have been excellent parents, however peculiar their lifestyle was.

"In the end, my lawyer proved that the State had no need of my children. That the State had been acting on reports the origin of which it would not reveal. However, in the interests of fairness, my lawyer thought it right to produce an additional witness, Mrs. Marjorie Greenpool, sister of Harriet Mickle Ross.

"The lawyer was masterly and Marjorie Greenpool tried to be. Yes, she said, she was the sister of . . . the accused. Yes, she lived on Old Forest Hill Road. Yes, the house did have fifteen rooms. But there were the dogs. And the staff. Yes, she was executrix of the estate of Matthew Mordecai Mickle, deceased. Yes, he had been deceased for some time. Yes, she believed a bequest was to be set aside for Harriet, but not until. . . .

"The Children's Aid Society left the hearing feeling rather definitely used. I left with an uncomfortable feeling that class had been used, and that Tom would disapprove. Sim left wanting to go to the bathroom. Madge was furious. The judge felt that he was bringing a family together again, and was pleased with himself for suggesting that Madge take temporary responsibility for us.

"It was awful at Madge's place," Harriet says, "but those two Jamaican women were good. They had Melanie trained in a wink, and they got Ainslie to eat. Sim had a fit when he had to go to a private school and wear a uniform, but it was beautiful to see him shining and in order. Sue just carried Mick everywhere in her arms–she had a kind of sling she made out of a big kerchief–and he quieted down like anything. I went out every day and got my life together. Madge, too.

"I was commissioned by the judge to look into the children's relationship with officialdom. It took some time. At first, the assistant deputy registrar for the province of Ontario was not amused; in the end, as the situation revealed itself as more and more baroque, she turned out to be a friend. 'I can't get over it,' she would say, 'I can't get over it.'" Her name was Adge Henderson.

Tom was not Sim's father, or Ainslie's. He was only perhaps Melanie's.

"It looks as if he just scooped up the kids nobody was doing anything with," Adge said.

"You can't put him down for that," Harriet had replied.

"I'm not, child. I'm looking for their papers. Look, the trouble with communes is, a girl goes to a government office with a baby and says, here is my baby, I want the baby bonus. In a commune situation, sometimes it's three or four girls, the same baby. B.C. is going crazy with them."

36

"Tom was before communes."

"Before communes, but not before communal living. You'd be surprised, I –"

"Look, Melanie's the spit and image –"

"I know, I know . . . " Adge Henderson had placated. "Roots, Mrs. Saxe. People are looking for their roots.

Looking not for roots but registration, looking, above all, for order and propriety, Adge Henderson slowly and with not much help but hand-wringing from me found that Simeon was born in New Mexico and Ainslie in New York. Simeon's mother was a classmate of Tom's at UCLA who had run away with a visiting philosophy professor from Missoula, Montana, already possessed of a wife and six children. He did not know what to do with her or with Sim, or with the six children. He committed suicide. She drifted back to California and said, 'Tom, you look like a good guy, take care of the kid.' Later she died on a drug trip, combination of something very sinister and speed.

"Ainslie's mother, Emily, was from New York. She was delicate, asthmatic and Jewish. When she was eighteen she met a boy from California and went with him to the land of sun and honey. *Her* parents followed, protested, petitioned. Her boy friend caved in, but Emily fled north with Tom to British Columbia, where, just before he came east, she died. There were half a dozen in that group, friends and lovers. They baby-sat for each other when they returned to the States to apply to be landed immigrants, but Tom was the only one who cared about the kids.

"He was enamoured of parenthood as no woman he met would ever be; Melanie's mum was a weaving-girl with a braid. When she got pregnant, she wanted an abortion, but agreed to bear the baby if Tom would take it away.

" 'Well,' said Adge, 'you've got 'em. Do you want 'em?' Adge was tall, thin, English, straight. Her ancestors ran India. She came over to Madge's and looked approvingly at Madge's carpets. Madge's Beetrice had brought in the scrubbed and Doctor Dentoned children to be kissed.

"I tried to be honest. 'I'm not sure I want them. I mean, I don't want the work of them. I can't do the work for them, properly, to Madge's and Beetrice's and your and the Children's Aid standard, and earn their living, too. But I love them. And I'll never leave them.'

"Adge leaned her neck back. Adge had been around a long time. 'You need money, honey.'

"'Even if I had money, I'd never be as good as Tom. I'm a working woman, Adge, like you. Domesticity isn't my thing. Mick's straightened out so much with Sue it's beautiful.' I looked at Madge, but Madge only glared. When she cleared her throat, the spaniels at her feet sat rampant, staring at me as if I were an edible threat.

"'What's my legal position, do you know?'

"'Mick's yours, of course; you can adopt Melanie and Simeon. Ainslie's in a different position.'

"'Have you been in touch with her grandparents?'

"'Your lawyer has: you're fortunate in him. You have good contacts, Harriet: don't knock that. It's what keeps most of us from going down the drain. Theoretically, we're all equal, and therefore all vulnerable, but it's the people who know good lawyers – and good assistant deputy registrars – who survive. Ainslie is very, very well connected.'

"'It's funny to think she's Jewish.'

"'Tom was, too, originally. There's a link there, probably. No, Ainslie's grandparents are all very, very powerful people. Two in New York and two in California. They're willing to let you bring her up as long as you give her the best of everything.'

"I looked at Madge again. Madge was turning into a statue. A painted statue. An awful, haggard, store-window model: the hag we fear. Her eyes glittered.

"'I can't give her the best of everything, Adge. I don't even believe people should have the best of everything. I couldn't live forever in this house. Quality stinks.'

" 'Did you get that from Tom?'

"Oh, be damned for a nickel, be damned for a dollar, I thought, I can't talk to Madge, I'll talk in front of her. 'The quality in this house is Beetrice and Sue. I can't afford Beetrice and Sue. If those kids spend much more time in this house they'll be corrupted ... they get a kind of love, a kind of order, from Beetrice and Sue, that I can't give. And Beetrice and Sue can't give it forever. They're nice to the kids and they know about kids from where they come from. But they'd rather have their own. Beetrice and Sue are only on lendsies, Adge.'

" 'So what will you do with Ainslie?'

" 'She's the one I could give up, isn't that awful? She's sweet, but she's also self-effacing. Sim's the oldest. Melanie's Melanie. Ainslie almost doesn't have a place. But I love her.'

" 'Come to the office on Monday, dear, and I'll tell you.'

"Adge left and Madge stayed in her chair like a statue.

"Monday morning early the lawyer, Pip, phoned to say that, even earlier, he had received a phone call saying that my father's estate was settled: I was to have my legacy with nine years' compound interest. I couldn't believe it when I heard the amount, I thought I was in clover. My lawyer told me to get a house: I got in here at the right time, and got two.

"I used to say the Lord was taking care of me but it wasn't the Lord, of course, it was me, and Pip the lawyer and Adge and Madge and the judge and the Children's Aid combined, though I've never forgotten that pallid little social worker who'd never seen downtown dirt before. At any rate, help just appeared: somebody sent a housekeeper for a month. Beetrice boldly ordered Madge's chauffeur to come down for Mick every afternoon: he'd get his free ride and be spoiled from one to six. It was what he needed then, and what he needs again, in a different way. Two years ago, he started believing he was a bicycle, and he's been difficult ever since. It's all that trouble he has with his palate.

"And finally papers came through so poor Sim could go to

what he called real school, not the private one.

"Ainslie's grandparents came up from New York. They were nice people, and she liked them at once, so I let her go. But in a month I had a distress call: she was so homesick it was affecting her health: would I take her back with an allowance? Oh, it was lovely to have her back. The middle one, the good one I'd never had time to notice before. But she had Tom's heart trouble so she's down in California with her father's people now. The allowance still comes. I suppose Tom wouldn't have taken it, but I do. I'm immoral about money now, Mrs. Saxe. I get it where I can and be damned."

Mrs. Saxe looks away from her earnest pedalling: "You were fortunate, Mrs. Ross."

"I certainly was. Adge moved to the street, as well. We had good times, in those days. But then she died and I was silly enough to marry Michael Littlemore. Do you like peanut-butter sandwiches and Campbell's soup? It's all I know about for lunch. I never have worked the cooking page."

"Oh, I should like to try it," says Mrs. Saxe.

"Peanut butter's an acquired taste, but you may find you like it, in the end. Here, I'll make you a sample. You can have it with jam, honey, lettuce or mayonnaise. Like it?"

"Delicious."

"There's cranberry sauce, too, left over from Christmas."

"Honey."

Harriet spreads with an experienced knife. Mrs. Saxe clears her throat. "Tell me, Mrs. Ross, Harriet, er, tell me about the child Sidonia."

"Oh, Sidi! You're right: I left her out. Why does one always leave Sidonia out? That's her trouble, you know, a kind of failure to root herself. Of course, she's never had a chance, poor lamb. She's my sister Babs's daughter – by adoption – and I meant to tell you, you mustn't leave your purse around, she's light-fingered."

"She's very beautiful."

"Isn't she? And I love her voice: there's a tiny lisp. If only

40

she wasn't such a bloody crook. She's here only temporarily. Here's your sandwich. Milk? Coffee? Both? Good; me, too. And for dessert we'll have mandarins, we're still using up the Christmas box.

"Well, anyhow: Sidonia. First you have to know about Harry and Babs.

"Babs is twelve years older than me, and quite a different kettle of fish from Madge, who's seventeen–years older, that is. Madge was always a trial but Babs has only started to be one.

"I used to admire her dreadfully when I was a child. She was tall and blonde and she wore her bangs in a roll like Betty Grable. And she was clever: she went to university and took a first-class degree, and was some kind of student activist and Sorority Queen to boot. And she could sing–during the war she sometimes sang 'The Bells of St. Mary's' at concerts. My father didn't like it because it was a Catholic song, but any-thing Bing Crosby did was supposed to be all right, so he let her go on. Anyway, she got some kind of volunteer job here in Toronto and she was the toast of the servicemen–one of her beaux was even the grandson of an English lord–and I thought she was the smartest thing that ever trod the earth.

"It took her quite a long time to marry, though. I don't know why . . . perhaps someone she was in love with was killed, or she was jilted, who knows. At any rate, she was a hoary old twenty-five when she married a man named Harry Prentice who wasn't a soldier at all: he was a businessman.

"My father was, of course, disappointed, he'd wanted her to marry one of the fine, upstanding young servicemen from our church. Harry was a dapper dan, a sophisticate, he went to nightclubs instead of church and I gather he played cards for money–it was years before I found that out, and I must say I was rather shocked, we were brought up against that–but Father had to give in and take her down the aisle. She wore a long white satin gown with a train–there was lots of material because the war was over–and she looked lovely.

41

"Well, they seemed to be all right, certainly they had a marvellous time and their names were always in the paper, but they never did have any children. Perhaps Babs was given to miscarriages, though there is no sign it's a family trait, I've never had one, and I get pregnant, or I did before I took care of that, just by looking at a man, but there were no children and of course Father pronounced himself disappointed, but at me rather than Babs, because he'd argued with Harry so much they just never came round to the house any more, and then I was gone myself. And Harry certainly did well in business: he'd started out in wholesale dry goods and furniture and he's all over the town now, he's a multi-millionaire. There was no sign that anything was wrong until about ten years ago Babs came to me in tears and said he had a mistress.

"I didn't know what to say, except maybe cheer up, they all do it in the end, the fancy dans. I don't quite recall what I did but pour her a drink and tell her to carry on, because she'd had no professional training, all her work had been volunteer and she'd no desire to leave him, she just wanted the mistress out of sight. But then she got this bright idea of her own: a month or so earlier, a business associate of Harry's had been killed flying his wife to a lodge in the north, and they had died without making any provision for their little girl: why not adopt Sidonia?

"It took some doing, because there were relatives who weren't in favour, and Harry and Babs were distinctly over age, but she got her own way in the end. And while she was waiting, she moved Harry out of their apartment into a huge house in Moore Park, with a yard large enough for a kindergarten and the most expensive swing set in the world; and she did up the child's room like a fairy princess's or like something out of a women's magazine. You and I know kids' real style is early dump, which is why they never let me near the propaganda department of the magazine I work for. And I feel guilty, sometimes I feel very guilty, working for an outfit that promulgates the foul gospel that houses nowadays, houses that belong to women who work outside and raise children both, should look like personalized showrooms. It's degrading; it makes us feel like failures in the end. Anyway, there was this white canopy bed and the blue wallpaper with white clouds on it, the white carpet, the cupboard full of educational toys and the revolving night-light–they *never* sleep with revolving night-lights on, it's a rule of the game–and into it went Sidonia.

"She was a beautiful five-year-old, blue eyes, blonde curls and all. Harry was crazy about her and lugged her around everywhere in her little white gloves and hundred-dollar coat–even a white rabbit coat for winter, for God's sake. I remember the first time she came here Mick thought she was so wonderful he flung his arms around her and he'd been working with finger paint. Harry nearly had a fit. And of course he never did bring her back, we weren't good enough for Sidonia then.

"Well, I'm sure you know the rest of the story . . . she had just lost her parents, and with them she must have been playing both sides against the middle from the day she was born. She was a charming, beautiful, pouting child, and ought to have had her bottom warmed every day.

"Harry and Babs catered to her. When she got to school and they found she had difficulty concentrating, they hired tutors for her. She drove the tutors up the wall. I've never seen a child so manipulative. I mean Mick tries, and the twins try, but nobody has any time for them, so they don't get away with it. But Sidi! Two whole adults and a million bucks to herself: her eyes were like silver dollars.

"And, of course, they didn't know anything about children. When she got up in the morning, it wasn't Babs in the kitchen, it was the maid. The chauffeur drove her to school. Babs and Harry got up good and late. Babs saw Sidi at tea, gave her her supper carly; then they'd be going out, so it was always the baby-sitter putting her to bed. They got her a dog but nobody bothered to train it, so it had to go. Babs tried to help her with her lessons but Sidi always conned her out of it. And meanwhile, Harry was getting tired of not being an only child, and meanwhile, they'd always drunk a lot – they were the cocktail-party circuit personified – and life with Sidonia was so tense that the alcohol started to get the better of Babs.

"Oh, they meant well, but they'd picked themselves a winner. I'm fond of Sidi, and she's always a pleasure to look at. I love that thick, thick, blonde hair, her dimples, her smile. I love her voice and the way she walks, but the fact is, she's a mess. She lives in a dream. She was picked up for shoplifting in a department store when she was ten; when Babs and Harry were splitting up, she ran away for five days and God knows where she'd been. She's had psychologists and psychiatrists by the score, and last year things got so bad that Babs, who has custody of her, went on a toot and Sidi tried to burn down the house – they'd moved to a smaller one after the divorce – and, well, Harry's living in the Bahamas, what does he care – and right now she's waiting for a special placement with the Children's Aid.

"Wasn't there a poem? 'She walks, the lady of my delight. . . .' I've forgotten the rest. You, too? I recall it as 'a wilderness of sheep' but that can't be right, but it's very graceful and I think of her – ah, that's it, a shepherdess of sheep; redundant, terrible line – but I think of her as a beautiful Dresden shepherdess. She's sweet, she's good-mannered, and when she doesn't get her amoral way, she's quite, quite mad. She's on the waiting list to live with a caseworker who's specialized in her kind of pseudo-saint. Because she doesn't even know she's real. She's amoral because nothing ever gets through to the real Sidonia. I used to think we could, but we're not trained and controlled, and of course we don't. There isn't a crack in her, we can't get into her mind. She's made up some kind of tale for herself to live in while she's with us – I suppose she's a lost heiress – and she's superficially compliant, but I know, for instance, that she

44

doesn't always go to school; I know she steals, and I know she isn't a virgin. I check up on her when I can, but if I do there's a terrible scene and it eats into the others like acid. She needs to go right back to her babyhood and start again, but she can't do it here. When she goes back to her mother she slits her wrists if she's crossed. The time she apparently burnt down the house, Babs had found her in bed with her boy friend, and she was only twelve. I just keep her on birth-control pills, clothe her and feed her, and pray."

Mrs. Saxe has sat through this recitation with her mouth open like a fish. She snaps it shut and says, "Modern youth."

"I don't know, Mrs. Saxe. I keep meeting girls like that in Victorian novels, except that not much is said. They're the poor ones who strangle their babies, or the consumptive beauties who die. But of course the rest of us feel better: how lucky not to have been beautiful, eh?"

"Heh!" Mrs. Saxe cackles. "No beauty, you or me. Clever girl, though?"

"Sidonia? Who knows? She's a year behind in school now. She was doing all right for a while, when she was in private school, but they couldn't handle her: she learned too early not to listen. Oh, inside, somewhere, there's someone who's very smart and very scared. Every once in a while she carves up her skin with a razor blade just to let that person out. I'd better phone the office now, to see if she went to school. She might have, because you're here, and she's already had an event for the day. And after that, it's time for our nap, wouldn't you say? I like the old ways."

"I know," says Marshallene. "I've known since the crack of dawn, when the twins came to tell me all. She arrived at midnight on a black bicycle and you're adopting her. She's a hundred and four years old and she has a mole on her chin. If you do that to yourself, Harriet, I think you ought seriously to think of taking in my mother, who's broken up with Norm again. She just got out of the de-tox unit in Owen Sound and needs somewhere to go. Come on in. I've just made some of that dizzy-making Korean tea: when I've heard from my mother, I go off the drink, she's that good for me. I woke up this morning to the dulcet tones of Peter and Pat, and then Sylvia rang up and let me hear, through that glorious instrument the telephone, the voice of her new baby macaw who can now lisp in numbers. I love my neighbours, you make me feel normal, secure and sane. Roger's running around looking furtive – you don't very often look out the front window, do you? You should, it pays off – and people are delivering the oddest parcels to his house; either he's refurnishing completely or he has an elephant coming to stay. The two dames in Number 11 have been fighting again, and Sylvia's been after Vinnie something fierce. She sure turns that relationship upside down. You'd think he was the one who put her in the wheelchair, the way she's been screaming at him."

"Maybe it's Sam."

"Not bloody likely; Sam's voice is sweeter. As a matter of fact, for a parrot he's got a good one. No, it's Sylvia, all right. Her nursemaid is letting her down."

"He gets tired."

"I bet he does. And if he isn't there exactly when he should be to do exactly what he ought to do, all hell breaks loose. I guess you don't hear them, but it seeps across the street from their bedroom window. If I were him, I'd moor her in the kitchen one day and disappear for the rest of my life."

"He's fond of her, really."

"He's got no sense, then."

"The trouble with Mrs. Saxe is I don't know what to do with her. I ought to show her around, but I don't think I quite have the energy."

"Oh, get the twins to take her up to the Science Centre on Saturday. That will do for her look at the colonies. Honestly, Harriet, I don't know why you're punishing yourself. You've enough to do. Finished the welfare article yet?"

"I don't think I can do another one."

"Well, you'll have to, won't you? The tax bill comes in February. But if you keep on taking on more and more people you'll prove you're just as much a masochist as Vinnie is."

"What's your mother going to do?"

"Go to the country home, for all I care. I mean, she left me at my aunt's when I was fourteen. I don't feel obliged. That time I tried to be all sentimental about her she tore my life apart. If she comes to Toronto I'll take her down to Grossman's and just leave her. She's a card."

"So are you. Well, I've got to get back. I put her down for a nap so I'd better try to write a line or two. Did I tell you about the woman I met who'd had her nerves out? *Maga* won't acknowledge that that kind of person exists."

"None but the middle class," Marshallene warbles. "Still, once you acknowledge, you have to take an attitude, and that might be dangerous. Look, I'm going to Simpson's tomorrow: I'll take your old lady if you like, then you can get on with it."

Harried nods gratefully and leaves. She remembers the day when she hesitated to let part of her house to Marshallene and shakes her head.

The wind is colder; the snow has crested and turned the deposits on the sidewalk into little peaks of ice, impossible to shovel: the child labourers leave a lot behind. Far down the street she sees Bob Robbins setting two shopping bags down on the pavement so he can open his door. His overcoat is too big for him, he looks lost and lonely, but he doesn't want to speak to her, or to anyone. He's been downtown to deliver his cartoon, she decides, and now he'll drink for a while, and then sleep, and then get up and start to paint again, to wipe out the guilt he feels at the way he earns his living. We're all crazy. She goes in and sits in front of her typewriter with an empty head. Maybe she had her nerves out years ago and nobody told her.

CHAPTER TWO

By the third day it becomes apparent that Mrs. Saxe's musical niece is indeed either non-existent or a victim of unpublicized spontaneous combustion. Harriet is used to being stuck with people but she feels ever so slightly abused when it happens unnecessarily. She goes next door to discuss the matter with Marshallene, but there is no answer so she trudges down the hill to the IGA discussing it with herself. "The old," she mutters to herself as she slips and slides (apparently nobody is responsible for the shovelling of this block), "take liberties as the young do; they have passed some kind of watershed. They feel free." She tries to imagine herself at Mrs. Saxe's age, decrepit, sucking her teeth, settling herself on Melanie or Ainslie, unrepentant, beady-eyed. She fails. "Mrs. Saxe is old," she says to herself, "and the least I can do is to take her in until her charter is due. I must ask her if it is three or four weeks. Nobody in England has money enough to travel overseas without a charter any more. Yes, I'll let her stay until her time is up, that's what I'll do, unless she has a friend somewhere else. Maybe I'll praise up Vancouver, or Montreal: in case. Yes, that's what I'll do, make it clear that she can stay, suggest other possibilities, be tolerant. I wish she didn't eat so much."

The IGA is always pleased to deliver Harriet's enormous order.

"Mrs. Saxe," says Harriet, shovelling cartons of spaghetti and macaroni and tins of soup into the cupboard, "when is your charter going back to England?"

"Pardon me, dear?"

"Your charter. Your flight. You know, your return ticket."

"Oh," says Mrs. Saxe, "I don't quite know, Harriet, dear. Whenever, I suppose."

"Didn't you come on a charter: a special group flight?"

"I don't recollect I did. I went to the Air Terminal, or was it the British Airways office, somewhere in Kensington, dear, and bought a ticket. I suppose it's good for a return."

"I'm sorry about your niece. You're welcome to stay here for a while, though."

"That's extremely kind of you, dear."

Harriet finishes plunking the cans in and throws the boxes down the cellarway for Mick to stack in his lair. She goes into her office and sits down and stares at the list of things she has to do. Mrs. Saxe follows her and sits on the exercise bicycle. Slowly, she swings a leg over. She begins to pedal.

"Mrs. Saxe, do you have any other friends in Canada?"

"Friends? Canada?" She does not stop pedalling.

"Do you know anyone in Montreal?"

"Montreal? Of course I don't know anyone in Montreal."

"Vancouver?"

"Oh, my dear, not since Ernestine emigrated in '06."

"Ernestine?"

"My daughter."

"You should go and visit her."

"Come to think of it, it can't have been '06. No one alive has a daughter born early enough to have emigrated-quite-alone in '06. She's dead. It was unfortunate."

"I should think so. It's a pity you can't see more of the country, Mrs. Saxe. I mean, I can take you around the city but I doubt if I'll ever be free to go many places. On the whole, you don't go anywhere when there are too many of you to fit into the car."

49

"Harriet, I am perfectly happy here with you." She says this with great sweetness and assurance, and then, staring fixedly at the wall, starts to pedal again. Harriet begins to work on her article.

It would be more amusing to see Mrs. Saxe as a kind of existential mystery, but the world around Harriet as usual refuses abstraction. Mrs. Saxe is the cousin of Fenella's Aunt Grizzel, with whom Harriet and Fenella once stayed in England, in a tarry, damp hut on the edge of a canal, which Fenella found charming. Harriet, after three days, got pneumonia, and staggered forth to deal with the complexities of the National Health Service. It would be nice to think that Grizzel's babies grew up to be hobbits, but seeing Mrs. Saxe, Harriet has put away that illusion.

Supper is surprisingly quiet, for the Ps have phoned to say that they have met Michael Littlemore, who is taking them to McDonald's instead of the dentist. It is a statement Harriet has dealt with before and will deal with again: he regards it as his right to stand outside the school at four and carry them off from time to time and regardless of their other obligations. If Harriet remonstrates about this, she has to see him; if she sees him, she has to lend him money, for she is not, and never has been, proof against a man who has devoted his life to borrowing. She simply takes a small, quiet supper as evidence of his devotion to the children and makes a new dentist appointment. And Sidonia is with her social worker.

During dessert, Harriet asks Mick if he will help Mrs. Saxe put her bicycle in the basement.

"Better in fron' hall," he says.

"No, Mick."

"Might get hurt in basement."

"No, Mick."

"Basement too small."

"No, Mick."

"Tell me," Mrs. Saxe says, "about the basement."

Mick gives her his worldly look: eyes aslant, mouth finally closed. "Sdark," he says.

Mrs. Saxe looks expectant.

"Sdirdy."

Harriet thinks wistfully of sending him for elocution lessons and giggles inside herself at the thought of Mick, slicked, on a platform, reciting "Norse am I when the first snow falls." His speech therapist knows no poetry.

A kind of inarticulate tug-of-war is going on between Mick and Mrs. Saxe. He scowls at her, waiting for her to run away. She is not adamant, not impervious, but as optimistic as a rubber ball. Sim puts down his spoon and stares at them. Melanie gets up and begins to clear the table, humming one of her pop songs. Mick suddenly pushes his chair back.

"Okay," he shouts, "so okay."

With much huffing, puffing and shoving, Mick and Mrs. Saxe persuade the big bicycle through the narrow house and down the stairwell. It is some hours before they are seen.

"How long's she staying?" Sim asks.

"I don't know."

"She's not too bad, considering."

Melanie sniffs. "She eats enough."

"Are you going out?"

"You should see the homework I have to do."

"Don't blast away on the phone all evening, then."

"Mother, you're a pig."

"Thanks, kid. And you'd better wash that green colouring off your scalp."

"Didn't I get it all? Fiona's hair's purple, now."

"You know what I think about that."

Melanie pitches her voice up to a nag. "I don't want to live with you while you're growing it out."

"That's right."

"You've really got it taped, huh? Everything for your own convenience."

"Try doing it any other way."

"Some day I will, believe me."

"Melanie!" She grabs her and holds her in a hug. Melanie wiggles away but is not unpleased. "Everything's going to be fine."

"Mother, I've got oceans of homework and I want to get it started before Sidi comes back."

"Go to, my love, go to."

Harriet settles down in her office and tries another version of "Welfare Women." This time she makes some headway, but she writes without enthusiasm. Every word is banal. Perhaps every word has always been banal: but now she sees it. More and more, she thinks, I am walking across the crusted snow of depression: if I step too firmly, I'll fall in. Up to my waist. And when I try to get out, the crust will crumble. Make a bigger and bigger hole around me but never get out, never. A mile away, snowmobiles will rumble by on a firmer surface. I'll feel the vibrations. I'll be left all alone. Writing about welfare women. My God.

The Littlemores slam the door and she feels her real life has begun again.

And now Harriet and Mrs. Saxe are going out for tea.

This day is grisly. Grey, grieving skies mean with half-frozen tears, drab snow humped at the curb to keep them from parking. Indeed, there isn't a parking place for miles. Babs's building, which is part of a shopping complex, is conveniently placed for taking the subway, but Harriet has had enough of puffing behind Mrs. Saxe up subway stairs. She holds Mrs. Saxe's arm to prevent the old thing from skating off in seven directions. She wishes she could persuade Mrs.

Saxe to buy some galoshes and stop stepping into roadways to startle traffic with her umbrella.

Closer to Babs's street there is even more traffic. Harriet wonders if they have moved the Symphony Rummage Sale to the plaza; but no, the street is plugged with police cars and ambulances. There has been an accident. As they reach the building, she sees, on the small square of snow-covered turf the apartment owners call a garden, a heap on the ground covered with a blanket. There is blood on the snow. Harriet clutches her heart. I am the old one, not Mrs. Saxe, she thinks.

Abandoning imagination for action, leaving Mrs. Saxe to follow, Harriet plunges past the policemen into the foyer of the building, and, after a prolonged struggle with her handbag to find her glasses, presses Babs's bell with a shaking finger.

"Yeah?"

Harriet wants to sink to the ground with relief, but not quite to get under the blanket. Mrs. Saxe is behind her, so she remains upright and righteous. The door buzzes. Harriet and Mrs. Saxe pass queasily through.

Babs lives on the thirty-second floor; there is time to exchange a word in the elevator. But Mrs. Saxe endures elevators with a strange fixity. Her eyes roll back in fear or, perhaps, ecstasy.

Harriet is still shaking. "I thought for a horrible moment it was Babs."

Mrs. Saxe nods wisely.

"Babs," says Harriet, "is . . . so . . . different."

Another nod. The elevator stops. Mrs. Saxe appears to be fascinated by the gilt and flocked wallpaper in the corridor. Harriet is not.

"Hiyah, hiyah, hiyah," says Babs, the Rock of Ages, at her door. "Harriet, you old bitch, I never see you except when you want something. And this is your friend. And how's my baby? Come on the hell in."

53

Babs is wearing a soiled and cigarette-scarred turquoise negligee and waving a bottle of gin. Harriet remembers, then, that she has forgotten to bring the tea. Standing on one foot, taking her boots off (though who would notice boot marks in the mess of crème de menthe stains on the rug?), she says, "Someone fell off your building. I was scared." Flesh. Splat. Her mind is full of ugly images. She thinks of boning chicken breasts, she thinks of blood and what it really is when it is not imagined.

"Harriet, I'm not as easy to get rid of as all that. Did you bring the tea?"

"Darling, I forgot."

"Good, you're the same old stumblebum as ever. Well, come on and sit down, Mrs. Saxe. Harriet said you were over from England and staying with her. How you stand that madhouse is beyond me."

Babs has been living in this apartment since Sidonia's fire. It is a very expensive apartment, as Babs's negligee once was very expensive, but it is showing similar signs of wear. Babs, too, looks like a haggard owl.

"Drinky-poo?"

"No," says Harriet.

"Yes," says Mrs. Saxe, eyeing, steadily, the gin bottle, which has a picture of Queen Victoria on the label. "With quinine water, if possible."

Babs turns in her kitchenette doorway. She is not, Harriet sees, as drunk as she is pretending to be, and she is holding her head in a manner meant to be fetching.

"Quinine water? Quinine water? Oh, tonic. We're out. Have to make do with lime juice, Mrs. Saxe. Or would you care for just a smidgeon of vermouth? Harriet, don't be a stick, join us."

There are noises of glasses and ice, taps running. Mrs. Saxe and Harriet look around the apartment. There is not much to be said for Babs's taste in decoration nowadays. It could be a hotel room.

Babs plunges huge tumblers at their hands and follows their eyes.

"Ghastly, isn't it? Harry took the pictures back. I don't give a shit for his damn pictures, anyway. Went to Zellers and bought some of those little kids with the big eyes, but hell, they kept staring at me. What's the matter with bare walls, anyway? How are you, Harriet? How's the mob?"

"Terrific," says Harriet glumly, thinking how much easier it would be if Babs were dead – but not horribly. Babs, in the flesh, is . . . Babs in the flesh; hiding behind a drink, pretending nobody is there. And the somebody who is hiding is as sharp as one of those nail beds little Hindus lie on in cartoons.

And the apartment is strange: there is not now an artifact other than dime-store ashtrays.

"Where are the plants?"

"Oh, Christ, spider plants. They were crawling all over the place. I got rid of them. Gave them to my cleaning woman. Creepy crawly things. I got rid of everything, Harriet, everyting I could. The way I figured it, Harry wanted the pictures back, and you know Madge always envied the majolica plates, they'd look better in her place than mine; and Sidi took her things. So I said to myself, Babs, who are you, really? Nobody. Well, baby, express yourself. So I do. Terrible, isn't it?"

Babs's neck has started to go, too. She lost weight one year and her neck corrugated itself; she put on weight again, but one is still aware of the hidden stripes under the chin, like lines on a sparrow's throat: now her neck is a consort of strings. The lines move upwards to bags under the restless eyes.

"I find it interesting to attempt to be impersonal," says Mrs. Saxe.

"You bet it is, Mrs. Saxe," says Babs. "Harriet, how is Sidonia? She hardly ever comes to see me any more."

"You hardly ever answer the phone."

"Mrs. Saxe," says Babs, "the story is this, in case you haven't heard it, though Harriet talks so much you've probably heard everything: Harry and I – my husband before he left me, I mean, not Harriet my sister – adopted Sidonia when she was just a little squawly baby, to keep our marriage together. It wasn't a very good idea. So she lives with Harriet now."

Mrs. Saxe sits as far forward as she can in Babs's plush armchair, so that her crossed ankles attempt to reach the floor. She sips her gin and smiles noncommittally.

"Babies," says Babs, "were more than I bargained for. I wasn't like Madge when she was first married, moaning and groaning for one. I was perfectly happy without a baby, but Harry wasn't. He said children would be the making of me, look what they'd done for Harriet. Not that I have anything against Sidonia, I got her when she was five, but my God, babies reek. If you don't change their pants every half hour, they positively reek. And they puke, just like Shakespeare said, they mewk – didn't know I was literate, did you, Harriet? – and even if I did take Sidonia late, I had that child to seven psychiatrists before she said, 'I want to go and live with Aunt Harriet.' Thank God for Harriet. Thank God for Sidonia's sense. I'm not cut out to be a mother."

"Babs," says Harriet, "the baby bonus. Hand it over."

"Harriet, you are a grossly covetous woman."

"I am not," says Harriet. "I am a firm and just woman, and I want Sidi's cheque. She needs new shoes, the taxes are overdue, and I have all those mouths to feed."

"Aw right, aw right, I'll go get it." She turns to Mrs. Saxe. "Tell me what you think of Canada, Mrs. Saxe."

Mrs. Saxe opens her mouth just a little and holds out her glass. I wonder, Harriet thinks, if I can turn her over to Babs? No. No. No. Turn no one over to Babs. Ever. It will take years to get Sidonia back in shape, poor kid. Cancel that thought, Harriet. Ex it out.

Babs hands Mrs. Saxe another drink. Mrs. Saxe takes it in

both hands like a baby bottle and sinks back in her chair. Her tiny legs stick out.

"Thank you," she says, in a plummy voice that Harriet, who has endured her company for seven weeks, has not heard before. "I am very fond of Canada. You have curious customs here."

"Such as?"

"Bodies fall from the air. There are displaced children everywhere."

"That's just Harriet. She collects them. Every time she gets married, the guy comes with two displaced communal babies, she has four more, he disappears, and she takes in two more orphans. I don't know how you stand it. You should come and stay with me. I'll show you Canadian civilization."

She must mean the television set, Harriet thinks. Or the view over St. Clair Avenue at rush hour.

Now Babs is standing over Harriet, waving Sidonia's baby bonus cheque.

"Heavy, heavy hang over thy head, what shall the owner do to *redeem* it? Harriet, have another drink; you're turning into a square."

"I have to drive," Harriet says glumly.

"Just a little," says Babs, handing Harriet six ounces of gin and a squeeze of lime juice over one bent ice cube. "Mrs. Saxe, we have curious customs here. I was a cheerleader once. Not a pom-pom girl. Harry left me for a pom-pom girl, but we didn't have pom-pom girls in Canada then. I was a cheerleader at the University of Toronto. I cartwheeled all over the place. 'Give us a T,' I yelled, 'Give us an O: Give us a TORONTO.'"

Suddenly Babs, gin, negligee and cigarette butts are flailing all over the apartment, flesh is falling again. The doorbell rings. Babs sits on the floor, looking at her glass of gin, which has not spilled.

"Christ," she says, "it's Madge. Our sister, Mrs. Saxe."

Harriet gets up to answer the door while Babs extinguishes with one corner of her negligee the coals that have fallen from her cigarette onto the rug.

For several years now, Madge has contemplated a trip abroad, but she has not quite managed to leave town. She is, as always, splendidly accoutred for travel. Today she is wearing a safari suit. She looks like Mrs. Macomber. Harriet wonders suddenly if she shot Stanley.

"Hullo, hullo," says Madge heartily. "Good to see you, Harriet." Marches into the room. "Babs, we have to have it out."

Babs withers and quails. She had been having a good time as a cheerleader. Mrs. Saxe's bird eye takes Madge in all over. Her little head shakes.

"I brought," says Madge, "the tea."

"Oh, no," Babs wails. "It means you're serious."

"Damn right, I am. I will not have you frittering away those. . . . "

"Marjorie, this is my invited guest, Mrs. Adeline Saxe."

"How do, Mrs. Taxe. Now, Babs. . . . "

Harriet puts down her drink, comfortable in the knowledge that Babs will not let it go to waste. Mrs. Saxe attempts to rise, but is too far back in her chair. Harriet gives her a hand. Remembers both being a Brownie and pulling her father out of his chair.

"Well, folks," she says.

"You're not leaving," Babs says weakly.

"Have to feed the mob, love. Sidonia's getting on fine."

Madge looks at Harriet with distaste, which look Harriet returns. Madge is better preserved than Babs. Her hair is dyed black. Elephant guns, Harriet thinks. She has come to discuss the estate.

"Harriet," says Madge, "next time that tribe comes to visit me, I want them all in real leather shoes."

"Sure," says Harriet, cheered, comforted and restored to the lower middle class by the vision of rows and rows of rainbow North Stars by the back door. "Sure, Madge. Take care of yourself, Babs. Bye-bye."

"See you next month, Harriet." Babs chews her words. "Bye, Mrs. Saxe."

Outside, all of the police cars but one are gone. There is blood on the snow, but the body is gone. How odd Babs doesn't know her neighbours. No, how characteristic. Harriet pauses a moment, in memory, perhaps, of those who fall through the air. She hears one policeman say to the other, looking not up at the building but up at the fir tree that justifies the tiny square of the apartment garden, "Who's going to pick the rest of her out of the tree?"

Harriet and Mrs. Saxe shudder and pass on.

In the car, Mrs. Saxe, who is gin-fuddled but apparently happy, says, "Regan and Goneril."

"No," says Harriet. "Nothing so interesting. Two middle-aged women with nothing to do. Flesh in the fir tree. Policemen get to pick it out. Once when I was . . . when Tom died, I wanted to . . . brrrr. They're going to discuss the estate," she says. "They control my father's firm."

"Is it large?"

"I have no idea. He took me aside one day and said, 'Harriet, it is not a disadvantage to be the least favoured.' He left me twenty thousand dollars' cash. Period. I was lucky. Once I got it."

On the way home, Mrs. Saxe subsides into ginny silence. Canadian customs, Harriet thinks. Give us a T, give us an O. Last time I saw Madge she was wearing an Arctic down parka. She looked like a walking blueberry. It's supposed to be brightness, that's it, that falls from the air. Not here. This thought keeps her warm as far as Rathbone Place.

"We're home," she says.

The first person at the door is Sidonia, who has, as she explains it, spent twenty dollars cutting off her golden hair. She is nearly bald, but the shape and the texture of her neck and head are elegant. Harriet hugs her, a new Sidonia, a sculpture against her shoulder. To hell, she paraphrases Babs, with the fact that she stole the money and forgot to sell the yards of golden hair: we're home.

Mrs. Saxe is curious about Indians. Harriet and Marshallene have a little think about the Native Canadian Centre and the Nishnawbe Art Gallery, and finally decide, on the dubious grounds that one of the Nahmabins, to whom one of Marshallene's sisters is married, might be there, to take Mrs. Saxe to the Silver Dollar.

"It's right next to the Scott Mission," Harriet explains, "where there are free breakfasts."

"A doss house?"

"Well, sort of Christian rather than, well, Dickensian. Though I've never been inside."

"And it's one down," says Marshallene, "from the Chinese funeral home that used to be the Jewish funeral home that everyone called Benjamin's but was listed under another name in the yellow pages, which made it hard for the Uncalled to go to a Jewish funeral. But that's moved north."

"And it's across from the Connaught Labs, where they used to make all the insulin and the vaccines, that used to be Knox College, the Presbyterian dovecote, which also takes in the old Borden stables, where they store radioactive materials very unsafely."

"And," says Marshallene, "it's right around the corner from the Clarke Institute of Psychiatry and the Addiction Research Centre."

"And across the street from the El Mocambo, where the famous groups play. Melanie's bitter because she's too young to get in."

"And Chinatown's moving there, though the art-supply stores are hanging in."

"And the Bagel and the Tel-Aviv Restaurant."

Glazed by a plethora of ephemera ("Spadina is the widest street in Toronto, if you don't count University Avenue and nobody does"), Mrs. Saxe wades into the Silver Dollar and the beer with Harriet and Marshallene.

"It's only an ordinary mead-hall," says Harriet, "but nicer than some."

"Decor: washable; space: as decreed by the government. Band: deafening."

There is only a sprinkling at first. Mrs. Saxe goggles to see which are Indians, which isn't hard after she has been told that they are the ones with the long, glossy black hair. They sit there and talk to each other, they sit there and drink beer. They sit there and stare hard at Marshallene and Harriet and Mrs. Saxe. "As well they should," Harriet says firmly.

After two hours of desultory conversation – because what, among people who live together, is there to say? – the three of them stagger out. Harriet and Marshallene, summoning a taxi (whose driver does not want to take them on so short a journey south), look expectantly at Mrs. Saxe for an opinion.

"They're very clean, aren't they?" she says in disappointment.

"You watch out for them Indians, Mrs. Saxe," says Marshallene. "They keep their coal in their bathtubs."

Mick's anger changes the shape of his mouth; it is a sidewise, mobile oval, like the round of an old key, plastic, red, loutish. Brutish, as he yells, "Fuck off, all of you mothers, go fuck yourself, sluts, buggers." He scrunches up his face until his eyes are slits. It's what he does now instead of crying. He's a baby, Harriet thinks, a baby in his highchair, beating his rattle against the wall, stiffening, rising in the straps, arching his back. He was the only one I had to strap down.

"Aieeeee, tayeeeee," ancient arcing screams come out of him. What is he now, some sort of leprechaun? An angry old

Irishman in a play? Out under the streetlight there, putting on his show.

"Aieeee." Then something begins thumping against the house. She clutches her stomach. She hears herself talking faster and faster, "I can't stand it, you see I can't stand it. . . . " He has his effect.

He has, somewhere, in the frozen outside, found mud. It is the wrong time of year for mud, but Mick is some kind of genius, Mick has found mud. Perhaps it's a mixture of snow and axle grease. Plunk. Plonk. On the white part of the verandah, where it will be stuck until spring. Fuck it, Mick, stop, she thinks, you know I hate cleaning. . . .

With a thud, a large clod hits the front window, which shivers the way it does when a truck goes by along Gloag Street. Stop, Mick, she thinks, stop, it hurts.

"Aieeee," he cries. The sound is high, sexless, alien, ugly. They are coming to scalp us, she thinks, they are. . . .

Patsy climbs over her to see what Bad Mick is doing.

"Look, Mummy, isn't he rotten, he's awful, he's ... crazy!"

Mick is feinting with a lump of clay at a passing car. He does not throw. Another hit on the living-room window. She thinks of London, the Blitz. But we have our lights on. She turns the front light out, goes to the door. He's doing all right, she thinks. He didn't throw at the car, he didn't break the window, he has that much control.

"Mick."

No answer.

"Mick!"

"Mick's really a problem, Mummy; you're going to have to send him away."

Send me away, she thinks. I'm the one who wants ... but they don't do that to mums, it costs too much in welfare. Get in there and cope, lady, they say.

From nowhere, Mick yells, "No. No. No, ya old bitch."

She wants to run to him, plead, concede. I did it, Mickey, if you'll only stop, I'll say I did it, whatever it is: bore you, bought you a house, raised you, felled you, failed you. Mick!

She even capitulated to him that way once. Much good it did her.

This time she says, "Shut up, Patsy, you'll get mad one day, too. Go upstairs and do your homework, clean your drawers, wash your drawers, piss along, now. Leave. He'll get over. . . . "

"No, he won't, Mummy. He gets worse and worse. This morning he. . . . "

"Get off with you. He's not a side-show." This eternal feminine need to be self-righteous galls her.

Clutching her middle, she retreats. He has taught me to clutch my middle, to be martyred, not to. . . .

Oh, no, it wasn't him.

Poor Mick, the black-tempered child. The hurt, stammering child. Why? Tom died just after he was born. He drank my anger, drank my tears. The shrink says he'll get over this patch. Will I?

Doctors always say, you had him, you had him.

Listen, it's only me, little Anne, speaking here from under the frying pan.

Swat. Wug. Clay always makes them feel better.

Harriet has thought herself behind the chesterfield. Papa is coming home. He hands his hat to Mrs. Deans. "Where's Harriet?" Thunk. Swat.

He could have used his cane.

Harriet on her knees to the minister, whose wife didn't want to let her in: "I don't know what to do with my father."

He listens with palms together, fingers making church and steeple. "You adolescents dramatise too much. Your father is a good man. See: honour thy father and thy mother, that thy days may be long. . . ."

"Shorter days, God," Harriet prays. "Shorter days."

63

Harriet did not have an angry adolescence. Her father had it.

Her sister Madge has told her that her mother died not in childbirth but in a sanitarium, where she was to be cured of drink. Soon after Harriet was born. She never asked her father what the truth was: she had some sense. And she knows Madge used to tell lies. Madge tried to send her to the reformatory.

Rage hit Mr. Mickle late, though how old one's parents were one never knew in those days. Still, he couldn't have been young, bringing up this third daughter. Harriet doesn't remember that he fought Babs and Madge the way he fought her. Perhaps she looked like her mother, all of whose pictures were destroyed.

"Harri . . . . et!" cries Mick. Harriet hides.

"Aieeeee."

It's not fair, she thinks, not fair. I won't have it. I've had it before. The sins of the fathers. Tom never raised his voice. I gave him a sucker instead of holding him: so I could work, write, raise the whole mob of them. They've always been so good.

Kids always say it isn't fair, it isn't fair, you give the others more. Sim and Peter were easy, but Mick was the one all along, raging, troubled. Only bicycles soothed him. I wrote, cleaned, cooked, changed a million pairs of pants, loved them all, I thought, equally – oh, this one had this charm, another that, there are inequities – but Mick, speechless Mick, withhold your rage . . . my father. . . .

He was an angry man. No one knew it but me. Mrs. Deans made the supper. Mrs. Deans went home. Babs went to university, lived in the sorority house. Madge married. There was only me, clutching the middle leg of the dining-room table. Mick, save me.

Nothing will save Harriet but Harriet. She is no longer young. And old Mr. Mickle, pillar of the community, grew to hate his wife for dying. Called the last child Harriet. Harriet hangs onto the leg of the dining-room table forever, white, teeth clenched, belly distended with undigested fear. "You don't eat," he says, "and your face is sallow. You don't do your homework."

Or: "You eat all the time, you're as red as a beet, you haven't curled your hair, you do nothing but homework, you're fat and spotty, nobody asks you out and no wonder."

Or: "You care about nothing but your face and that . . . Kevin. Kevin's a Catholic name. You do no work. . . . "

"Honour thy father and thy mother," says the minister, making a church and steeple. "We have no idea what they have done for us; their compromises, their sacrifices. I dare say it's hard for the two of you alone together, but you must make the best of it. I hear you're difficult about helping Mrs. Deans with the housework. You don't make things easier for yourself, do you?"

"Harriet," says Mrs. Deans, "if there ever was a girl with two left hands and two left feet it's you. Go and do your Latin, dear."

It was not because she had courage that Harriet left school and went to work early.

When she got the job on the magazine, old Mr. Mickle raged and tore, and jumped up and down like Rumpelstilt-skin. She should have been inured but she wasn't; it cost her, she thought then, all she had. But she stood her ground. She was nearly eighteen.

For Christmas, she bought him a kitten. At first she thought he was going to strangle it, but the kitten was agile and saucy and captured his heart. He called it His Nibs and they lived happily ever after.

"Mick, come on in. It's cold now. It's over."

"Shuddup."

"Okay." She goes away. If all he is saying is shuddup it is over. Her belly and teeth have not quite yet fallen out.

Sim barrels into the house. "What was that all about?"

"Mick's in a rage again."

"Don't let it bother you." Sim is still fair but he is big now, golden, bending over her.

"Of course it bothers me."

"He'll get over it."

"Live to kill."

"I don't think so. I like our Mick."

"You know, Sim, you and the girls are okay, and Patsy and Peter. He was the only one who didn't know his father."

"You worry too much, Ma."

"It's Gehenna."

"What's that?"

"Something in the Bible. A burning lake."

"Glad I missed all that stuff. Just tell him to clean up the mess in the morning."

"He won't. You would have."

"If I did it, sure. I'd be ashamed. Isn't he?"

"He has no conscience, Sim. No conscience."

Sim gets a bottle of beer out of the fridge. He is old enough. He straddles a wooden chair, puts his bottle down, thinks, stares at her. He is very beautiful, our Sim, she thinks. Nearly twenty.

"Ma," he says, "he does have a conscience, okay? I know that kid. I grew up with him. He has so much conscience he can't bear to think of what he's done, that's Mick's problem."

"Thanks, Sim."

Infinitely, youthfully, adorably condescendingly, Sim lays a big, raw hand on Harriet's head. "It's going to be okay, Ma."

"Fetch him in, Sim. Fetch him in."

"Naw, leave him out. He'll sneak in the cellar window when he feels better."

She wants to put her head in her apron, she wants to sob on Sim's shoulder. She sits back, closes her eyes. Sim lounges up (you can lounge up only when you're big, boneless and nineteen), and she mutters "Oh, love," but so he

66

cannot hear. You take your little pleasures where you find them.

He hands her a shot of something – Marsala – out of the kitchen cupboard. She begins to sing, slowly, in a high, quivering voice, a hymn she remembers, one they used to sing at night. It reminds her of old necks, quivering bits of ostrich feathers on hats, sadness: "The darkness deepens, Lord with me abide...."

"Ma," says Sim. "Snap out of it. Snap out of it."

"What do you want me to do, Sim? Go upstairs and pick scabs?"

"Ma," says Sim, leaning towards her (Sim, you are growing up and you had better soon go away), "Ma, Mick's in love with Sidonia, see? And Sidonia's living with us now, and we all know Sidonia is disturbed, so he doesn't figure he can do anything about it. And Sidonia's putting it out; my God, she runs around upstairs like a stripper. Melanie's running around in her underpants, too. It's really tough, Mum. Even little Patsy's getting sexy, see? He's only turned fifteen, he doesn't know what to do with that stuff, and you tell him to do his homework ... so of course he blows."

She thinks of her father and his household of burgeoning girls. No wife. No matter what happened to her mother: her mother died. Mrs. Deans was all white starch to Harriet, Madge and Babs, but what was she to Father? And himself a decent, honest, upright man, elder of the church.

"Sim, what do you mean by putting it out?"

"Well, I guess I'm being metaphorical. I don't think she and Mick are really doing it. But she would if he would. She's real jail-bait, Mum."

"I know. That's why I brought her here. She couldn't stay with Babs the way Babs drinks."

"She's hitting Mick hard, Mum."

It's true, Harriet thinks, she goes around half naked all the time. Melanie doesn't – just an occasional long dash to the bathroom with her hands over her breasts. I must talk to Melanie about her breasts. She feels very frightened of those lovely new breasts. She's not teasing anyone. She feels too bad. But Sidonia. . . . No, I won't have that. There's no need to put up with her. I took her in as a favour.

"I'll have to get rid of Sidonia."

Sim looks down at the table. Tilts his chair back, raises one knee and one arm, and gets a new bottle of beer from the fridge.

"If my father . . . " he says.

"Sim, I love her, too. She's so pretty and so needy. But think of the rest of us."

"Yeah, I guess so." He rips the cap off the beer bottle and catches it in his other hand.

The front door clicks. There is the sound of someone walking on the heels and balls of his feet quietly and successively.

"Hi, Mick," Harriet says in a weak little voice. (I am always deduced and seduced and traduced by my men, and maybe, after all, I love it.)

"I'm sorry, Ma."

If you have a husband, Harriet thinks, you can threaten to leave him. If you have an ex-husband, you can ship the kids to him. But Tom's a-cold and what right-thinking person would hand a child to Michael Littlemore?

"Sim," she says, "reach me a beer, will you? Want one, Mick?"

"Sure."

"There are a lot of things I could say, but I won't. But somebody wrote a couple of good lines of poetry once: 'And malt does more than Milton can to justify God's ways to man.' "

Mick looks at her from under his newly bushy eyebrows, trying to focus. He is wearing his blacks today: satin, denim, leather. Sim is all blue and gold like the Swedish flag. I bet they've never heard of Milton, she thinks.

"Cheers," she says to them.

"Cheers," says Mick, blowing on his fingers. "Some cold out there."

I am an immoral woman. I sue for small pieces of peace, Harriet thinks. But when I get them I am very happy. Her eyes water.

"Hi," says Sidonia, tall, thirteen, tossing her head, as if she still has long golden hair, from the doorway. "Can I have a beer, too?"

Mick hunches down into his satin shirt, tense, waiting. Sim slides over to make room for her.

"No," Harriet says, home again at last, and to her real home, home. "But we'll always love you, no matter what happens."

CHAPTER THREE

When peace sets in after the front door has slammed for the last time the next morning, Harriet rereads "Welfare Women." It is dim and uninspired but competent, containing all the information she has obtained about these women's lives that the magazine – delivered free in wealthy suburbs – will be able to print. There are things about all of us that nobody wants to know, she thinks. More and more she is haunted by these things: the existence of warts, moles, pimps, debt-collectors, cancer, socially unacceptable lovers (well, she thinks, not all of us find socially acceptable lovers, there was a gypsy . . .), repressive welfare workers, permissive welfare workers, networks of missing nerves. . . .

It's over, though; she has slain the succubus, removed its clinging, dead, sticky footpads from the back of her neck. She can pay attention to Mrs. Saxe. I've got everything upside down, she thinks, work is more important than Mrs. Saxe.

Nevertheless, Mrs. Saxe is in the kitchen, hopefully scanning the *Globe and Mail*. Whether she has sociological interests, interests that Harriet inevitably assigns to everyone because she has them herself, is moot: but she is here and willing to be entertained. The car, Harriet's brown bomber that Sim now has a half interest in, sits under six inches of snow in the back yard and Harriet looks at it dubiously.

"We'll have to take the bus," she says.

"Eh?"

"I'll take you downtown today but we'll have to take the bus."

"Lovely."

"Perhaps," says Harriet, and is saved by the telephone.

"Harriet," says Sylvia, "come over, I've got something to show you. Come over right now."

Harriet is dubious of Sylvia's enthusiasms, but an invitation is a command. "Can I bring a friend, Sylvia? Is there anything you need?"

"Come over" – the high voice shrills through the instrument – "right now!"

"Sylvia," says Harriet, "is my neighbour in the wheelchair. She's excited today." Putting her coat on gloomily, helping Mrs. Saxe with hers. There are things that don't bear saying about Sylvia. "You'll like the birds."

Mrs. Saxe waits on the top step while Harriet sweeps the snow off the porch. Then they walk Indian file across the road, up Sylvia's ramp, and through her wide front door.

The house is like Harriet's, but seems both wider and smaller because of the alterations to its proportions for the wheelchair, because of the tiny lift that runs up the banister of the stairs. Sylvia appears, wide-eyed, pale, her fair hair scraped so tightly back from her face that it seems to hold her eyes too far open. Harriet introduces Mrs. Saxc but Sylvia pays no attention at all.

If the front half of the house is like Harriet's, the back is like no one else's. Sylvia has two things in her life, three if you count Vinnie (but no one does much, except Harriet): she makes costumes for figure skaters, and she keeps birds. Therefore, the right side of the kitchen has been enclosed in wire to form an aviary, and what used to be the counter is a large sewing table over which are suspended plastic tubes that hold finished costumes, half-finished costumes, boas, braids, lengths and concatenations of satin and swansdown, and hanks of sequins, beads, and marabou. To enter the kitchen is to fall headfirst into a whirl of colour and sound, over which Sylvia's high-pitched scream says, "Harriet, but Harriet, look!" And she takes out of her shirt pocket something that looks obscenely like a cluster of boiled chicken wings. "His first appearance, isn't he wonderful, look!"

Closer up, the object is clearly unboiled; raw, in fact, and featherless. Sylvia tenders him in both hands; the knot of skinny elbows writhes, shifts, and reveals a hideous head.

"Joey," Sylvia nuzzles him, "Joey, you are so beautiful."

"Splendid," says Mrs. Saxe, "oh, I say, splendid. One of yours?"

Sylvia looks at her gratefully. "I can never impress Harriet with birds. She won't look at anything that isn't wearing a baseball cap and a Cheap Trick button. This is Joey, son of Mala; he's beautiful, isn't he? I've been bringing him along by hand. Mala doesn't want to have anything to do with him, do you, wicked old Mala, your own little boy and you don't do anything but hang on your wire and screech at him. Harriet, at least you can take your friend into the aviary and introduce her to the birds, it's time for Joey's feed."

Harriet, full of fear and wonder, skitters across the room and shows Mrs. Saxe how to work the catch on the aviary door. "They're quite wonderful and they expect visitors to pay attention to them." The big cage is full of smaller cages and smells mealy and clean today. "It would be nice to say they could be free, but they're different species and they fight. See, at the end, the little ones are Mexican parrotlets. They're the prettiest, I think. I love the way they twitter and tumble. And these two, they are Grand Eclectuses. Sylvia, do they really come from New Caledonia—I'm sorry, New Guinea? They're called Sam and Olive for some reason; and these are the lories, beautiful colours, aren't they?" The lories, in response, quietly and watchfully prune their ruby, emerald and sapphire feathers and shed their liquid droppings tidily. "And here's old Mala and her man Bill. Mala, I'm surprised at you for being a bad mum, wanna cracker?"

"Harriet, never say Polly wanna cracker!" Sylvia warns.

Too late. "Polly wanna cracker," Mala says.

"Mala cracker, Mala cracker, Mala cracker," Bill takes up the cry. Soon the whole aviary is imitatively twittering. Sylvia turns and glares at Harriet. "Syl, Syyl, Syyyyyl," cry the African greys, and Mala begins to cackle and shriek and roar.

"Oh," says Mrs. Saxe, "splendid."

Sylvia is feeding Joey with a dropper. He opens his great, pallid beak, stretches his withered neck, and receives gouts of a mixture that looks like egg yolk and pebbles.

"Lovely baby," Sylvia coos.

"When does he get feathers?"

"When he feels like it."

"I'm sorry, Sylvia. Beauty's in the eye of the beholder, I guess."

"He's a miracle, a downright miracle, an accomplishment. A victory, Harriet!"

Harriet feels duly reproached. She does not mind being reproached but she is left apologetic, wordless, and she knows she will hold this against Sylvia and there is already enough.

"I don't always go for babies, either," she says. "It's the baldness, I guess."

Sylvia sniffs. "And you married that character Littlemore."

You bitch, Harriet thinks, you know his secret, don't you? Can't see him without undressing him to see if he's pink all over. But I don't need to undress birds. She tries not to look daggers at Sylvia, looks instead at Mrs. Saxe, who is deep in mysterious conversation with the lories. "Krrrrr," she is saying. "Cheeerup, cheroo."

"Tereu," says Harriet, for want of a nail.

"Where'd you get her?"

"England. Cousin of an aunt of a friend of mine."

"Permanent?"

73

"God, no. Good company, though. Likes everything."

Sylvia whistles. The Grand Eclectuses whistle back. Mala squawks.

She joins Mrs. Saxe and Sylvia in the aviary, steeling herself against the laying out on the table of the skating costumes in all her least favourite fluorescent colours. There are times when her Puritan ancestors rise up and haunt her. She wants to weep.

Mala sticks her head out of the bars of her cage and pulls Harriet's hair.

"Hi, baby," she says. "Wanna cracker?"

The correct reply to this, Harriet thinks, according to the household I live in, is "Fuck off, pervert." Mildly, she scratches Mala's head, pities her for her lack of maternal feelings (she'd make a sensible mother, she knows an ugly babe when she sees one) and stands polite and silent, dreaming of Montezuma, as Sylvia explains the birds to Mrs. Saxe.

For how many years now – five, six? no, longer, since things started getting tiresome with Littlemore – Harriet has been seeing the Man from Montreal twice a year, when he is in town, for something he describes as dinner and a little whoopee, to rhyme with "Molly Whuppee, gin ye 'ere come back again." These are usually, as Harriet describes them with a giggle in her mind, bang-up occasions. Tonight, she has put a red semaphore triangle in her bedroom window and dug out her little black dress, which is more than a shade too small.

The Man from Montreal looks like an American football player, which he once was. He is a prominent businessman of the sort all socialists wish to avoid, has short hair, a gold tooth, and rimless glasses. Harriet met him when she was asked to interview him, years ago, for *Maga* on the subject of women. What she feels about him is that he is on many levels a mistake – married men are, after all, the same mug's game

74

they were thirty years ago – and on a very important other one, twice a year, a delight.

Good food, good wine. "You know, I always think when I'm with you, Harriet, that if I could solve my problems with Maudie, and you weren't living with that menagerie – how many you got at home now, six, eight, ten? – we could make it, we could really make it: the marriage to show them all."

"It's easy over a dinner table, Ewie."

"Especially in a restaurant and nobody's spilling their milk. Have a little butter on that potato, Harriet, live it up for once."

"You've no idea how I love being corrupted."

"You should see your face."

After dinner they dance – and this is something Harriet never does with anyone else; Roger is the only man she knows who is the right height to even think of dancing with, and Roger's generation doesn't dance – to old, slow Rodgers and Hart, to the restaurant band. It's corny and, on some level again, corrupt – how many people are dancing in Cambodia to Rodgers and Hart? – and they are doing it for one reason, the same reason: because they did this, once in a while, when they were young. The other dancers are middle-aged as well.

Slowly, they stagger back to the hotel, young, vaguely guilty, vaguely giggly.

"I don't know if I can still do it," he complains. "I'm fifty, now, you know, Harriet."

"I have a friend you can practise on if you're not sure."

He turns and throws a pillow at her. He can still do it.

They lie in bed smoking till two, three in the morning. His body is broad and hot, Bermuda-tanned. She moves away from him to cool herself. He notices: he notices everything, always.

"None of that stuff, love."

"I'm not used to it any more."

"What?"

"Oh . . . propinquity."

"How many years have you been on your own?"

"Six, seven now, I guess."

"What do you do? Other women? Lovers? Yourself?"

"Less and less anything."

"That's bad for the complexion."

"I'm getting old and stiff. I guess it's having to see the kids through their stages."

"Your body's uptight now. It didn't used to be. No love for how long?"

"No trouble-free love, that's it."

"I get spooked by these women who go for women."

"You want two at once, greedy one, that's why you think about lesbians. No, if you want me to tell, I have an arrangement, but I feel it, shall we say, drawing to a close."

"Go to the health spa, drop ten pounds, get another."

Harriet watches his smoke rings and wonders if she has the energy to get another.

"It's what it's about, Harriet. There isn't much else: everything lets you down in the end, but the body gives pleasure."

She doesn't want to say anything, stays silent. He flops over and butts their cigarettes. "I know, it's late, you're tired, *aprés un certain âge* bed is for sleep. I can go out and ask for it, you can't. But there's always luck, sweetheart." He begins to get dressed. He always puts her into a taxi at the hotel door so she doesn't feel like a tart, creeping away, leaving him. But now that sadness has crept into the bed with them: will they see each other again?

"I'll be back in April," he says as they part. "You're a fabulous fuck, honey. Take care of yourself."

On the way home she runs through the evening in her head. A lot of what was said went on in silences, for his silences are more intelligent than his words – you can tell this by reading about him in the *Financial Post* – but now, every time she leaves him, she has a vague sense that all they are doing is using each other. Why not? her modern self asks, when it's making love that makes you want to go on living? But an old, deep voice is louder inside her every year and it says, "This is a worthless adventure, Harriet." Is it her father, spoiling her uncalculated pleasure again? Is it the voice of the *zeitgeist*, misanthropy?

She pays the driver, scrambles into the house, undresses carelessly and ploughs her face deep into her pillow. Whatever it is, it stops when she falls asleep.

Michael Littlemore holds no grudge against Harriet. She took him, used him, sucked him out like a lobster claw, threw him out, threatened to put him in jail for not paying maintenance, maligned him to the children that she had extracted from him with such wiliness: but no, he doesn't hold grudges. Grudges are a waste of energy, and he is the inventor of the conservation of energy.

Michael Littlemore is lying in bed, in the snug warmth of his old room at home, which is unchanged except for the waterbed that cradles his weak back. Well, he thinks, he was a bit bad to take the housekeeping money to play the horses, but up to this point he has had no luck with money, no talent for making it.

Soon the bad times will be over, though. He wriggles his toes and sinks his large body in the flannel and vinyl and warm-water world that cradles it. I'd better take the Ps to the flicks soon, he thinks. God, they're growing. In about a week they'll be so big I'll have to pay adult for them: three bucks, even in the afternoon. Highway robbery.

He doesn't like thinking of money, he has no talent for it, no luck. He lies on his back and wriggles his bum into the warmth beneath him, better than newspapers on a park bench, good old Mum, light on the ceiling, yellow and white like fried eggs, even in winter: always the same; ring of rust round the old stovepipe hole. Had it good with Harriet, used all her contacts. Well, wasn't so bad for her: these scurrying,

77

efficient women, all elbows and practicality; human calculator, Harriet: this one has this much a month, that one so much, she has to earn so much to make up the difference; Michael, too. Hell, they didn't need all those bicycles. What normal kid got a bicycle just when he wanted one? And new clothes instead of passing them down. Trouble with Harriet, she didn't know how the other half lived.

God, she worked, though. Scurried around just like his Mum: up at six making juice, eggs, toast. You came down and sat at the breakfast table, she'd plunk a plate in front of you and, if you looked young enough, cut your toast in strips and break your bacon up. Wasn't so good the year she decided bacon was too expensive. Flying plates and elbows, and her as little as his Mum. He tried presenting himself once, twice, thrice (as she had presented herself once, twice, thrice: God, she loved it. Had gone without, though, after Tom died) and it was true, every time he sat down again she plunked a plate in front of him until she finally noticed and laughed like a drain.

That was one of her phrases: I laughed like a drain.

Well, she got what she paid for, he thinks. I screwed her and I made her laugh. Dunno why she turned nasty: mind like a cost accountant's, buzzing-around fascist lady pretending to be earnest, a Good Mum. Never knock Harriet, her brother-in-law Harry, the one who ran away, said, she keeps 'em all fed and dressed, that's an accomplishment this-day-and-age. Never knock Harriet, Harriet never-nox, the old gasbag.

I'd have never met Sue if Bing's Fancy had won that day. Proves what Ma says, you've got to take the bitter with the sweet.

It is early; the lower windowpanes are still frosted with feathers; the low sun slants up and dapples the ceilings without warmth; Michael Littlemore, all three hundred soft-skinned but not flaccid pounds of him, wriggles his toes. He hears his Mum get up and patter to the toilet. When he was

78

little, she pulled out the chamber pot and he woke to the soft piss of it. Nobody but the two of them remembers there were houses with just earth closets in Toronto in those days: right down here where the new developers are having raptures over the age of the brick. The all-cotton crew who've just discovered the world isn't made of polyester. Not on your Nelly, he thinks, and when the old lady's gone (sigh) we'll make a packet out of the street. Just like a bloody English cottage, house with its nose bang on the sidewalk. He can see them ripping out baseboards still furred with old railway soot, excavating the lovely pink roses his Ma papered the whole upstairs with once. Funny, he thinks, I'm always attracted to energetic women: she'd paper the house all weekend and on Monday go out to clean. Me, it took me all weekend to chew one eraser off my school pencil. Bet she's going out today. What day? Tuesday. Mrs. Magee, that'll be. Used to bring me back little pink cakes from the bridge parties. For her poor orphan.

She had wanted him to have an education, but he was preternaturally the wrong shape. When he was sixteen he ran away to sea and learned that Conrad's vision was officer-class by stoking boilers in the North China Sea. But he learned his true vocation in the ports, and the fineness of Oriental skin. He manages now, gets by. Soon he'll be more than getting by. Sweet Sue.

He smells bacon. His Mum's a bit screwy now. Afraid of losing him again, though he's said nary a word. In his way, he takes care of her. He knows his place, knows she needs him. His job is to thump on the floor when he has a hangover (though he doesn't like drinking much), say about once a month, so she can still feel useful and martyred and bring up the racing form and his early morning tea. Hell, she did it for his father. She's the last of a fine old race, thinks the male of the species is to be indulged. It makes her happy.

When he was living with Harriet, his Mum didn't know what to do with herself. She got herself an old golden tomcat, but she said it wasn't the same, he wasn't much of an eater, he just liked that dry, cat-food stuff. She was glad when Michael came back. Though work is as thin as she is now and he has to find ways of slipping her a few dollars now and then. She doesn't feel it's right to take money off him (not like Harriet!) but it's necessary. You don't get social benefits if you're a cleaning woman, you work till you drop. You're happy enough to pretend you've absentmindedly overlooked a twenty from one of your ladies in the bottom of your old black purse.

Michael smiles and rolls over for his cigarettes. He doesn't approve of smoking in bed; for the first one in the morning, he always sits on the very edge of his bed with his pink satin comforter over his shoulders. After he stubs the fag out he throws the comforter off and pads to the bathroom for a long, slow piss.

"Michael?" his Mum calls feebly from downstairs.

"In a minute, Mum."

He buttons a plaid shirt over his belly, pulls on his jeans, buckles up, pads downstairs in his scarlet health socks. His overturned plate is keeping the bacon and eggs warm in the frying pan. The tea sits steeping under a cosy that is a crocheted Anne Hathaway's cottage, a thing of beauty and a joy forever. He puts his big arms around his little Mum and holds her close. She leans against him for a second (you couldn't lean against that old gold cat) and says, "Sit down, now, you."

He does. He lets his tea be poured in his father's moustache cup. He laces it with sugar and milk. His father was a coalman and died when Michael was three.

She serves him three eggs, five strips of bacon, two bits of fried bread and a tomato. She came over from England, was a Barnardo's girl. He is all she has. Before, she never dreamed of having anyone who was her own.

She sits down with a cup of black tea and a bit of buttered toast. (Not gyppo any more, she has trouble with her heart.)

She shouldn't be out there cleaning, Michael thinks sadly. But there isn't anything else for her. I'd better talk to Sue.

She stands up, unties her apron, runs her hands through her funny short white hair, gets into her good black coat and prepares to go to Mrs. Magee. Things have been thin since Mrs. Bourne sold her house and moved into an apartment and Mrs. Newell's children put her in a nursing home. I've got to think of something, Michael thinks, watching her bony fingers push buttons through holes, feeling the same cold, bony fingers on his chest, dressing him when he was small.

"Not too cold this morning?" he asks.

"Not too bad at all," her long nose sniffing and twitching, preparing for the cold air.

"See you, Ma. Have a good day."

"Goodbye, son. I'll have supper at six."

"I might not be here."

She stiffens. "I've a pork tenderloin. I was going to make dumplings, too."

"There's a man I have to see about a dog. He suggested dinner. I'm sorry, Mum."

"Fiddlesticks. You'll do yourself no good with all that tearing around. I don't know what's to become of you."

"It might lead to something, Mum. I'd better go with him."

"Mind he treats you well. You're easily deceived about the nature of people."

"I'll do all right, Mum. Don't worry."

She shuts the door very firmly indeed.

Michael grins and clears his place by putting his dishes in the sink. Then he sits again, pours himself another cup of tea and re-opens the paper. It's only half past eight, for God's sake.

When he finishes his tea he trundles upstairs with the paper under his arm. Sits down on the can, opens to the sports page. Grunts, pushes, turns pink, stares at the newspaper. Nothing occurs to him.

He is forty-four, an awkward age for a man. If he hadn't met Sue he'd be thinking of himself as a failure. Certainly none of his jobs had lasted. No luck. He was a short-order cook once, a good one, but the owner said he was too fat for the galley. Wrote a few articles when he was living with Harriet, pretty good for his grade eleven education, but somehow her editors hadn't cottoned on to his tales, they wanted women's stuff instead, and they were damned suspicious of him, seemed to think that because he used her typewriter he used her head, though they admitted the writing was his own.

After she gave him the heave-ho, the bitch, he went down to Montreal for a while and lived with a French girl but she was a bust, too; it took him a while to catch on to the lingo but not as long as she thought: she'd sit there and boldly insult him to his face, thinking he didn't know French. He worked as a bouncer there for a while but it wasn't his style: he was big enough but he didn't like playing the tough guy. In Montreal it was wise to get out if you had a mug as English and hair as red as Michael Littlemore's.

So he came back here and drove a hack for a while – twelve hours a day. All right if it's a good day and everyone pays, but jeeze, the drunks in the middle of the night. Did pretty well on the horses for a while after that, got a decent wardrobe together, did badly on the horses, lost some of it and then, just as his luck began to run out, met Sue.

Good old Sue. And a fine figure of a woman, as they used to say, too. Well, more bust and less butt would suit him, but beggars can't . . . .

But she's straight about that, he thinks, she's straight about that. She knows I don't have anything. I've never had her opportunities: she understands. Not like Harriet, always screwing out a nickel here, a nickel there, I wonder she didn't ask me to pay for it, but, well, Sue doesn't have to run a typewriter like some awful mill of the gods, she's loaded and she knows it.

Michael Littlemore rises from his throne, pulls up, turns,

82

flushes, zips, turns again and washes his hands. He goes into his room and stands at his old dresser, bends his knees to see in the mirror, brushes his whiskers and his thinning hair. He changes his plaid shirt for blue broadcloth, the forget-me-not shade of his twinkling eyes, and puts on a tweed sports coat he found at the Salvation Army. It's a bit too small and hangs back from his belly like an old-fashioned cutaway coat. His scarlet vest is at the cleaner's.

He rummages in the closet for an unoppressive tie. Preens in the mirror. Thinks, and adds his father's Masonic tie tack. There, it hangs better: and he is a period piece. Grow the sideburns to muttonchops, she'll like that. A lot of trimming, though.

He is halfway downstairs when he realizes he is still in his jeans. She wouldn't like that; he'll hate giving them up, they feel like satin when you've got them worn just enough, but no, jeans are not Sue's style. Not polyester slacks, either. He rummages in the closet for his old navy serge and hopes he hasn't put on weight again. Yes, he'll have to dress better, but he's levelled with her and she's said she'll pay. Knows which end is up, he thinks, not like Harriet, the bitch. Must be panting for it.

His toilet complete, he turns out the kitchen light, leaving the dishes in the sink. It upsets the old lady if he lifts a hand. He sets the front door on the lock, takes his duffel coat from the hall stand, and goes out, slipping the toggles through the bits of frayed rope that are supposed to hold them. The sun is shining; he squints against the light; no warmth in it. Next winter, he sighs, we'll go south.

He decides to walk. Save sixty cents, and get at noon to the place he wants to go: Forbush Enterprises Limited. He wishes he had a gold-headed cane to swing as he advances towards the future. It is going to be a very good day.

The degree to which the city is increasingly non-Anglo-

Saxon, to say the least, continually agitates Harriet. It tests her poor, thin, Mission-Band liberalism and she wonders where it is taking her to. One way to deal with it would be to move to the suburbs, but she doesn't like suburbs. Forest Hill was a suburb when she grew up there, and it always felt wrong to her, too far from corner stores and the muggy reality of railway tracks she remembers only vaguely from their first house. If you live in a city you ought to be able to feel its texture, and how can you do that when the main concern of the neighbourhood is the quality of the lawns? The attempt to reproduce the playing fields of England implies forgetting they were planted and rolled by serfs.

But here, on the Gloag Street bus, there is no forgetting. When she and Mrs. Saxe get restless they go up and down on the bus, up to the subway, down to the King streetcar by the Massey-Ferguson plant.

"Our aristocracy came from manure spreaders," she says, "and tedders and harrows and the instalment plan. It always comes from the land, doesn't it, and making land pay?"

Mrs. Saxe's eyes bulge on the bus and what Harriet likes is that, when she sees anything she likes, she's as expansive as a melting Mr. Freeze running down Peter's or Patsy's face: she drools at the black babies encased in shocking pink artificial fur, in snowsuits that would be vulgar on pasty white ones but are luscious against brown skin until they've been two or three times to the laundromat. Her eyes bulge at Rastafarian braids and she takes delight in ballooned peak caps over woolly heads and accents that wobble in and out of English, students shouting to each other, "Mon?"

And on the buses there are so many others, too: prim-voiced ladies in saris, turbanned Sikhs looking wary, slouching or preening in their confusion at having become the new Jews; and the stout, winter-sallow Mediterranean people, hoarse-voiced, and women matronly among mobs of children, all possessed of burning, resentful black eyes.

But what's best, Harriet thinks, is that it's so hard to make generalizations. The blacks are obviously the most beautiful, the browns next; a busload in this neighbourhood is a busload of disseminated pride, territory, joy, despair, hope, resentment . . . flying feelings. Weariness, defiance: that child will not shut up, that mother will not move over so I can sit down (does she think I'm a tourist here?), the black kids on the way home from high school jive in the aisles, the Greek girls giggle and are all called Effie (Euphemia? Ephigenia?) and talk about boys – brothers and fathers included – the Portugeezers, as Mick calls them, are gap-toothed.

Some of them handle winter badly, dull and half-dead in grey and brown Canadian coats, braving puddles of salt slush in ugly, cheap boots (which last longer than the expensive ones – there is some fairness in the economy after all). Only the teenagers have life in February, the rest are as slack as Harriet and why not, coming home from the factories with bags of cut-rate groceries and gewgaws, dying, in their tropical love of colour, for something other than this greyness, which we were born to.

"It's hard," she says to Mrs. Saxe, to whom it is all a gorgeous travelogue, "not to think of us and them."

Mrs. Saxe nods her head towards two stately girls of banal colour and unknown origin, dressed in coats of Russian cut, buttoning up the side, trimmed with Persian lamb, real or imitation, from hem to neck. Wearing little square hats, looking magical. Until they open their mouths and speak another language, of origins undiscernable by Harriet, who has not taken nearly enough in school, and giggle in the accents of any high school in town.

"Melanie could tell us all about them," she tells Mrs. Saxe, "but they're neither disco nor punk and they don't look like Central Commerce either."

They shut their mouths and are two Russian princesses again, nodding, aristocratic, vaguely benign.

Harriet shudders, just a little. "We freed up the school system," Harriet explains to Mrs. Saxe, "so anyone from any neighbourhood could go to school anywhere. Except, of course, the Catholic schools, because that changes your tax base. What happened was that class settled in schools, not in neighbourhoods. Melanie won't go to the local, Sim went to North Toronto for the enriched program, the privileges go to the kids whose parents know the ropes. The Chinese are the ones who are winning, which is okay in its way, but confusing."

Homogeneity exists only in the very old. After a certain age, all the ladies are bag ladies. The hair is white. A few trembling WASP-ladies of uncertain status, hair cropped and curled in uniformly respectable bobbles and dyed a uniformly strawberry blonde, attempt to cut the world off because it's changed too much, but the rest, democratized by age, exchange nods and courtesies.

As with buses, so the bank. Harriet and Mrs. Saxe, behind the red cordons (Harriet twitching, hating the padded ropes, a new excrescence, that say, "Nobody who isn't respectable is let in," but having to admit they make the lines move faster), stand patient as oxen on Fridays, Harriet depositing or withdrawing, her mind cautioning her, "Provide, provide," Mrs. Saxe changing travellers' cheques in small, time-consuming amounts for a personal use that has never showed up in Harriet's accounts. The banks are a better racial index than the buses, for one hears the languages, the requests for interpreters, the whispered addresses for money orders for abroad. Sees the waiters' cheques, envelopes from restaurants Harriet will never dare take Mrs. Saxe to, the settlement of long telephone bills, queries over calls to England, Hyderabad, Jamaica. Even the Vietnamese phone each other now, she tells Mrs. Saxe, separated by charity, station-to-station all over the world.

The mean ones are the ones left behind, and they are now on the verge of being called poor white. Their teeth are bad, their age is showing, all they have is their long residence in the neighbourhood and how is the bank manager, who changes every year now, to understand that?

They sigh, they mutter. They see themselves surrounded by menials. Oh, yes, they have done this work, too: but it has bought them, in the end, not privilege but poverty. After five generations, their will-to-struggle has come to an end. They are sad, and if they were younger, they would fight.

"I'm only beginning to see the city now I've stopped driving the car," Harriet tells Mrs. Saxe. Dreaming of summer cottages and trout streams, virgin camp-grounds (when they went tenting with their father, it must have been as things were in India, but without a syce), anything to escape this crowding.

Then it is her turn to put the wages of Depressed Housewife into her account, removing from it first the burgeoning sum the support of them all requires.

CHAPTER FOUR

They were both blue-eyed, tall, handsome. So handsome, in fact, that they each, separately, learned to manipulate their beauty so that it would not be so great as to offend other people. They were called Roger and Olivia; they had both been at Oxford, though not at the same time. Roger, a Canadian, went there after his undergraduate work was finished, on a Rhodes scholarship. Olivia went, at seventeen, because her family expected her to go, and she was good at school. They met in Toronto.

They met in Toronto in 1968, they fell in love, so much in love that they raced around the city at night chalking R LOVES O and O LOVES ROGER; in 1970, Roger bought a house in Rathbone Place; Olivia moved in with him. Being Olivia, however, she maintained a toehold on sanity, and kept her old flat. Being Roger, he thought that a fine idea. He liked women who knew what they wanted, especially when they were Olivia and wanted him. They made a glorious couple, glamorous, Olympian, not too fashionable, either. Harriet used to see Roger and Olivia at serious outings, campaigns against foreign wars, fund-raisings for the restoration of old buildings, civil rights protests, not cocktail parties. They were beautiful, but not frivolous, Roger and Olivia, lanky, handsomely but inexpensively dressed, serious, side by side in the evenings, reading, in their horn-rims; well-matched, Economics and Statistics.

After seven years, however, cracks began to show. Olivia was not, after all, Canadian. She found Roger's political friends and their homemade wives dreary, and she lost patience with hiding the fact. Roger, who believed seriously and serenely that all people were equal, even Roger, remonstrated with her.

"Angela Kitron is not as good as me," Olivia flared back. "She stammers, she has bad breath, and she's fat. Harriet's dirty kids drive me up the wall. Damn it, Roger, you're as pious as a Methodist."

Olivia's aunts were always leaving her money. Roger had good ideas for the disposal of such gains. Olivia would have none of them. She bought not stock but mortgages. She didn't care whose mortgages she bought. If the payments lagged, she foreclosed. She did it all through a broker whom Roger disliked.

Olivia's Aunt Rose left her not only money but furniture. Olivia haggled with the customs broker and got most of it into the country free, as antiques. The house was suddenly crammed with what Roger called Regency Tat.

"Regency Tat," Olivia howled, "you and your Canadian country values, and you've never mucked out a pigpen in your life. At least I looked after my own bloody pony." Olivia bought her own house, decorated it beautifully to suit the Regency Tat, and moved in. Roger began to enjoy sleeping crosswise on his bed.

They remained friends, however, and lovers. There was far too much between them now – time, taste, proclivity – for them to separate. Even when they tried, they found themselves in the same parades and theatre queues. They lived a life of constant and tender reunions. They throve on it, were handsomer and more Olympian to their friends than ever.

One day last August, however, Olivia phoned Roger to

meet her for lunch. "And not in a health-food place, either. Let's make it the Courtyard Café. I feel like the Courtyard Café today." There, in the ferns, as Roger disdainfully scraped the sauce off his pâté, Olivia told Roger she was pregnant.

Roger beamed.

"Oh, damn it all to hell, Roger, I just thought I'd tell you before I got rid of it. I don't want a baby." She burst into tears in her brown linen table napkin. Several businessmen were severely affected.

"Never mind, darling, we can get married . . . anything you want."

"I want an abortion," she sobbed.

"I don't."

"It's my body."

"Your body is housing my child."

"How do you know it's your child?"

"Is it?"

"Yes."

"Well, that's that, isn't it? Your body is housing my child."

"We're fighting. We've been fighting for years."

Roger sat back, took a deep breath, and ordered them both hard drinks, something he seldom did at lunch. "Look," he said, tapping the table with his forefinger. "This is serious, Olivia."

"Of course it's serious. I don't want your child. I don't want anybody's child. I hated being a child and I don't want to be tied down to one for twenty years. I feel as if I had a growth or something."

"You're really sure, are you?"

"I had a rabbit test. Not frog, rabbit. Poor damn rabbit. I'm killing things already."

"I think you should take the afternoon off and go home and lie down and think it over."

"What do you think I've done the past six weeks but lie down and think it over?"

"You're looking marvellous."

"I always look marvellous. It's a kind of curse."

He was surprised at the depth of his instinct. "I do not want you to let that child go."

"It isn't a child, it's a foetus. But we have to do something, Roger. It will be a child soon."

"When's it due?"

"February."

He stopped eating and stared at her. At her broad forehead, now blotchy; at her long nose, now red at the tip; at her wide, beautiful long hands. English, he thought. Blood stock. Brood mares. Though actually her father was a doctor in Yorkshire; the aunts were Scottish: not rich, frugal. Everything women have said about men is right: I want you because you are beautiful, I want to breed on you.

"Let's have lunch again tomorrow," he said carefully, "and I'll be able to tell you then what I really think."

"I won't change my mind, Roger. I've never wanted a child."

"You'll give me time to form an opinion, though, won't you?"

She looked at him carefully, as if he were very dangerous.

"I guess so," she said, in a little, wilted voice.

They finished the meal in silence and went their separate ways.

After work, he went home and collected a bottle of Dubonnet and went across the road to Harriet's.

Just the sounds in Harriet's house at supper time are enough to drive an ordinary mortal crazy, Roger thought as he opened the door. Already he heard toilets flushing, chairs scraping, doors slamming, boots on the stairs.

"Hey, Ma, Roger's here!"

From the kitchen the sound of a spatula tapped on the side

of an iron frying pan, a child hawking and spitting, someone else calling, "Oh, no!", a milk jug picked up, gushing forth, plunked down again.

"Hi, Roger!" Harriet called.

Roger waved the bottle at her.

"Super. Go into my office, huh?"

The chair in her office had a sound, too, a gusty sort of sigh. He listened as he leaned back: a stereo was playing somewhere, a radio somewhere else. A tap was running, or was it the upstairs toilet he tried to tinker with for her? White noise, he thought, what you need is a tape of white noise, drown it all out.

"Whoosh," said Harriet, sweeping in. "Here are glasses, lemon peel. You're a genius, to bring a drink. I always think I'm impervious to them but I'm not. It's sausage night. What's the politico-economic outlook today?"

"Not bad."

"You look beat. Seen Olivia?"

Without meaning to, he stiffened.

"Sorry," she said, "didn't mean to pry."

Roger played with his fingers. "Tum," he said. "Tum-te-tum."

"Da, da, di dah. Well, if you don't want to talk we can always drink."

He tried to think of all their names. "Heard from Ainslie?"

"Yep. Last week. Gosh, I miss her. But her letter begins, 'Dear Ma, I love being a poor little rich girl in California' so what can I say? She's well out of this mess and she knows it."

"Harriet, why did you have them all?"

"Heck, Roger, I only had half of them, remember. The rest were Tom's."

"Well, yours, then. Why?"

Harriet put her hands in her lap and stared at the ceiling. "Not for any good reason," she said. "Honestly, I think it was just because I was mad smack in love with their fathers.

You don't have any big intellectual reasons for having a family, Roger; intellectual reasons are no darn good. Irrational reasons are the only things that get you through. God, that doesn't make sense, does it? See me in the morning if you want me to make sense. My head's a sieve by this hour. Another little smash?"

He stared at her. The din in the kitchen had lessened to a quiet munching. "I see," he said.

"If you think you do, you don't."

They finished their drinks. He excused himself and left the bottle with her.

"You tell me about it when you feel like it, huh?" she said as she saw him out the door.

Sidonia, the beautiful one, was coming up the walk. Only thirteen and far too able to wrench a heart.

"Hi, Roger."

"Hi, Sidi: you're looking well today."

"Like my new hat?" She brandished a sailor's cap with a gesture fit to set a man at her throat. "I ripped it off!" And skipped in, beaming over her shoulder at him.

He stared after her, thinking of something Harriet said once when he had evidently shown a snobbish displeasure at the children's rowdiness. "They're not kids, Roger, they're people. From the day they're born. Think of them individually, not collectively. By name. Then they're human."

He went home, read the agenda on his desk and made four phone calls. Then he went into the kitchen, and carefully slitting and slotting vegetables with a chef's knife, wrapping dishes in clean tea towels and packing them in a wicker basket, trimming a leftover of his own *pâté en croute* and roasting a chicken he had picked up at the last of the real poulterer's the day before, prepared a picnic. He phoned Olivia and asked her to meet him at noon on Philosopher's Walk, poured himself a cup of coffee and went into his study to think.

The baby is born on the third of February. Roger goes to collect both of them four days later from the hospital. Olivia looks pale, a little frayed, her hair still in a long hospital braid. She holds the baby almost maternally to her bosom and smiles at her in the car. She comes into the house and sits gingerly down on the armchair. Roger puts her hat on the coffee table.

"Did you check the list of supplies?" she asks.

"I think I have everything."

"Let's go over it again. She can't go out for a week, so if you run out you're stuck. Enfalac, bottles, sterilizer, vitamins, cotton balls and stuff, okay?"

"Okay," he says, watching her uneasily. The baby is in her lap, almost falling between her knees. She isn't looking at it.

"Lots of nappies, Roger, that's the real thing, lots of nappies. And don't be an ecologist and fart around with cloth ones, huh? The disposables are a lot easier. Come on, button," she says to the baby as she picks it up. "Well, Roger, here's your daughter." Holding the bundle out to him.

The bundle. He holds his arms out for it gingerly. Receives it awkwardly. Takes the small, light, grunting thing in his arms. It has a red face and a mop of black hair. It gropes towards his bosom. He feels rough and awkward. I must find something softer than a sweater to wear, he thinks. Its face will break out if it nuzzles up to a Shetland sweater.

Olivia looks at her watch and stands up. "Well, I've kept my part of the bargain; you keep yours, now. I'll call my taxi. I must wash my hair and put a face on before I get on that bloody plane."

He sits there, stunned, staring at his daughter. Olivia dials the taxi number. He realizes he can't drive her home; he has to stay in with the baby.

"Ten minutes to wait," Olivia says. "God, I'm out of shape. Bermuda will not be at all bad. I'll let you know my address when I'm settled in Montreal. I don't want to see her but I want to know if you're all right, okay, Rog? What are you going to call her?"

He is still staring at the baby, who has just managed to insert a minute thumb in her mouth, and opened her dark blue eyes in the process.

"Call her?" he says weakly, "I don't know. Olivia?"

"Don't be foolish, she'll be called Liver in school. Think of a name you like. Think of a person you like and call her that. You had a lot of good aunts, too, didn't you?"

That so small a creature should have a name seems beyond him; but names are important, surely, he has to find one and find one at once, in order not to show Olivia his terrible weakness, his writhing fear, the defeat of the hope he had had that she would not be able to bear to go, after all, as she had planned all the time; he had hoped that the maternity leave would run into holiday leave and then separation leave, and she would have had two months' holiday before she installed herself, svelte, in another city, another job. He stares at the baby, looking for traces of Olivia's will. Why, he wonders, did I never notice Olivia's enormous and determined chin before? The baby is lost in a mumbling dream and the blue eyes he raises to Olivia's are his own.

"Name? Name? Not Olivia? Anne? I've never known an Anne I liked. Aunts? Bettina? Never. Ha! Winnifred. That's good, isn't it? I can call her Winnie and she can be Fred, if she wants, on her own. Winnifred in one piece when she achieves dignity. Winnie, yes. Wyn with a *y* if she wants to be smart. Hello, Winnifred," he says, looking down and smiling.

"She gets her feed at four and don't let her get off schedule," Olivia says sternly. "The nurses have her perfectly trained. You do know how to change her? You'll find the tapes a merciful change from pins."

He remembers with a shudder sticking pins in his sister when his mother left him alone with her in the bedroom.

95

He'd got a beating with a hairbrush for that and resented it and his sister for years.

"Maybe Molly will help," he mutters.

Olivia sucks in her breath. "Oh, no, Roger, don't pull that one. Don't you just dare. You wanted a baby: you have a baby; you can look after her as women do, all by yourself. Here's my cab. Goodbye, you two." She goes out without looking back, her red fox cossack hat bobbing out down the walk towards the black and yellow taxi.

He sits there, stunned. Olivia has done what she said she would do, given birth and given over and gone. Without a smile, without a tear. Gone to Bermuda, and from Bermuda to Montreal. "There's no mother's instinct," she said. "Just doing what you've decided to do is enough. You'll get on fine, Roger, just fine."

He unwraps the baby from her shawl, and lays her out in his arms again. Her head fits neatly in the palm of his hand, her feet do not reach his elbow, she is not, in spite of her mother's height, a large baby. He traces her small mouth with his finger. She makes a snuffling kind of moan. Then he puts her down on the floor in the cot Olivia has told him to buy, instead of the old pine cradle he coveted ("Roger, your back!"). He gets a cup of coffee and a cigarette; then, thinking the baby should have something, too, unfolds a little flannelette blanket from a package he has bought (it had been a struggle finding good, plain baby things without bunnies on them). A little fist struggles out and hauls the corner of the blanket to the mouth.

He sits and contemplates the future. Olivia has made him promise to cope on his own for the first week, cancel engagements and get the feel of staying home and looking after her. Then a woman is coming, though she doesn't seem very satisfactory, from eight-thirty until four. After that he'll have to either take the baby – Winnie – with him or hire babysitters. It is going to cost a lot. Well, he thinks, it sounds very simple if you're organized, though no doubt it isn't, there's always a new thing in life to get your face rubbed into. "It's a twenty-year obligation," he hears Olivia say, "and I'm not into twenty-year obligations. I don't like kids and I don't want any. I wouldn't be having one at all if I hadn't gone all feminist about the pill. Teach me."

The baby, Winnie, coughs and begins a struggling sort of cry. He puts his coffee down and stoops to pick her up. Already her face is covered with lint from the blanket, and the little sort of jump suit she wears is drenched. Well, there is a card table laid out in the living room (Olivia has insisted on a downstairs changing place, as well), with all the equipment on it. He'll see what he can do.

He remembers his orders and goes first to soak a small blue washcloth in warm water. Then he puts it and the baby on the table and begins, with fingers that grow more and more enormous, to undo her clothes, wrestle the finger-sized arms out of the tight little sleeves. She doesn't like it, she doesn't like it at all. By the time he has her half-naked she is blue with cold, and he tries to work as swiftly and determinedly as Olivia, but his fingers are too big. He gets the top off without, he hopes, dislocating her shoulder and whips her legs out with a finger each, firmly, and rips the wet diaper off.

"Come on, Winnie," he mutters, "we'll get through this together."

She is howling, scarlet with rage, as he wipes her bottom, which seems to consist, unexpectedly, of an exaggeration of the female parts. He supposes she is too small to have any buttocks and wonders if boy babies are as blatantly male.

Winnie doesn't want him to wonder. He remembers the nurse at the hospital saying some babies hated being naked, felt insecure: Winnie is obviously one of them. He grasps a new diaper and slings it crookedly, too loosely, around her, fumbles among the clothes laid out on the table by Olivia, and chooses not an elasticized suit but a long flannel gown. It has rosebuds on it. He slips it over her arms, then remembers she needs an undershirt and begins all over again, Winnie squawling, himself determined but afraid of the weight even of his fingers.

By the time he has her dressed he is trembling. He holds her against his shoulder and sits down, heedless of what is to be cleaned up behind him. He feels the little heart against his shoulder (somewhere in the midst of the operation, he has taken his barbed-wire pullover off) going pit-a-pat, pit-a-pat, slowing a little, as the squawling that was not yet a sobbing stops. He strokes the little body with his free hand, and it soothes, it loses its anger that was fear, it calms. Slowly, he turns his head to the little scarlet face and puts his lips, more tenderly than they had ever touched Olivia, on the little face.

When she is quiet, somnolent again, he puts her back in the cot, and divides the soiled clothing between laundry hamper and garbage can. Looks at his watch. It isn't time yet for a feed. Olivia has told him to warm the bottle under the hot tap. He wonders if the formula is a duplication of Olivia's milk, or of mother's milk in general; dismisses the former theory because of what he knows about analysis costs, and sinks down to stare again at his charge.

He sees himself, then, what he has been and what he is going to be: no longer the tall, sure man who lectures, organizes, mocks, prompts, chairs, chides, but an unsure creature, gangling and awkward and coy as one of Harriet's teenagers (they'll come in useful, he thinks, and then, avoid Sidi at all costs, God, think of Sidi with a baby!), unsure, half drunk with fear and discombobulation, pram-pushing, vague, milk-scarred, forever fumbling in his Doctor Spock. He begins to laugh. No, he won't be that bad. But I'll be bad, he thinks, I'll make mistakes. You can't plan this trip. Theories don't work, you don't turn out a John Stuart Mill by changing its diapers. She's going to be like the other babies I've known, sticky and awkward and the bane of order. And he sees the two of them, himself grieving over the cradle of the feverish one, then, slowly, a fat forefinger spelling out words – no, that was too far ahead (but I will buy the cradle, he thinks, as soon as I can get out again, she's gone, I have a strong back, I will buy the cradle, so I can rock her as I read). He sees, now that he has washed and awkwardly dressed her, that his dream before she had been born had been a father's dream, a dream of formation, of education; but before that can happen, he now knows, there will be a period of sheer and servantile tending merely to keep her clean. (Yes, she is covered in fluff again, everything must be washed, washed again to take the lint off.) But by the time that is through, they will be a unit, Roger and his Winnie, so close. . . .

He closes his eyes for a moment, swallows, wonders if he had been wrong. She could have had an abortion. It was her business, not mine to interfere. Her business; not my body, hers. Yet I had to insist, whether she went or stayed. And she's gone. I feel so lost.

Children are not pets, he says sternly to himself. Children are individuals, citizens. This one doesn't like to be awkwardly, roughly peeled out of its clothes: that's what I know about her now. In ten years, I shall know more about her than I have ever known about anyone in my life. I shall know (and this gave him a surge of power) the thing women know.

And in fifteen, another voice says inside him, you'll know nothing at all.

He sleeps for a moment then, his head lolling back on the chesterfield. A faint, chugging sound wakes him. She is sputtering like an outboard engine that won't start, moving out of sleep into hunger. He tiptoes into the kitchen and puts a bottle of formula into a pan of water, as instructed, and holds it under the hot tap.

Then picks her up again, less awkwardly this time. She is wet. Well, she'll be wetter after she feeds. He loops the flannel blanket around her torso so she won't be cold and carries her over and turns the thermostat up. He finds he can do things with one hand while he carries her, she is so small.

99

Later, he supposes, she will wriggle more. Later.

She sputters and coughs as she tries to drink from the bottle. She drinks with her eyes closed, like a new kitten. It takes half an hour to get her two ounces down. Then he sits her up and taps her back as he's been shown; a lot of it comes up. More clothing to change.

By nightfall, he is exhausted. He carries her up to his room in the little portable bed – surely she is too small to sleep alone in a crib – and lies half-dressed on his bed until it should be time to begin the routine again. She snuffles piggily in her sleep. He thinks of Olivia, how she had been so strong, strong enough to defeat even that last stray hope of his that, in spite of the papers he had signed to make the child his own without requiring Olivia's presence, in spite of the plans she had made to change countries, change jobs, she would, at the last moment, wilt before the presence of the child, and stay. But Olivia is that rarest of creatures, he thinks, a woman of her word: when Olivia has decided – off with their heads. No wonder women like that are feared. It's because she's English and of the old, upper-middle-class school: she has that confidence they have, that feeling that it was right for them to own the world and tell the rest of us not only how to live our lives but even how, from their point of view (which to them is the only possible point of view, no weak relativity for them), lives in the past were led. So that they incorporated our pasts while they were manipulating our futures.

Yes, he thinks, you'd have to be very sure of yourself to leave Winnie. And yet he wonders. There was a shadow on her face, almost a nicker of pain, as he named the child: when she said, "You'll have to give her a name," or whatever she did say: and he said, "I shall call her Winnifred." She went to say something, then shut her mouth, and the expression on her face was almost one of pique, something Olivia isn't given to. She saw what she had lost then, he thinks: the

100

power to name. The power to be the be-all and end-all for the child.

The child, Winnie, snuffles again in its cot, four days out of the womb, accommodating itself to a lifetime of finding hidey-holes. He lies on the bed, smiling at his weariness, thinking, my hands are just too big and I'm still afraid I'll break her; but he sees himself growing as she grows, finding himself growing or shrinking like Alice, mentally and physically, to encompass or finally lean away from this new existence. It seems to him, for a moment, that he has become a garden, changeable, flexible, weather-vulnerable; no more the great male rock he is supposed to be, consistent, unchangeable. I will, he thinks again, know the things that women – no, parents – know. And he feels flooded with a great and almost political peace before he falls asleep, knowing she will wake him soon.

"Harriet," says Madge firmly, almost prodding her in the eye with an outstretched pinkie as she drinks her tea, "we've got to do something about Babs."

"I think Babs ought to be encouraged to do something about herself."

"She won't."

Mrs. Saxe's eyes are travelling the living room. Her feet are engaged in fending the spaniels off.

"She won't do a thing I tell her," Madge complains. "She's as bad as you were when you were a teenager."

The room is chilly and Madge is wearing an elegant ski jacket.

"I have a feeling alcoholics need to hit bottom and realize what they are doing to themselves."

"Think what she's done to Harry! To Sidonia!"

"She was hardly drinking at all when Harry left."

"Nonsense, they had cocktails every night."

"And I think Sidonia did it to her."

"Sidonia's a dear child. Her mother corrupted her. We must put her in the Clarke Institute, Harriet."

"It's pretty hard to commit anyone under the law as it stands now, Madge."

"Liberalism has gone too far. The woman is destroying my reputation."

"How, Madge?"

"Everyone knows she drinks!" Madge's eyes flash and she clashes her cup on its saucer. "Father will be rolling in his grave."

Harriet sighs. They've been through this before, talked to doctors. Only Babs can save herself, and Babs doesn't want to. "All we can do is refuse to talk to her on the phone."

"That's ridiculous. I can do much more. And I will."

Madge ushers them to the door and snaps it after them. Mrs. Saxe scuttles down the walk with Harriet in fear of her life.

"Babs," Harriet says, "she's after you again. Straighten up."

"I'll do whatever I bloody well want."

"You can't say I haven't warned you."

"Lotta good that does. How's my girl?"

"On the surface, very well. But I think there's a lot going on underneath."

"How can you tell?"

"I just feel it."

"Oh, Harriet, I'm sure you'll manage splendidly."

"Have you been out today?"

"Of course not."

"Pull yourself together, Babs."

"Why?"

"All you have is you, frankly; you ought to take care of it."

"Kee-rist," says Babs and hangs up with a bang.

"I've made it worse," Harriet says gloomily to herself.

"What would a good shrink do? Push her to a crisis?" And she wishes with all her heart that she had never had to meet one.

"She's at it again," says Madge. "Phoned me at three in the morning, raving. I'm going to have her locked up. Come at once."

"Melanie has the flu; I'm staying with her."

"You're shirking your duty, Harriet. Shirking. Mickles never shirk."

"If you can do it at all, Madge, you can do it yourself."

"No wonder she's out of her mind, with all the help she gets from you!"

"Just go over there and keep her company. Talk to her about when you were girls. Or something."

"You're soft, Harriet. You spoil everyone."

"I've got to go. Melanie's very sick."

"I'd like to see Aunt Madge in a pilot's helmet," Melanie gasps. "Like Snoopy. Oh, here I go again. What did . . . I do to deserve . . . this?"

"Nothing," says Harriet, "and you'd better remember that: a germ is a germ."

Sidonia comes back at eight and checks into Harriet's office, smiling like a rose.

"How's it going, Sidi?"

"Oh, beautifully, thanks, Aunt Harriet. We had such a lovely time."

"I bet," says Harriet. Whenever Sidonia is gushing, disaster is in sight.

"Is Mickle home?"

"He's down in the basement with Mrs. Saxe."

"I don't want to go down there."

"Go do your homework then, Sidi."

"You don't mind if I wash my hair?"

"Homework first, dear."

"Oh, dear, I'm a sight, but I'll do my French."

"Everything, Sidi, you'll do everything. It's like eating your crusts up to make your hair curl."

She makes a moue. "Oh, if you say so, Aunt Harriet dear."

"I do say so, Sidi."

"You couldn't possibly, could you, dear Aunt Harriet, do something about the noises Melanie makes in bed?"

"She snores, does she?"

"She . . . she farts. It's very upsetting."

"I suppose it is."

"I thought perhaps if I moved to Mickle's room?"

"Mick, dear, we call him Mick. He hates Mickle."

"When I say it, he loves it."

"Stop trying to melt me. No, you can't move to Mick's room. Yes, you have to do your homework. After that, if the bathroom's free, you can wash your hair. Okay, kid?"

"Tell me more," Mrs. Saxe says, "about Michael Littlemore."

"Michael Littlemore," says Harriet, "is, in his way, a greedy darling. Turn him over, he's a vampire with a mother. Michael Littlemore is big and fat and pink and round, a personal solution to the energy crisis – he radiates heat. I was a fool to marry him, but a lonely fool, and he kept me company.

"But when I was in the hospital having the twins my doctor leaned over suddenly and hissed, 'Get rid of that man.' I later discovered that Michael, the Authority on Everything, had told him how to deliver babies. While I was home recovering and nursing them, Michael went out to my magazines and told them how mistaken they were to hire me instead of him. He got assignments but, because he was at the racetrack, he somehow failed to produce. And once, when I was tending the children and somehow not quite up to making his bacon and eggs, he blacked my eye. I threw him out.

"I can't still quite say he's a bastard, Mrs. Saxe, although technically he is. He's as warm as a wood stove, but if you get too close you get burnt. He's a man so possessive he calls love into question, so sure of himself he calls self into question. I was angry at the doctor, I couldn't believe I'd made a mistake, but he's a martyr-maker, he makes you cry out, 'I've worked my fingers to the bone for you and what are you?' and that's bad for civilization. Because, though it's right to work your ass off for children, or for a roof over your head, a grown man who takes the Christian work ethic and bends it and twists it like a paper clip and takes the profit and the baby bonus to the race track. . . . And yet still sometimes I accuse myself of a failure of love."

CHAPTER FIVE

Marshallene phones and asks her for a drink.

"No, it's the Task Force meeting tonight," Harriet replies.

"You're going to vote with Roger, as usual," Marshallene says sourly.

"I'm going to vote as I was asked to vote at the Ratepayers' meeting. I'm going to vote on the tenders for removing the mattress factory. Roger will be in the chair."

"But you'll do what he wants. You always do."

"I'll do what I see fit."

"I don't see how you can go along with that crowd."

"What crowd?"

"Roger and his colonialist buddies."

"What colonialist buddies?"

"Look, I've told you a million times it's a bad project, a colonialist cop-out, and you keep stringing right along with them. I don't know what to think of you."

"My city has asked me to be on the Task Force designing a housing project for my neighbourhood. I've accepted; that's it. We've discussed it before, Marshallene. I am not part of some neo-socialist-capitalist cop-out; I'm a member of the mayor's Task Force, that's all."

"And who asked you to be?"

"The mayor."

"And who told the mayor to ask you, silly?"

"The Ratepayers' Association."

"Fuck it, Harriet. Can't you see a manipulation right before your eyes? We've been over this again and again and you never understand. It's Roger the do-gooder sucking you in."

"I believe in doing good. We need low-cost housing."

"What does Roger know about being poor?"

"Marsh, I'm late for the meeting."

"Harriet, you're copping out again."

Harriet puts down the phone, sighs, answers four homework questions and locates Mick's hockey pads, flies out the front door, fuming. Again and again and again. Every time she mentions the Task Force. And every time she doesn't mention the Task Force.

Marshallene, who is not active in any political party, hates Roger, who in a small way is very active in city politics. Harriet does not hate Roger, though when he is in high gear he frightens her, as people with IQS over two hundred do. Marshallene plays into her fear by telling her she is being manipulated by Roger. By the time she arrives at the meeting she is a pulp. If it were anyone else she would kick her, but she does not want to kick Marshallene. Oh, I do, she thinks, sliding into her seat breathlessly, I do want to kick Marshallene. I just want, more, to be superior by not kicking her.

"Now that we're all here ..." says Roger.

Mr. Green moves that the seats be changed so that all the smokers can sit together and leave himself, the non-smoker, isolated. The motion is carried. The meeting and the musical chairs have begun.

Harriet is seldom in the mood, when she first rises, to contemplate the subject of adultery, but today she wakes up, for no reason she can yet perceive, thinking that it would behoove her to do so. Nothing she can bring precisely to mind has led her to this conclusion: whatever it is, perhaps some fleeting corner of a dream, remains; like a tea towel flicked in the eye by a quarrelsome child, it has left a teary sting which will bother her all day unless she works it through; so she takes her coffee into the living room and tries to think.

Well: it's adultery, then, and there's no way around it, new morality or not. For six months she has been committing adultery with Vinnie. She has justified it on the grounds that, since Sylvia doesn't provide sexual services for Vinnie and Vinnie purports to want sexual services, she, Harriet, might as well provide them. Put coldly, it's that way. If he were single, it would only be fornication.

Of course, if you put everything coldly the world collapses in vilification.

Still, there is no glossing over this: by now it's a lump in her craw, best vomited or swallowed. She is doing something she has not been able to eliminate from her own morality as wrong; by doing it, she is making herself guilty and, because she is guilty, she is beginning to hate Sylvia: that's what is wrong.

But I've never really liked Sylvia, something desperate and childish inside her says.

No, Harriet, you've never much liked Sylvia, but you live across the road from her, she'll never move and you'll never move, and for years you've sent all the kids across to the aviary on the pretext that they might run errands for Sylvia; and you've sent little, dry bits of cake across to Sylvia, though she doesn't need them, and gone for coffee with Sylvia, never liking her much and hating her silly birds. And now you're sleeping with her husband and beginning to hate Sylvia.

Well, Sylvia isn't everyone's cup of tea: she's rude, she's malicious and she makes glitzy skating costumes.

Glitzy skating costumes belong to taste, not morality. You are in the wrong, Harriet.

Vinnie's very good in bed. He doesn't look it: but he's very, very good in bed.

Now you're closer to it: who wants to give up that comfort, that wondrous feeling in the middle of the night: the feeling that this is it, this is why we are alive? And face, probably, at your age, never finding it again? You're closer, Harriet. But you're still crooked.

I don't want to give it up, but it's making me uneasy.

You are now more than sixteen years of age.

When Sylvia looks at me, I see in her eye a larcenous gleam.

Bang on. Sylvia wants someone to pay for her accident. If she can get you to pay, why not? She is as bored by your children as you are by her birds: and face it, her birds are better looking. You're going to get in trouble, Harriet, if you don't watch out.

Damn it all, I don't want to hurt Vinnie.

If you know, Vinnie knows, Harriet: there's that much between you. If you don't treat him like a person, he's a sex object, Harriet.

Harriet narrows her eyes against the smoke trailing up into the dusty living room from her cigarette and thinks about Vinnie: his beige, conservative self unreeling into her body; neatness translating itself into deftness until she feels like a small animal balanced on the end of his prick. It is an act without emotional overtones, but singularly efficient in the production of happiness. But is it worth ruin? Nothing but the children is worth that, that's the truth of it.

"I have to give up Vinnie," she says to herself. Damn it all, there's something brewing, and Vinnie will have to go. She feels like whimpering. She feels the way Mick did, when he was the smallest, stammering out, "But isn't there anything left for me?"

She could tell herself it's better for the children that she has no lover, but she won't. Damn the children. They will have lovers, why shouldn't she? She could tell herself it's better for Vinnie: if she gives him up, he will have to confront his unhappiness with Sylvia. But she won't. She has to tell herself she is violating a rule–the rule that you should do something about a rat the minute you smell it.

Adultery is against the Bible; even if you don't read the Bible any more, it is also still against the legal code, of which Vinnie is a part, and probably against her own and Vinnie's generation's morality: she sees the lot of them trotting off to espouse what they think is twentieth-century morality, and ending up huddling together later in tears, all single and depressed. We don't do it gracefully, she thinks, because we were taught it is wrong. The fact that it is also human we can't deal with.

So is murder, Harriet.

This isn't murder; it's convenience.

Sylvia knows, Harriet, and she doesn't like it. Sylvia has you on the hip.

Yes, that's it; nothing to do with morality at all: a simple dislike of being on Sylvia's hip. Disgusting how things boil down to personal prejudices.

Wiggle out of it quick, Harriet, before it's too late. Vinnie can take care of himself.

Mrs. Saxe is in the office, pumping away on the exercise bicycle. She must have thighs like an ox, Harriet thinks. Damn it all, why does everyone have more character than me?

"I've got to work," she says brusquely, wading to her typewriter. Depressed Housewife is going to maunder on about adultery today. She won't have an affair: she never does anything she wants to; but she'll think about it, and much good will it do her.

On Tuesday the fourth, Mick has invited his psychiatrist to tea. Harriet gets up early and tidies and cleans the whole house, in case Mick decides to give the man the royal tour. She slices up cherry pound cake and makes two kinds of sandwiches, all the while telling Mrs. Saxe the story of her Aunt Edna, whose talent was slicing in half slices of sliced store bread. She gets more and more tangled as she explains this, and is in a panic at four when, with a great skid, Mick gallops his bike right up to the front porch. He takes a whirling tour through the house, slicks up his hair and answers the front door. Dr. Munster is prompt and courteous, the most beautiful man Harriet has ever seen. Mick gives him an affectionate look, marches into the kitchen, and piles all the tea things on the big tin tray they use when they are sick.

"Come on upstairs," he says to Dr. Munster.

At five minutes to five he brings Dr. Munster into the kitchen to say formal thanks for the tea and to be introduced to Mrs. Saxe. He sees Dr. Munster to the door and returns to see Harriet.

"Next time no tea bags," he says.

"That was for all of us, Mick," says Harriet, watching wistfully as Mrs. Saxe bags the last sandwich on the plate. "I'm glad you took him upstairs and not to the basement, though. I didn't get round to tidying the basement."

"Loose tea next time," growls Mick. "That wasn't home-made cake."

"Stop sounding like Michael and do your homework."

Mick stomps upstairs again.

"Maybe he talks better with his mouth full," says Mrs. Saxe, bursting into bubbles of laughter.

Harriet sits and glumly contemplates the return of the young to Utopia—clothes that have to be ironed, loose tea that browns the sink, real food cooked in non-atomic ovens. She vows to live, in her retirement, entirely on delicatessen sandwiches. With Dr. Munster, who makes her feel better.

The twins are doing their homework. Gradually Harriet becomes aware that their accompanying hums have words to them.

"Daddy has a girl friend," sings Peter.

"Yes, he's going to marry her," Pat replies.

"Is she nice?" Harriet asks finally.

Patsy looks up, blushing. "She's rich."

Peter says, "She has a Mercedes-Benz."

"He's fallen on his feet, then."

"He's going to work for her father's company."

"What one is that?"

"Forbush Precision Industries Limited," they recite, "manufacturers of patterns and stampings; tool-and-die cutters."

Harriet, foreseeing the fate of Forbush Precision, shudders and turns back to her work.

Harriet knows that nearly all of the children – the Ps are perhaps too young – have experimented with drugs; she has a strong feeling that, around the corner from the house, Melanie takes the pearl studs out of her earlobes, using Bob's silvered window for a mirror, and installs safety pins. She knows that Sim, for all his kindness and balance, has experimented with LSD and that the marijuana plants in Ainslie's room were never there for botany. Then there was the time Sidonia knocked herself out with nutmeg.

But what of Mick? she wonders. What's he snorting in his basement lair? When she goes down to clean it she finds dirty little cigarette butts and stacks of *Penthouse* magazines, safes (has he been blowing them up like balloons? Is he old enough to use them?), and what's this little brown bottle for, Rush?

Damn that Timothy Leary, she thinks, pushing drugs as a shortcut to change. Sure, something had to give, but why did it have to be the kids? Mine have missed the speed generation, thank God, but what else are they fooling around with? You can't tell them it's bad for them, they want to find out for themselves, and what are they doing to themselves?

112

Angel dust on the street corners, MDA, if it isn't the same thing, in the locker rooms, and half the high-school population dropping out because math is impossible from a marijuana dream. Red eyes in the sunset and only some of them will pull through. Five per cent of kids are a wipeout anyway, but I'm as unwilling to let any of mine collapse to fulfil the curve as I am to die to solve the population problem.

And the ones who aren't doing drugs steal or drink because, gee, Mum, we aren't doing drugs. Shit.

Down there in the dungeon, she hates Mick for hating himself. And comes upstairs, feeling ashamed.

"Well," says Marshallene, "what about treating alcoholics with LSD? Apparently they can see themselves, then."

"That's medical. So's heroin for cancer patients. Fine."

"I don't know what Toby's into in India. I figure if he still writes he's doing what he says he is."

"I hope so."

"People have stopped going to parties with little spoons around their necks."

"Hell, Marsh, I feel stupid about it all: square. When I see a cocaine spoon I see a stack of unpaid bills, and then I think how square it is to pay bills and push kids through a system that probably has no meaning any more."

"It's all we've got, though."

"Even you go along with it that far?"

"Even I do. I get mad as hops, Harriet, when I see you propagating it, but I don't see what the heck we can do but put up with what we've got unless we foment some kind of revolution, and none of the other ones has really worked."

"Some people say China has."

"I met a Chinese woman at the Writers' Congress who'd been four years in jail; she translated foreign books. Her son committed suicide; her husband was in longer than she was. What I figure is, I'm a writer, and where they jail writers, I don't go."

"When I went to France there were tanks in the streets

113

and machine guns outside the post offices. During Algeria. It's people without any kids who fool around with the idea of revolution, anyway," Harriet says gloomily.

"Without change, we stagnate."

They push their coffee cups aside, feeling foolish because they'll never solve the world's problems this way, though they won't solve them, either, by writing articles or film scripts or novels or Depressed Housewife.

"I'm dying for the spring," Harriet says. "I can get out in the garden. The only person who's come up with anything like a solution is Montaigne."

"You forget the inventor of the paper-clip dispenser," says Marshallene. "I'm off. Don't brood."

Well, thinks Harriet defensively, brooding, the Holy Spirit broods, too, doesn't it, or he or she?

The first whisper that Roger has developed a child is dismissed by Harriet as a juvenile rumour.

The second gives substance to the first and she begins to watch his house. But there is no sign, still, of any activity at an unusual hour of the day, and it isn't the season for baby carriages.

Mrs. Saxe, who persists in cycling in slush, claims to have seen a white-capped nurse at the front window. Harriet holds her peace. It is supremely interesting to find out what is going on in the street, but not always dignified. Certainly Melanie hasn't been asked to baby-sit.

On the third Thursday in March Roger is called from the chair of the Task Force meeting to the telephone. He returns brusque and rather white. He asks Harriet to take the chair. He has been called away.

At midnight he calls her at her house. "I ought to have told you this before," he says. "I've followed your example: Olivia and I made a baby, and I've adopted her."

"I heard something was going on, but I thought I'd wait until you told me."

"I didn't want to go around showing her off. Anyway, Harriet, she's sick and I need some things."

"How old is she? Can I come over and help? Is she feverish? Have you called the doctor?"

"I need a vaporizer and some baby aspirin. She's on antibiotics already. The doctor's away. She's almost seven weeks."

He is calm and businesslike. Harriet discovers she wants to hear a note of panic.

"I've only got five-grain aspirin; you can give her a quarter of one if you really have to, though some people think it's dangerous. I'll dig out the vaporizer and be over in a tick. I'm dying to see her, Roger."

She sees a red, struggling face under a mop of black hair, hears a seal bark.

"Oh, Roger," she teases, "your first croup."

"Do they do this often?"

"Not if you're lucky. Where's Olivia?"

"She's moved to Montreal."

"Poor baby."

"Winnifred, her name is."

"She's lovely, Roger. She's going to be just the right age in the summer. I mean, if they're too little they have a terrible time in the heat."

"I don't like this croup."

"It's ugly, but it isn't dangerous any more. Tetracycline's still red syrup, eh? You're marvellous to take her, Roger. You must be nervous as a cat."

"I discovered that I didn't believe in abortion."

"Winnifred's lucky you talked Olivia around. You'll have your moments, you know."

"I'll be late for meetings now and then."

"Her fever's not bad. She'll be right as rain in a day or two. You have a nurse?"

"Quite a competent woman."

"I can't volunteer to pull you out of all your flaps, Roger, but we're always here. Melanie's good with kids."

"She's awfully young."

"So's Winnie. Anyway, you can keep the vaporizer, I haven't needed it for years. When she's better, bundle her up and bring her over for an hour. She's less likely to make strange if she sees a few people." She looks up at Roger, trying to read his face. All she sees is a kind of benevolent weariness. She knows he's too proud to ask for help except in an emergency, but that's all right, she thinks: if we lived in each other's pockets nothing would get done.

Winnie begins to cough again. He puts a diaper on his shoulder and holds her tight. She squawls. She has little tight red fists. Harriet feels the first twinge of baby envy she has felt in years and fights it down. In no time at all she'll be telling the cat to fuck off, she thinks, letting herself out into the cold black of the night.

Depressed Housewife is not doing well this month. Harriet, in a good mood, has trouble acting out her dilemma. So what, the car's broken down and the dog needs to go to the vet and they're overdrawn again? She has no patience with Depressed this time: she ought, long ago, to have replaced the dog with a healthy cat. Much less trouble unless, like Smoke, the cat's purring around your feet for some unexplained need, like a different brand of cat food or a raw egg or a tidbit or what *do* you want? she asks, pushing it away.

The doorbell rings but someone else gets it, probably Mrs. Saxe, who's in the front room.

Mrs. Saxe, now at Harriet's door, announces, "There's a Mrs. Littlemore to see you."

Harriet nudges the cat and stands up, dusting the ash off her sweater as Smoke curls away. She follows Mrs. Saxe down the corridor and finds Mrs. Littlemore still in her worn black coat, fingering her old black purse and her tam on the settee. She introduces her to Mrs. Saxe, who for once volunteers (is it the age of the guest?) and says she'll put the kettle on.

"Is there something wrong, Mrs. Littlemore? It's always good to see you, but you do look upset."

"Have you seen Michael?"

"Oh, Mrs. Littlemore, I haven't seen Michael for months. The twins went to a movie with him last night, so he was all right then. Has he disappeared from home?"

"He disappeared from his bed last night and all there was on the supper table was a note saying he was unavoidably going to be absent. And I had a veal cutlet in, his favourite. I've learned to cook them the way they do in the restaurants, all for him."

She looks up at Harriet; she's a little girl whose dolly's been taken away. Well, thinks Harriet, he was my teddy bear.

"You know, Mrs. Littlemore, he does have a life of his own. I'm glad he left a note for you."

"It's not so much that, it's the not knowing, like, whether he'll be back and when: it makes me so nervous, Harriet."

"Mrs. Saxe is making tea. Let's use him as an excuse to enjoy ourselves."

"She's an English lady, is she?"

"Yes. I stayed with her cousin's niece when I went over there long ago, so she's staying with me. She's very nice."

"You can tell she's a lady. Shall I help her with the tea?"

"I will. I'll be back in a moment. You just hang your coat up and I'll make sure we have a nice cuppa."

Mrs. Saxe has managed with the teapot but is having a time reaching the good cups. She's no taller than Patsy Littlemore. Harriet gets them down, dusts them with the tea towel, and hunts for a decent sugar bowl. Mrs. Deans would have had cubes and tongs. Mrs. Deans was the sort of person Mrs. Littlemore would have approved of.

"We must be kind, Mrs. Saxe," says Harriet.

117

Mrs. Saxe brings the cream and sugar, Harriet the tray. They set it in front of Mrs. Littlemore. Harriet leaves to get the bit of frozen chocolate cake, which she cuts so thin it will thaw on the way down the hall. She hopes.

"Your son is Patsy's and Peter's father," Mrs. Saxe begins.

Mrs. Littlemore, who has never quite taken this in, looks as if Mrs. Saxe is accusing her of something, then recovers herself.

"Yes, he is," she says, "and he's gone away, and I don't know where he is, so I thought perhaps he'd come here."

"Young men are thoughtless."

"Oh, no, Mrs. Saxe, he's usually very good. Why, even when he was with Harriet he came and stayed with me. Sometimes a week at a time. He's been wonderful to me, my Michael. But lately...."

"Absent?"

"Absent."

They breathe in unison, meditating on the wickedness of sons.

"My Ernest," says Mrs. Saxe, "would go down to London to stay with his friends. Perhaps your Michael is in town."

"I live in town!" Mrs. Littlemore says fiercely.

"Ah, Mrs. Littlemore, there's town and town; that's it, you know, there's town and town: bright lights, green eyeshades, billiard cloths, tailors' bills: town and town, if not town and gown. Or town and gone. Never mind: he'll be back. Bad pennies."

"Michael is a very good man."

"A manner of speaking."

"I see."

Harriet returns to ply her with thin slices of cake. The paper napkins say *Merry Christmas*.

"My Mrs. Gore had those this year."

"How is Mrs. Gore?" Harriet asks.

118

"Failing, failing. You know, Mrs. Newell's people have moved her to a home. Mrs. Magee isn't doing at all well. Mrs. Fortune broke her hip."

"Mrs. Littlemore is kind enough to look after these ladies," Harriet says.

"Very good, oh, splendid," cries Mrs. Saxe. "I didn't know there was anyone left."

"I've been with Mrs. Gore for thirty-eight years," says Mrs. Littlemore, "and Mrs. Magee for twenty-two; we've promised each other we'll see each other through."

"Let's get the kids down," says Harriet. She bellows at them from the doorway. Mrs. Littlemore quails, and is soon engulfed in her grandchildren, who are old enough now to put false piety on. They finish up the cake and she gives them a quarter apiece and they fade without asking for more, to Harriet's relief.

"Well," says Mrs. Littlemore, "I'm ever so much better, now, Harriet. You have so much experience, I must say."

"Mrs. L.," says Harriet. "Michael comes and Michael goes. What happened to the cat?"

"He wasn't very affectionate. I was thinking of a bird."

"A parrot?"

"A nice canary, it would be more cheerful, like. Well, I must be going now. I'm sure you're right: he will come back."

Fortuitously, Sim comes in the back door. Harriet grabs him and asks him to drive Mrs. Littlemore home. Alone of the children he's old enough to respond to an eyebrow.

"Sure," he says, "I'll bring the car round to the front."

They pack Mrs. Littlemore in. She is frail, a little tearful, but relieved, safe with Sim.

"When I was first married to Michael," Harriet tells Mrs. Saxe, "that woman used to come round and clean, just to make sure he was properly taken care of. Who's exploiting whom? Give me a hand with the teacups and I'll get back to

Depressed. I can't get interested in her problems with the vet:
I mean, money can't be the only thing, though we sometimes
think it is."

Monday morning and, for a reason deeply hidden from his
mother, Tom's Mick decides that he will not only not go to
school but he will make a scene. Since unjustified absence is
in violation of an agreement she has with the school principal, Harriet routs him out of the basement by the shoulders, threatens to expose his privates by undressing and
dressing him in the kitchen in front of the others, and, finally,
slaps him. Mick howls and jumps up and down. The Littlemores grab their lunch boxes and flee. Sim is already gone.
    "Mick, don't be an ass," says Melanie, and gets a bowl of
cereal in her face for her pains. Sidonia is still upstairs, brush-
ing her beautiful short hair. Harriet wipes Melanie with the
kitchen towel and the table with the dishcloth.
    Mick takes a swipe at Melanie, taunting, "There she is,
the old slut!" Harriet straightens up, blood in her eyes, and
goes for Mick, who dances away from her with his fists up,
yelling, "A mother was chasing her boy with the broom."
Upstairs, doors slam as Melanie routs Sidonia from the
bathroom. Harriet grabs Mick with all her strength and holds
his head under the kitchen tap. She wants to stuff his nostrils
with Shredded Wheat and his ears with Rice Krispies and his
ass with Cheerios and kill him. He struggles away from her,
affronted.
    "You damn near drowned me."
    "Dry your head and go to school."
    "You could have killed me, you bitch."
    "Stop swearing at me; dry your head and go to school."
    She looks desperately at Mrs. Saxe but Mrs. Saxe is still as
a bird, an interested observer. Mick boots Harriet in the shin
with his bare foot and disappears down the back stairs for his
clothes. Harriet sinks in a chair, clutching her heart. She is

not sure if this is theatre or not, but if it is theatre it is better than running after him with the butcher knife. The house is shaking with temper now, doors slam and windowpanes shiver. Mick tears upstairs, hisses at her and runs out, without his lunch. To school, she thinks, or somewhere. Melanie thunders down.

"Mother, look at my hair, and Sidonia won't let me have the hairbrush!"

Slam, clatter, the hairbrush comes down the stairwell and lands on the telephone. Melanie rips at her hair, grabs her lunch and runs out. Slowly, in state, ten minutes later, Sidonia trails out, beautiful in her dignity.

"Bus money?"

"I don't need any."

"Nannies," says Mrs. Saxe, when the house is empty. "Nannies and boarding schools. Even after Mr. Saxe's reverses. We were fortunate."

Harriet says nothing. She still wants to kill Mick and she should be over being shocked at this and she never will be over it. She wants to dismember him, she wants to gouge out his eyes: the effrontery! She is all the witchy old women in the world who chase little boys and she hates herself, hates Mick, hates the world.

"If you're free today, Harriet," says Mrs. Saxe, "I should so much like to see the Science Centre."

"Mrs. Saxe," says Harriet, "I am going to take a sleeping pill and go back to bed." She stalks out of the kitchen, leaving a circle of bowls and puddles of milk and spoons and cereal boxes and Mrs. Saxe behind.

In bed, with the covers over her head, she thinks, this will pass, drat you for dying, Tom. Sim was never like this, Tom's Mick is the one. Whose temper is it? (Though she knows.) And oh, God, I can't stand another week of it. This is what death is for, getting out of it, and if there's an afterlife there's more of it and who wants it. And he scared all the others, or I did, and I. . . .

Now she remembers why she married Michael Littlemore: because they were all so dreadful at that age and she needed. . . .

But Michael Littlemore whacked Mick half-unconscious once, and that was the end of it.

Mick's been some use, she thinks, and I hope to heaven he's going to school and not peddling his ass down Yonge Street. Though she sees him in fragments, still and glaucous as jellied eels, murdered, dismembered by a vengeful mum. How did I get here? she wonders.

Her stomach is grinding and her teeth are going at each other like rivals but somehow she manages to fall asleep. She dreams she is in bed with Tom and it comforts her.

Harriet is not devoted to floor scrubbing; however, as Mrs. Saxe is drinking her four o'clock tea, she takes it upon herself to exorcise her guilty rage at Mick by cleaning up the mess around the cat's dish, which is beside the kitchen register. Sidonia's silver tones waft through the opening.

"Mickle, dear," she begins.

"Wha?" says Mick, dropping a wrench.

"Mickle, what are you going to do for money?"

"Gessum summer."

"What's that, dear Mickle?"

"Getsum sumwer."

"Haven't you any idea where?" Moving closer.

"Hamme that. Gimme thother."

"Is this what you want? Your speech is really becoming much clearer. How horrid for you to have had all that trouble. Really, the adults don't know what they're doing to us, do they?"

"Not er fault. Mouf's bad, thasall. Twoperations."

"Oh, yes, but she doesn't help, really, does she? Always fussing about this and that and talking about money all the time. And my mother's much, much worse. Driving my father out like that."

"He jus lef."

"My dear, she drove him to it, with all that whisky she drank."

"Ma sezzits gin."

"So déclassé. Mickle, we just have to get away, and I think I know how to do it."

Mick's beloved wrenches drop on the basement floor, and, on hands and knees by the register, Mick's beloved mother listens very carefully indeed.

"Yesterday, in little Peter's room. . . . "

"Whatcha lookin for in there for, money?"

"Oh, no, dear, an eraser!"

"Keepya fucking hands off Sim's things."

"Peter has the loveliest revolver, Mickle, it looks just like a real one!"

"So?"

"Well, really, we could solve all our problems by just taking it to a bank. We could put nylons over our heads and wear jeans, nobody would ever know. And really, Mick, nobody else will help us, so we have to help ourselves!"

"Gerah!" roars Mick. "Get outa here . . . you wanna fuck me up like you did your dad? You wanna spend your life in jail?" In rage he is articulate at last.

"Mickle, people who have money to put in a bank got it by ripping people off. Nobody really works, you know: it's just a legend. They just go around ripping each other off. So we rip them off and. . . . "

"You're crazy."

"I'm not! All this talk about honesty your mother gives is bullshit. What does she do to get money? She just types out a few words about women and she gets enough to keep us for weeks except, of course, she spends it all on herself."

"All?"

"Cigarettes, and all that sherry she gives her friends. Last week she had *two* new pairs of tights."

Silence.

"Getta hell outa here. Don't want you back again, see?"

"Mickle ... darling ... we're lovers; friends, cousins. You just let me manage you and—"

"Wanna monkey wrench in the face? Outa here!" He roars like a lion. Harriet would swell with pride if she weren't straightening up to show she hasn't heard.

Sidonia comes through the back door shaking her head.

"Really, Aunt Harriet, I am distressed about the condition of poor Mick. He just threatened me with a big black wrench."

"What did you do?"

"Why, nothing! I mean, I just have to stand there looking, well, like a girl, and he explodes. It must be the age he's at. You should talk to his psychiatrist. He's in a very delicate condition."

Mrs. Saxe, munching on cornflakes, mumbles, "Hoyden."

"Oh, Mrs. Saxe," says Sidonia, "you do overstay your welcome. Could I have some cornflakes too, Harriet, dear, or will they spoil my figure?"

"All you want," Harriet says, shoving the box towards her and putting out a bowl. "Excuse me, now. I have a phone call to make."

Returning to the problems of her old sustainer Depressed Housewife, Harriet wonders if she shouldn't, perhaps, give her an affair. But *cui bono*? And where would Depressed meet a man anyway? She's imprisoned by the demands of her elderly crippled mother and her asthmatic child: it is hard enough for her to get out once a month to lunch with the people she used to work with; so hard, in fact, that the luncheon meetings become great balloons of fantasy before they happen, thus are always disappointing. And there aren't any men at them, except perhaps waiters, and who picks up the waiter at lunch? Someone Melanie's age, not Depressed.

What are the men, other than her hard-working, snappish husband, in Depressed's life? Her son, the furnace man, the telephone repair man, perhaps; the man who collects for the cable TV? He comes in the evening and would be paid by Jim. The grocery delivery man? Nonsense. There aren't any more icemen (and Harriet always admired them, their great biceps frozen against their sack-covered loaves of ice) or milkmen – well, perhaps in the suburbs. But of course Depressed is middle class, and anything like that would be infra dig. Or would it? Has any of Harriet's friends ever confessed to running after the milkman? Not even Marshallene.

Harriet realizes that she herself rarely meets new men. Oh, the odd soul on the Task Force, but the Ratepayers' Association is practically a church Couples' Club, and down at *Maga* the men are either skinny coffee boys or portly executives beyond the reach of female charm. No, you have to go out and work with people to meet men, or do what Marsh does, grab a friend and go out to a bar, replenishing your glass from a mickey in your purse when you're broke. *Maga*'s readers ought to be let in on that trick.

Back to Depressed and her son, Marshall Prout. Something's gone wrong with the wiring in her freezer and she has to get Marshall out of bed to help her save all that meat. And of course the chill makes him wheeze.

Oh, give her some fun if she's not having a lover, Harriet thinks. This chronicle of domestic dreariness has been heavy as pudding for years. Cheer her up. One year she kept parrots – just a few little Mexicans, not Sylvia's menagerie – another, she tried to train a dog. (Marshall was allergic and it had to go.) What can she do now? This time of year is dreary enough for any living soul. You don't dare wash the windows for fear of what you'll see outside.

She hears the mail slide onto the floor. Ha! The seed catalogue; that's it, the seed catalogue, and all those beautiful names. Hosta and vinca and bellis and Astolat delphiniums. Shall we have clematis Nelly Moser or Gypsy Queen? Zephyranthes, otherwise known as fairy lilies. Tuberoses (what books were tuberoses an issue in?), Gerbera, Clivia, Montbretia and all the expensive, lovely amaryllis. Lilies and day lilies with their Pearl Buck names – Black Dragon, Destiny, Green Magic, Imperial Silver, Lady Inara, Pink Heaven, Distant Shore, Wild Wine. Oh, yes, let her lay out her garden: a mass of pink here, a scarlet to orange bed over there (Siberian coral bells, marigolds, miniature canna, calendulas and gaillardias): something, let her succeed at something. Shades of all the lady gardeners in English detective novels, and why not? Everybody's got to have something.

Harriet has a black thumb herself and finds it a dubious proposition that lilies are of more value than love affairs. But if Depressed loses Jim, who's not apt to tolerate bad behaviour – in fact, he doesn't tolerate any behaviour at all – she's in a fix Harriet can't get her out of, and Harriet loses her living. Hemerocallis, then, and clematis up the front porch. They'll die, too – everything dies on Depressed – but not yet; give her a little dream.

It's a bright day, a cheerful day, and the world has oeen responding to the weather by ringing at Harriet's telephone and knocking at her door. Roger pops in for a cup of tea before relieving Winnie's nannie.

"How's motherhood?" Harriet asks.

"Hello, Mrs. Saxe. Harriet, the world's greatest invention is not the wheel but the disposable diaper."

"When you start forgiving mums for being late for meetings, that's when I'll know you have changed."

"I'll start taking her to meetings soon."

"There's a poet in Montreal who takes his daughter everywhere; but I dunno, Roger: they always squawl just at the moment when the chairman is reading out the motion. She'd be better home in bed. Heavens, who's that? It never rains but it pours."

It is Bob Robbins, who slouches into the kitchen with his head forward and his chin farther forward. He glares at Mrs. Saxe.

"Yep, I knew she was harbouring you. I knew it would be her." Pointing his finger at Mrs. Saxe, who smirks and squirms. "The little old lady who's been using Mick's viewy-hole. I said to myself, she's got an eye like an old poached egg, and the only person who'd harbour a creature with an eye like an old poached egg is Harriet. So here I am."

"So you are," says Mrs. Saxe, with a titter.

"My work," says Bob, "is an intimate thing with me. I chose to share it with Mick, not you. I beg you, madame, to desist."

"That's better," breathes Harriet. "Tea, Bob, or instant poison?"

Bob pulls out a mickey. "A little orange juice? A little ice?"

"Sure."

They sit in silence and Bob doctors his drink with great seriousness.

Finally Harriet asks, "How's Fred?"

"Fred who?"

"I don't know . . . Fred. You know, your Fred."

"My Fred." He looks innocently around, a boy who has stolen an apple and will not confess. "Oh. Fred. Well. Sometimes."

"Sometimes what?" Roger asks crisply.

"Roger to you, goo."

Mrs. Saxe offers him a breath mint. He takes it ceremoniously on a dampened fingertip and places it on the end of his tongue. Curls his tongue, swallows gustily.

"Reparations." He washes it down with his drink. "Fred is not what he ought to be."

They contemplate the nature of Fred, again in silence. The front door slams with the beginning of the avalanche. Patsy bounds in.

"Hi, Roger. Hello, Mr. Robbins, Mumsy, hello, Mrs. Saxe. Hey, guess what? I need a math tutor. Miss Fulcher says I need a math tutor."

"Sim will help you."

"No, she says you've got to hire me a math tutor."

"She can say what she wants. Sim can help you. Or Mick, or Melanie."

"Mum, I have a *right* to a math tutor."

"Let's not argue about it now, dear."

"Mother, she said, 'Patsy, you need extra help; I'll call your mother and give her the name of a math tutor.' If you don't get me a math tutor you're depriving me of a right to an education. And in the year of the child!"

Bob Robbins turns and looks at her sourly. "You're fat," he says.

Patsy, thunderstruck, blushes, and opens her mouth. No words come out.

"You're fat and self-righteous and ugly, and you've been sneaking looks in my viewy-hole too. The year of the child! You're not a child, you're a judgement on Harriet for indulging in foooooor-nication. Who said you had rights? Somebody put you up to it. You're not smart enough to know right from left. Buzz off, kid."

"Bob!" says Harriet.

"Mother, are you going to let this man insult me in my own house?"

"Patsy, I think you'd better leave us alone. Bob isn't in a very good mood today."

"I'm not fat," Patsy cries. "I'm not self-whatever-it-is. I'm not stupid. I need a math tutor and it *is* the year of the child. If you don't do something about Mr. Robbins, I'm going to sue you."

"Go to your room, Patsy. I think I'll have some of that

128

vodka of yours, Bob, if you don't mind." Blast the bastard for airing his tonsils. "Roger? Some for you?"

"No, thanks," Roger smiles. "Are they giving civil rights lectures in public school now?"

"She's picked it up from somewhere. Bob, she's only a kid, you could lay off."

"She's a fat, stupid kid."

"Not stupid, if she's talking that way. Think back to when you were ten, huh, and I'll tell her to leave the viewy-hole alone. You should close it up, anyway." Though she knows he won't; he needs that much of an opening, no more, to give him enough to complain about.

The clouds roll over the new spring sun. The kitchen darkens. The tea is cold, Roger stands up to go home. Harriet shakes her head.

"I smell trouble," she says. "Funny, it creeps up like the beginning of a cold in your chest: like fog in the lungs."

"I've got to get home."

"Try training Melanie to look after Winnie instead of taking her to meetings just yet. That's the best way to do it."

"When I'm old enough."

She sees him to the door. When she gets back, Bob and Mrs. Saxe are raising fresh glasses to each other. "To the year of the deer," Bob is saying. "And the year of the ape and the gnu and the camelopard and the poetaster, but never. . . . "

"Lay off, Bob," says Harriet, failing to hear the rest as the tribe comes thundering in.

CHAPTER SIX

In the motel doorway, Michael stops, turns, takes the key out of Sue Forbush's hand, reinserts it himself and turns it, shoves the door open, and picks her up.

"Oh, Michael!" she squeals.

"You don't need women's lib now, baby. You've got me," he says. And holds his breath, because he has almost dropped her on the floor.

Vinnie Palmer is, above all, a man of regular and healthy habits. He leaves the office precisely at five, and when the weather is good, he walks the two miles home. Because he is a disciplined man, he checks the tendency of his mind to turn this walk into a mental ramble by picking, before he leaves the office, something to think about. Sometimes a case he is working on, sometimes something in his personal, emotional (though he does not call it his "real") life; sometimes he plans alterations to the house or the aviary. Tonight he has decided to think not of the eavestroughs or the lories' enclosure or the Standish-Devening suit or the Prsytasny hearing, but about sex.

He has decided to think about sex because tonight he has a feeling about sex: there is a tide moving in him like the tide that washes the alcoholic, guiltily, against his conscious will,

130

to the liquor store. Vinnie does and does not want to make love, but he knows he is going to make love. Ordinarily, because of the circumstances of his life, Vinnie accepts this ambivalent impulse with what he hopes is wry humour, but lately it has come to bother him so much that he knows he has to carry out what he describes to himself as a Thinking Project about it. He is aware of many of the ironies involved, but not sure that he is aware of all of them. He steps across Bay Street and it is potholed with the possibilities of sex. He marches down University Avenue, declines to count the green-budded tulips. I must think, says Vinnie to Vinnie. And he thinks.

There is nothing wrong with the urge to make love, he decides; he decides that he has always known this. There is nothing wrong with the urge to make love's occurring weekly on Thursdays. He is a creature of habit, after all. He does not scorn himself for being a creature of habit, because the development of habits is what all education and all psychiatry tend to. If you are trained at an early age by a kind mother who was once a kindergarten teacher to go potty at precisely the same time each day, which is precisely half an hour after you rise from the bed that you will neatly make, you are bound later in your life to become a creature of habit. If it makes you want sex on Thursday, well and good. Vinnie would be more worried about himself if he did not want sex on Thursdays. He is only thirty-four.

What is it, then, that is causing this unease, this feeling of armpits and sandpaper, that he finds hard to bear? He does not resent being a creature of habit, true. He does not resent wearing pleasantly ironed cotton shirts (blue and white striped, today) to his office, and neat, knotted ties (he wears the knitted, narrow ones, which are harder and harder to find, but comfortable), because he knows he will get on better if he does what is expected of him. He went through a stage of trying to be a hippie and this was a failure. He felt wrong; therefore, he looked wrong, and he found that his life

131

went badly because he was not dressed to go to court at a moment's notice. He decided that the beards and ankhs should be left to his friends who were beard-and-ankh types; that he was square; that he did not mind being square. He was a successful product of a successful mother. He would have felt worse, he decides now, if he had one streak of rebellion in him. Sometimes he thinks, those chaps know something I do not know; but he knows that they are no happier than he is. He is, in fact, with his habits, his narrow ties, and his Thursdays, probably happier than they are.

No, that is too big a generalization; he is happier than A in the firm, who has to have blondes and fast cars but has not, now, quite the energy to keep up with the demands of his desires; he is happier than B, who wants to be a Famous Barrister and can find no way to be one. But there is something in himself that he disrespects, something that this Thursday sexual impulse emphasizes. That's it, he says, looking at the orderly flower beds beside a quite amazing white and bronze monument to a distant mutiny, there is something: it makes me feel like Pavlov's dog: I am drooling.

He has a wide mouth and a long, bristly blonde moustache: fairer than his hair. He rubs his fist along his mouth and feels no drool. No, I am not Pavlov's dog; but close enough, and do not want to be. He turns along Queen Street and pokes by the antique stores, browses through stalls of used paperbacks; sheers past new chi-chi restaurants. And do not want to be.

I want sex; but I don't want sex always on Thursdays; it turns me into Pavlov's dog. It is normal to want sex, and it is normal not to want to be Pavlov's dog. What now?

Further, he says to himself, further. Vinnie: dig further, harder, badger yourself. What do you want?

I am going home, I will therefore picture home, he thinks. Sees himself walking up the ramp to the house, opening the always-welcoming door. Setting his briefcase down in the hall, hanging his raincoat up. Rambling into the kitchen. He sees Sylvia is at the sink, peeling the vegetables. He lifts the back of her hair and pecks her neck. The birds are singing. He goes to the aviary. He talks to the sick ones in the isolation cage first, moves on to Joey, who is already jealous. He tells Joey how his day has been. Joey forgives him and lets him stroke his beak. "Poor Vinnie," Joey says, "poor Vinnie." He opens the cage door and puts his shirtsleeve through (having of course taken off his jacket and put it over his kitchen chair) and waves to the lorikeets, who flurry round him, making their Poor Vinnie noises as best they can. Then he bows formally to the lories, who bow to him with all their dignity and emit their liquid droppings. If there is anything new he leaves it alone; you've got to give them time. Finally, knowing himself to be watched and discussed and much criticized, he moves on to Sam and Agnes, who, with eyes as old as turtles' and beaks sharpened to needle points, are waiting for him.

"Sam, Agnes, good evening."

"Garp."

He turns back to Sylvia, who is blondely wheeling her chair to the stove to pop the vegetables in boiling water. He gets the martinis out of the fridge. He does not mind routine.

Some people mind routine, he thinks, turning up Spadina; Harriet minds routine very much. She even minds the routine inside herself, the tendency things have to become routine. She wants everything new every day; with six – or is it seven, now? – children, she manages to get it, but her minding routine has not been good for the children, though she can never see it. "It drives me to distraction," she says, making another timetable, sighing over a new schedule of assignments that will never come to fruition, "the regularity with which all these things have to be carried out. The number of times they have to be *fed*. Food is bad for you. Food makes you fat. Food gets stuck in your breathing tubes and chokes you. Food has too much roughage or too little, too many calories or too few, and every time I pick up the paper I read about how bad it is. I just wish there was a machine to mash potatoes for this zoo.''

Every night the children get hungry at five-thirty; she puts them off for an hour so she can try to find someone to mash the potatoes. Finally, sulkily, she does it herself. She hates routine. The tendency of all things to become shepherd's pie.

He thinks himself back to home now, watching Sylvia turn from the stove and reach out for her martini. His mind is wandering. He turns his mind strictly back to the subject of conversation: Vinnie *v* Vinnie, for the night: sex. What is it I do/do not like about sex?

This brings him back to Sylvia. When he and Sylvia were first married, they indulged in a number of acrobatics. After two years, Sylvia wrenched her head around and said, ''Yuk.'' He could not help but agree. He could please himself but pleasing Sylvia was complicated and undignified. Now, on Thursdays, unless she has a committee meeting or an interview, he wanders over to Harriet, who has never been known to say yuk; acrobatics are not, with Harriet, necessary. And, since she has no husband, the arrangement is extraordinarily convenient: guilt-free, neighbourly, not without affection. Vinnie's presence in the house does not scare the kids; Vinnie's visits to Harriet do not scare Sylvia: neat-o, a phrase he picked up in Harriet's house.

But it rankles, it rankles; a piece of thistle in a waistband, a nettle sting.

What do you want, boy, passion? This voice comes to him from the wise old beaks and horny eyelids of Sam and Agnes.

If I wanted passion, he thinks, if it were passion I wanted, if there were . . . a face looms up before him. He tries to wipe it away. It recurs.

''Vinnieeeeee,'' a big voice cries. He seems to wake up, blinking like a bird, in the arms of Marshallene. ''Vinnie, you old sod, you were crossing against the light, you almost got. . . . '' Marshallene is handing him his briefcase. She has a suitcase in her other hand. Her hair is cut short and frizzes out around her head. There are white hairs like wires forcing their way through the black.

"Marsh. Was I really? What a clod."

"Thinking about women again, you horny old bastard. You moved right out against the light. If I hadn't grabbed you, you'd have been a goner."

"Gee, thanks, Marsh, I guess you saved my life."

"You bet I did."

For a big woman she has small teeth. Her big round eyes are as green as gooseberries. Somehow he feels he has come to the crux of his problem, but that it is not a crux that would please Marshallene. My neighbour, but not, thank God, my spouse. Here stands, having saved his life, all that bothers him about Woman.

"Jeeze, Vinnie, you should take better care of yourself." Bad language.

"Where are you going with that suitcase?"

"Down to the bus station. Going to this island for the weekend. Thought I'd walk until I got tired. That kind of day, isn't it?" Prescience.

"Island?"

"Bunch of women: feminist colony. You wouldn't like it. All big girls and no brassieres. Feel good, look like jelly." Vulgarity and, more maddening than that, vulgarity backed by truth.

"Well, gosh, I hope you have a good time." She brings out the gulping adolescent in him. Makes him feel gawky, all knees and Adam's apple.

"Listen, it's early yet. Don't you feel you need a drink?" Manipulation.

"No, actually."

"Well, you owe me one." Brash truth.

"Maybe I could ... ?"

"No promissory notes, Vinnie. We're a block away. I'm going to haul you into the Paddock Tavern." Cavewoman.

She was Miss Sombrero Township in 1951 and it tickles

135

her and she never lets you forget. She is enormous now, in her forties, big, or as she will tell you, large as life and twice as natural. Hungry and thirsty and not after righteousness. Harriet's kids have two words for everything, gross and neat-o. Marshallene is gross.

"I'm going to the island," she says, in the dark, sour room, "but I don't know if I want to go."

"Oh," he says, receding a mile a minute. As she drinks, she grows: she swells like the face of the Cheshire cat; her eyes are greener and greener, her curls are aggressive pubic tendrils, her little teeth are pegs. This, he thinks, is the writer who has been called "a sensitive and, what is rarer still, energetic critic of Ontario society," and "a poet of super-consciousness"; this–creature–sitting hunched, like Sam with pneumonia (Sylvia got him through), this . . . paragon of literary art, this woman who makes Harriet call herself "not a real writer" (and what is a *real* writer?), is saying, "Well, you know, I split up with Gord and I cried all over Ev and she told me I was male-centred so I. . . . "

Vinnie abstracts himself, hunting a greener field. Marshallene plucks his sleeve. "Vinnie, you goddamn square, listen, there's something I've been wanting to. . . . "

Vinnie gathers his whole body into a wince. Marshallene, as if she had taken a course in interpersonal relations, fixes him with a bonnie eye. "Fuck," she says.

It's not, Vinnie thinks, that I object to women without brassieres. It's characters without brassieres that bother me: ooze and jelly. I am, whether I want to be or not, a neat man.

"What is it?" he asks.

"Never mind. Just get me another and bugger off home and do whatever you do to Sylvia. You're not on my wavelength. You can't stand me. Toby. . . . "

"Toby?" Her son.

"Toby writes from his ashram that I represent cultural indelicacies."

Guiltily, Vinnie tries to think of something to countermand that.

"The trouble is," Marshallene says, "that I know damn well I do."

Vinnie tries to think of something to say.

"If you don't get out, Vinnie, in another minute I'm going to ask them to play 'Melancholy Baby.'"

Just don't ask me to love you, Vinnie thinks. I never liked dates; Mother was so excited when the war ended, she said we could have dates. Then he remembers that this is not something his mother said to him; it is something Marshallene said her mother said to her: how, when the dates came and there were camels on the cellophane, she thought it would be heavenly and it wasn't; they were sticky and sickly sweet; it was the first time she understood "there's no accounting for taste." She is rewriting his autobiography by existing and talking too much: damn her. He orders another.

"Tell me about this island."

"I haven't been there before. But when Gord broke off with me I phoned Ev and she said.... What the hell do you care?"

"Not much. You're always breaking off with people and phoning Ev."

"Nobody's perfect."

"I want to hear about the women in floppy T-shirts."

"Not unless you tell me what you and Sylvia do for sex."

"Not on your.... "

"Don't say Nelly. She's a sacred name in the Movement."

"How can you be a writer and belong to a movement?"

She opens her mouth to reply but does not; sitting like that, one fist curled about a drink, she looks as tough as a longshoreman in a left-wing movie. He wants to say, "Tell me about Sarnia and the longshoreman's strike in 1948," but he thinks again and says, "Doesn't it affect your work, the whole feminist thing?"

Her eyes pop back into her head; she closes her mouth; collects herself. If she talks about her work, she'll be okay, he thinks. Work is safer.

"I mean," he says, as carefully as he can after much dreaming and three drinks, "I mean, politically oriented people are even less able to see what you do, probably–which is presumably write what you feel you ought to write or want to write or must write, for your sake or its own sake and no one else's–than even me. I don't read much fiction, but at least I don't have an axe to grind." He hesitates again, gulping, wiping his moustache with the back of his fist. "Waiter, two doubles for the road. And what they want is some kind of party line, which you are tempted by because party lines are beautiful simplifications, but at the same time simplifications bother you because you have led–haven't you?–a complicated life; so because you are honest, you can't write that way."

Something happens now. She looks pleased and proud, and in a strange way, she starts to soften: not melt at the edges, as he has presumed she would, but sit up and become thinner and prouder.

"I don't read much fiction, as I said; but I read your book about the pioneers. You didn't pull any punches, did you? You didn't accept the clichés. I felt you pulling yourself up by your bootstraps. . . . "

"That was what was wrong with it, and. . . . "

"No, listen, I felt you pulling the material out of the ditch. I felt you wringing it out and worrying over it, and I felt, this is the only thing I've read about my ancestors that isn't bullshit. That was good, Marshallene."

Tears spring to her eyes. He is afraid she will say, "Vinnie, I didn't know you cared."

She says, "Thank you."

He gets up. He puts his hand, thin and wiry, on her long plump one. "Have a good weekend."

138

"Sure, Vinnie."

Squinting his eyes against the sun again, he thinks, I said it so I wouldn't need to fuck her.

A kind of cleaver falls onto his head: sun and whisky. He reels. Mother, I didn't mean it.

Mother, I did.

I want to go home.

I want to hold onto myself, my respectability. Any more of this and I will . . . wet myself.

He hails a cab.

Sylvia is at the sink. "Good day?"

"Not very."

"You've been drinking; I smell it. Joey and Sam and Agnes won't like it."

"I met Marsh on the way home. She claims she saved me from walking in front of a car. I took her into a bar. Rejoice that I am alive and inedible."

The birds smell his breath and won't speak to him. He thinks of having a little nap, but the vegetables are in. Gingerly, he sips his martini.

"What do you think of Marshallene?" he asks.

"She's pathetic," Sylvia snaps.

"Why?" Perhaps we can both be brisk, it will take the fuzz off my mind.

Sylvia knots her fingers in her lap in the chair. She is wearing one of the thin cotton maternity tops she likes because they bunch up in the front and make her look more substantial.

"She wants it both ways. She wants to insult a person and be loved for it. She wants to hate people and be loved for it. I read that book about the pioneers. It was disgusting."

"Why? I liked it."

"They weren't like that, they couldn't have been like that,

it was all about greed and pride and . . . ."

"Surely, greed and pride come into it: all that virtually free land. . . . "

"She's a crass woman and she reduces everything to appetite."

Vinnie turns his head and catches Sam and Agnes glaring at him. For a small moment he wishes they could swish their tails like cats.

"I won't argue," he says, because he knows that he is above all a decent, disciplined man and, to a degree, a coward. "I don't particularly admire Marsh, but tonight I liked her."

"She saved your life," says Sylvia tartly, swivelling around to drain the vegetables. With the speed and co-ordination of a very good badminton player she distributes them on a platter with the veal. Vinnie turns around to the fridge and extracts the wine.

"Sam looks off colour," he says for something to say.

"His beak is out of joint."

"Sylvia, you're a card."

"He's been in a bad mood all day. Meat done enough for you?"

"Does he think I've been making passes at Ag?"

"Mmmm? No, I don't like this wine: I think we should go to the twos; dry is only a fashion, isn't it? Eat up and I'll tell you my secret."

"Secret? Is it a surprise?"

Sylvia half-closes her long, fair-lashed eyes and smiles mysteriously. She has the face of a Siamese cat. "You'll see."

Vinnie's head is spinning but he attempts to retain control; Sylvia's mood is fragile. Anything, he feels, could happen.

"You look disgusting when you're drunk," she says. "Your moustache droops."

"You make me want to apologize. For my moustache drooping."

"Your moustache is drooping."

140

"Hell, Sylvia."

"Hell, Sylvia," Joey says suddenly.

Vinnie places his fists on either side of his plate where his knife and fork should be. It is his form of aggression.

"I'll do the dishes," he says.

He helps her upstairs and places her in a position, in the bathroom, from which she can make her ablutions. He goes downstairs, rinses the dishes and loads the dishwasher. He pulls the curtain on the aviary without saying a thing.

"Vinnie!" says Joey.

"Shuddup," says Vinnie.

Sylvia is through in the bathroom. Vinnie wheels her into the bedroom and helps her into bed. He doesn't mind routine.

"Vinnie, I don't know what's got into you," she says.

"Hard day at work," he mutters. "Gonna read the *Globe.*"

"It's on the coffee table."

"Sweet dreams," he says.

"I sure hope you get over it."

"Sleep well, pet."

It isn't what I wanted to say, he thinks. It isn't what I wanted her to say. Doesn't anybody ever forgive anyone for anything in this house? He looks at his watch. It is barely nine. He knows how to punish her on a Thursday night.

Harriet's house is quiet when he goes there. They talk long and earnestly in soft voices—a relief from the stridency of children and lawyers and birds—about Marshallene. They come to the conclusion that she is funny if you want to take her that way. He wants and does not want to make love; he goes through his elderly ritual: asks her to marry him first. It is a joke, an impossibility, a kink. They both know that. It preserves his divine desire to be respectable.

After the eldest three have checked in, they pad upstairs in their socks to make love. He wonders, when he begins, if he is tired of her; afterwards, he has not a doubt that he is not. Respectability is missing, and that odd phenomenon that one

141

calls passionate love; but they make love with all the knowingness of old friends. There are words he has to say, formulas he has to go through to preserve himself to himself as a good boy; she understands that.

"I thought for a moment," he says, "I was turning middle-aged and promiscuous, going to start chasing secretaries. But oh, God, Harriet, now I feel I'm home."

Harriet runs a finger down his back. "The lights are still on in Sylvia's room." Their bay windows face each other.

"She was mad at me for drinking with Marshallene."

"You were mad at yourself."

"Yes, but . . . I dunno, Harriet."

"Shhhh," she holds up a finger in the dark; he seizes it with his fist. "Somebody," she says, "is riding the exercise bicycle in the dark."

He likes that idea. He traces his own smile with his own finger, tickled by his own moustache. Chuckles to himself. Remembers something else. Sits up fast in horror.

"Jeez, Harriet. She said she had a surprise for me."

"Oh, God, run home fast and ask her. If she asks you if you've been here, you lie. It's always all right to lie about who you sleep with."

"I hope it is."

He dresses grimly. Kisses her, pads down the stairs. There is everything wrong with her house but the stairs don't creak. Maybe it has something to do with the fact that they are made of bad wood. He remembers his father pacing the basement with shims to stick under beams where his mother's surgical shoes squeaked against their good oak floors. He closes the door.

"Gotcha," comes a voice from below. Some kid.

Never having imagined he would be free to father them, he has not sorted them out. They like being ignored by him.

His own door makes a lot of noise, but not as much as his footsteps on the wheelchair ramp. He pads up to her room

142

and hesitates theatrically outside the door. Knocks. There is no answer.

He goes downstairs, noses around the kitchen for a snack. The birds hear him and shuffle and whistle. When he opens the fridge door he hears an odd noise on the top of it. He turns on the overhead light and sees the most beautiful pair of blue and scarlet lories. Smooth, iridescent, healthy-eyed, and smug in their inquisitiveness. He puts a finger in their cage and discovers they are quite, quite tame. He puts a tea towel over them and understands why Sylvia has been angry: lories are more important to her than Marshallenes, and this is a pair of kings.

He lies on his lonely bed, dozy and somehow happy. Everything with Sylvia will always be incomplete, he says to himself. He closes his eyes and remembers the white breasts and iridescent backs and tails of the magpies at home in Alberta.

The summons to Madge's house comes from Beetrice and must not be ignored. Mrs. Saxe can act as a buffer again. Harriet looks eighty in her good tea dress, but she puts it on.

"She's probably going to talk about putting Babs in an institution again," Harriet groans. "Nevertheless . . . ."

The living room is as grandly theatrical as ever, and Madge is wearing something ominously like a stewardess's outfit. But she is thinner and smaller and somehow bent. Harriet waits for her to have her say. But she makes small talk about the children, appears to be generally interested in their progress while making it clear that Harriet doesn't work them hard enough, and is cordial to Mrs. Saxe.

"Was there anything specific you had on your mind?" Harriet asks.

Madge looks up at Harriet, and in the afternoon sun filtered through the leaded windows, Harriet sees that one of her eyes is clouded with cataract.

"No, Harriet, I just felt a longing for your company."

Then they tour the Royal Doulton figurines with Mrs. Saxe.

At the door, Beetrice whispers, "She's not well, Mrs. Ross."

"Call me, Beetrice."

"If I can."

On the way home, Harriet wonders if the dogs are gone. There's something different in the atmosphere. She'll be told in Madge's own good time.

As a journalist, Harriet is inclined to pomposity, and to cure this ugly condition she annually puts herself through a number of exercises designed to take her away from sermons and back to the territory of real speech. She, for a period, eschews her tape recorder and makes her rounds with an old-fashioned pencil and notebook instead, making sure she copies down, increasingly painfully, the exact words her subjects utter. When she writes things down she remembers them; when she relies on the tape recorder she remembers, instead, the room, the painful voices, the emotional tatters in the air, and these settle on her prose like a swarm of pre-Raphaelite roses, which will not do.

It was during one of these periodic punishments that she first noticed what they have all since come to call air lock: at a terminal point in a statement, the rich, the poor, the articulate, the inarticulate, almost everyone not speaking from a prepared text–you can see it in television interviews, too–indulges in a kind of hesitant drawing-to-a-close, which requires physical as well as verbal explication: arms wave in arabesques, mouths stammer, noses twitch, eyes wink: the hesitation of a door trying to close on an air lock. The degree of the demonstration varies, of course, with the personality;

the very nervous become almost spastic, the simplest and surest resign themselves to a mere nodding of the head and crossing of the fingers.

What does air lock mean? "I am almost finished." "This ordeal is nearly over." "All done now." "All clear." "My house is my own again." When she is tape recording, Harriet is at this point watching dials instead of people. But when she returns to scribbling she sees, again and again, these amazing demonstrations of ambivalence towards completion.

For a time, she attempted to put them in writing, but it was all in vain. In words, air lock is a failure. "Hands groping at the air, she says . . ." is no more effective than, "With a final groping for the right word, he. . . . " It does not belong in the text. It is every individual's tap dance into the death of the sentence, and must be left alone.

They all crowd at the doorway to see Sidonia off. She is brave and tearful.

"I'm sure," she says, "that as Aunt Harriet says, this is all for the best. I have to learn, sooner or later, that there just isn't any room in this family for me. I'll be far better off in a house where I can have my own room and be far from bed-wetters and snoops and nasty little boys. I'll come out of this, and into my father's money, and I'll build a mansion bigger than Aunt Madge's on an estate larger than Disneyland, and you can be sure that even if you come in rags and begging, I'll be far, far kinder and more tolerant of other people's weaknesses than any of you Rosses and Littlemores has ever managed to be. But I excuse you for your small-mindedness, for I know that life has not treated you well."

"Goodbye, Sidonia; take care of yourself."

"Thank you, Aunt Harriet. I know you try to do your best. Oh, Mickle, I hope you get away soon."

She goes down the steps like a bride, with her social

worker, a pleasant, expressionless woman who moves stiffly and correctly but does not seem unkind. The family turns and begins to shuffle inside, deflated.

"Bitch!" says Melanie.

"She can't help it," Harriet says, automatically making peace.

"Sure she can," says Mick.

"I don't think she was very nice about bed-wetting," Patsy says, "considering I haven't done it for six months."

"Nice isn't the word," Sim says. "Pete, can you leave me alone for a while while I get my calculus done?"

"Sure, Sim."

"Mrs. Saxe, it's time for our ride," Mick calls.

"I'm sitting for Elaine," says Melanie, "I've decided I like her after all, and she's gone up to a buck and a quarter. I can't afford not to. And Pen has decided it wasn't my fault that Eph chipped his tooth. So everything's okay."

"We're helping Sylvia clean the aviary out," say the twins. Like a scattering of shot, they are all gone and Harriet is alone. She phones Babs to tell her.

"Do you think it's the right thing, Harriet?"

"It's the only thing, Babs."

"God, I drank myself pink the day I signed the papers."

"She's a very, very difficult child, dear."

"I feel so responsible."

"It's too late now."

"Oh, Harriet, how have things managed to turn out this way?"

"Ten years from now it'll be different, Babs." Hanging up, wondering. No wonder the ancestors talked about bad blood: it was easier.

CHAPTER SEVEN

It is Saturday afternoon and Pen and Elaine are in the middle of a fight; Elaine's kids, to relieve the tension of it, are running back and forth, back and forth in the upstairs hall, banging their bodies against the shut doors, making a clatter that will soon cause the new people in Saskatchewan House, to which they are attached, to remonstrate by banging on the walls.

But Pen does not mind. There are points to be made, and perhaps now is the time, or perhaps it isn't, but they go through this period when the air has to be cleared, when one must submit to the other or the other to the one, when positions must be changed, chaos unravelled.

It began at five in the morning when Elaine's children, delirious at the thought that this was Saturday and they were free of the day-nursery and would have their mother more or less to themselves, burst into the bedroom and began to tickle her, poke her eyes, bounce on her. With a shriek, she sent them downstairs to get bowls of cereal and watch television.

"Elaine," Pen said sleepily, "we agreed that wouldn't happen to them any more. It's imprinting them with nastiness."

Elaine, in the madness of disturbed sleep, rushed downstairs, threw the television over, and yanked at the cable cord, failing to extract it from the wall. The children rushed

147

up to Pen and cowered under the covers with her.

She, resentful because she had to go to the store at nine and needed her sleep as much as Elaine did, ran down and found Elaine sobbing. She comforted her, picked up the vile machine and found that it was not broken, and began to make breakfast for the kids. When they were having coffee afterwards, she said, "Look, it's just that we have to make rules and keep them, El."

"They're always your rules, never mine," Elaine said like a sulky child.

"You can't let Eph and Claudie soak themselves in that stuff day after day, it over-excites them; besides, it's dumb and corrupting."

"They're too young to sit in bed and read."

"Look, I don't care whose rules they are, rules have to be kept."

"I thought they were there to be broken."

"You'll drive them crazy with your inconsistency."

For Pen is the large one, the strong one. Soft, yes, in her heart she is soft as butter and her friends are the little ones, like Elaine, the distressed ones. And it is simple for her to live: you set out to do things, you do them. You don't dally on the way like a child trying to absorb the whole world on the way to school and getting lost in it, you do what you plan to do and do it well.

Things are different for Elaine: the path is overgrown with thorn bushes and poison ivy and the most seductive flowers; she has to hack her small way with a large machete; everything tires her, worries her, except the occasional smiling flower, or a bright toad hopping. And she has the children: they are hers, hard-produced in labour rooms, hard-won in the courts. And it is easy for Pen to make rules when it costs her nothing to keep them. Pen is stronger, but there are a lot of things she doesn't know. People who walk in seven-league boots miss a lot of detail.

"Pen, I know they shouldn't watch it but I get too tired! At least it keeps them from crayoning on the walls."

"Look, there's no point in having kids unless you agree to bring them up really well."

And they go on and on, until the children, restless, clamour for Elaine to get dressed so they can all go to the market, as they have always planned to do. And Elaine does so sulkily, because it's a lousy day for the market and they don't need much food this week, they ran out in the middle and picked up things on the way home from work. Pen shrugs in despair and begins the breakfast dishes, wondering if Elaine will get around to the kitchen floor while she's at work. Finally, they pile into the car and drop Pen off at the store, where she will work until three, leaving Hazel to lock up at six because there's no point in their both hanging around in the dead hours.

And when she comes back, the air is still thick with reproach. Elaine is guilty for her tantrum, but she won't admit it, she's taking it out on Pen. And the jobs aren't done because she lay down for a little nap when she put the kids down.

"We'd better rearrange the job list," Pen says.

"You're so damn rigid. I'm dead these days, I need my sleep."

"Hell, Elaine, I'm not your boss, I don't need excuses. Let's get down and do it now. You keep the kids busy while I. . . ."

And Mrs. Saxe is at the door. They know her. Once the Task Force gets its work done and the mattress factory comes down for the new housing project, the street will be a through street; but right now, they're all jammed in each others' faces, they know more about each other than they need to know. Mrs. Saxe wasn't at Harriet's for more than a day before the twins told Claudie and then Marsh came over to complain that Harriet had taken one too many people in.

"I came to call," says Mrs. Saxe. And they invite her in to tea because they have to.

Elaine whisks in and puts the kettle on. Pen seats her on the brown settee. Mrs. Saxe looks around bright-eyed, interested in the variety of designs available on the street, wishing she could get into the decorators' house, Saskatchewan; odd to have two families so unfriendly. Elaine comes back from the kitchen, sees Mrs. Saxe's little legs sticking out like pegs from the wide-bottomed sofa and says, "Oh, she's put you there, has she? Really, Pen; come and sit here, Mrs. Saxe," indicating a little plush velvet chair.

Eph and Claudie come and are introduced. Pen sends them off to wash and comb their hair. Elaine scowls.

"Pen was well brought up," she says. "It doesn't always show, but. . . . " She departs to unbox the baking she bought in the market. Pen is slicing the bread very thin and helping a newly kempt Claudie arrange macaroons on one of the good plates. Elaine gets the good cups out and begins to dust them. Eph returns and is sent to rummage in the cupboard for the silver tray. Eventually a tea of great grandeur is produced.

To everything there is a function, Pen thinks sadly as she comes back to Mrs. Saxe, having fruitlessly tried to move her to yet another chair as the velvet seemed somehow inadequate. I am about bossing people around, animals are about eating, Mrs. Saxe is about taking tea. Elaine?

Elaine is very quiet now. Is she happy or merely luxuriating in her small victory? She is on the settee and the children are curled up beside her, quietly peeling the host paper off the bottom of the macaroons.

"Well," Mrs. Saxe is saying, "what a spread, ho! My, I never dreamed."

Pen thinks, we'll give them an early supper and let them stay up and watch television. Then catches herself and grins.

"Do you like television, Mrs. Saxe?"

"Oh, yes, lovely. I watch it with Melanie and Mick."

"Is she Melly's aunt?" Claudie asks.

"More or less," Elaine says. "I guess you could say that."

"Melanie's a nice girl," Pen says.

Mrs. Saxe, having heard of the Great Babysitting Dispute, tries to narrow her eyes but cannot; she is swallowing a piece of gumdrop cake. She nods pleasantly.

"Harriet does well with those kids," Pen goes on.

Elaine bristles competitively. "She's got more than anyone should be able to cope with."

"Well, nobody could be expected to cope with Mick."

Mrs. Saxe smiles graciously and wipes her lips on her napkin.

"My goodness, I do recall I have an engagement with Mick. He's a particular friend of mine." She says her thank yous, gets herself up and goes.

Elaine closes the door on her, turns to Pen, and bursts into helpless giggles. Pen, not knowing what to do, loads the tea tray up and carries it to the kitchen, hoping Eph will not choose this moment to try to wiggle between her legs. It's that long since they've had the good china out.

"What's the matter, El?"

Elaine straightens up under the kitchen lamp. "I don't know. I guess I needed to laugh. She's just . . . funny, Pen. Or maybe I spend too much of my life with children. She's like Harriet, isn't she, short and stout and all eyes?"

"I'd have said Harriet was all mouth, but never mind."

"I'm sorry about this morning, Pen. I guess I just get so tired of routine at school, and I want to loll."

"Five is a bit much. We'll keep them up later tonight so we get a good lie-in tomorrow. You're looking positively merry. What bird flew across your mind?"

"I thought of teaching Eph to knit; that's what we used to do in the mornings when we were little, can you believe it, we'd sit up in bed and knit!"

Pen puts her arms around her and thinks of long ago, Sunday mornings with Renie, leafing through Eaton's catalogue, trying to decide if the horse-harness pages were better than

151

the delicious appellations of material by the yard.

– The butcher flattening a pork tenderloin with the side of a wide meat axe: smack, smack, smack.
– The sucking sound as the jelly flops onto the dish out of its mold.
– The Littlemores' eyes regarding the jelly.
– Mrs. Saxe's small round O.
These effects compensate satisfactorily for the night even the cat wouldn't eat the dinner.

Most of Harriet's lunches pertain to business, but this one is personal and serious.
"How's Babs?" Harry asks casually.
"Bad."
"Drink?"
"Everything. All day alone in an empty basement."
"Sidi?" Harry never ages, though his skin is drawn a little around the eyes. Debonair, you'd say, handsome. Some tension there? He never ages, but he's gone out of fashion, like a forties bandleader. Still the wheel continues to turn, soon he'll be in again. Sixty, is he? Sixty-three or four. Ten years older than Babs. I always liked him better than her, more's the pity. Easier to be in a room with.
"Sidi's with a Children's Aid therapist and doing much better."
"Wha-at?" Real surprise here, shock. She mustn't have written.
"She got in real trouble last year. I had her for a while . . ."
"She told me . . . "
" . . . but she was impossible, Harry. I finally got in the Children's Aid because our shrink couldn't take her. She's with a special caseworker now."
Harry's face freezes as she speaks. He looks like a man

152

who's been worked over by a plastic surgeon. He swallows and gasps. "Get her out," he says.

"She's doing really well."

"But I can't let that happen to Sidi."

"She's in a one-to-one treatment situation, Harry. It's the best possible thing."

"There's nothing wrong with our Sidi."

"Harry, she lies, cheats, steals, manipulates and has twice attempted to peddle her ass. Aside from that, she asked Mick to help her rob a bank. There's nothing wrong with our Sidi."

"Look, Harriet, when I went away I left an address for you, you should have told me all this."

"When you went away you knew darn well Babs was drinking and Sidi was messed up. There didn't seem to be an answer for Babs, but there is one for Sidi."

"Get her out, Harriet."

"I can't. I'm not in charge."

"Who is?"

"The government."

"Really?"

"Really. Do you want to hear about Babs?"

"No."

"You'll have to. She lives alone in an empty apartment. She doesn't appear to have any money, but she still drinks. She used to phone me, but her phone's been cut off for some time. There are no pictures on the wall and she has six glasses, two plates, two forks, two knives and one spoon. What gives, Harry?"

"I send her what I always did."

"How much is that?"

"The rent."

"What is she supposed to raise Sidi on?"

"She has money, Harriet."

"What money?"

"Why, the estate. I offered her an allowance for Sidi, and she said she had the baby bonus and the estate."

"The baby bonus is twenty-one fifty a month now, Harry. She used to give it to me, somewhat unwillingly. Tell me more about the estate."

"Why ... Madge."

"Harry, you know Madge wouldn't part with a painted nickel if she could help it."

"When we went to draw up the separation agreement, Babs said she wouldn't take anything from me because she had your father's interest in the cheese factory."

"Harry, you believe what you want to believe, don't you? Babs doesn't know a thing about money. The only job she's ever had was pushing a library cart in a hospital, right? And you ought to know that the estate is a myth."

"Jesus."

"Madge is as crazy as a coot, Harry. She's not giving Babs anything."

Harry sits very still, swallowing. His Adam's apple travels up and down his neck like an elevator.

"I'm beginning to hate lawyers," Harriet says, "but I think we ought to do something."

"No lawyers, Harriet."

"I know what you both think: if we give Babs money, she'll drink it. But she's got to eat, too."

"I ... I didn't know."

"So the phone's cut off, the pictures are gone, the silver is gone, she's probably not even drinking, Harry. She's just sitting there waiting to die."

"She should have gone out and got a job."

"How can you start at the bottom at fifty when you've lived at the top?"

"Other women do."

"Women are falling on their faces all over the place."

"You've managed."

"Because I went out to work at nineteen."

"Seventeen, Harriet."

"When she wrote to you, did you ever answer?"

"The letters were indecipherable."

"So you send Sidi presents."

"Which she never acknowledged."

She wants to rage at him, tell him he's five years old and the Bahamas and the dolly-birds are a wonderful place, but she can't, it's too important for anger. "Do you want to see Babs or do you want to see my lawyer?"

"Business is bad, Harriet."

"I can help her get welfare but you know darn well that's wrong; one of your dependants is on the dole: do you want them both to be?"

"Tell me more about this business with Sidi."

"Sidi was fouled up when you got her. She swung between the two of you like a pendulum. Finally she started swinging her own way and it wasn't a good way. Didn't you even keep their medical insurance up, Harry?"

"I've been in another country."

"So you pay the rent."

"It isn't cheap."

"Come and see, Harry."

He doesn't want to, but he goes with her. The building is silent but for the eternally pissing fountain in the lobby. Babs answers the bell and buzzes to let them in. When she answers the door (they have been silent in the elevator, totally silent), wearing a neat, cheap little housecoat, Harriet recognizes an educated eye and the dime store. Her voice is hoarse.

"Babs, I've brought Harry."

Harry steps in and bows his head, a chastised schoolboy. "Hello, Babs."

Babs can't speak.

Harry looks at the spotted carpet, the empty coffee table. The bare walls and threadbare chairs. At Babs, who is thin, who is old.

"Why?" he asks.

"Pride goeth before destruction."

"You could have told me."

"You'd have said I'd spend it on drink."

"Doesn't Madge give you anything at all?" Harriet asks.

"She used to bring money in the tea tin. She's not going out any more."

"Babs, I never suspected you had this . . . dignity."

"I'm allowed my secrets even if I am a lush."

Another silence.

"How's Sidi, Harriet?"

"She's doing well. In another month she'll be ready to come home a bit."

"She can't come here! She can't see. I don't want her to see."

"You look nice, Babs. You've been out shopping."

"I thought about trying to get a job."

"That's good, Babs. That's really good."

"Just because Madge can't go out I'm not a prisoner."

"Madge has been very bad."

"I was supposed to get half of Daddy's estate."

"Where did it go?"

"I don't know. She'd show me bits of paper and take them away again before I could figure them out. I was never good at figures, was I, Harry?"

Harry is still quiet. Then he sticks his chin up like a bird's. "I think you were, Babs, I think you were."

"You never wrote, Harry."

"I did. You never answered."

"You've been had, you two," Harriet says. "Do you want me to help you work things out, or do you want me to go to?"

She stays.

"I always liked Harry," she tells Mrs. Saxe, "and I wasn't wrong. They're not exactly going to get married again and live happily ever after, but she'll have some sort of home. He

156

wants her to join Alcoholics Anonymous, but she feels too exposed. We'll just have to take a risk on the drink. He's going to see Madge about the money; maybe she'll talk to him, she has no opinion of us, we're her baby sisters, we can't manage anything. For all I know she'll give everything she has to Harry."

Mrs. Saxe cackles wickedly.

Harriet whirls on her. "What happened to all those men on white chargers, can you tell me that? They were something somebody made up, weren't they, to keep us in line? Harry will help Babs because I told him if he didn't I'd write to all his directors, I'd write articles, I'd expose him in every way I could. He said I was a man-hater. Why have we all been such fools?"

Mrs. Saxe, self-absorbed, says nothing; pumps away at the exercise bicycle like a toad on a stool.

Harriet, left on her own, is furious because she has no one to talk to because she has got what she wants: solitude, the desideratum. Everyone is busy this afternoon; no one has time to talk to her. It's as it should be, it doesn't suit her. She plunks a piece of paper furiously into the typewriter and starts to write about Depressed. But Depressed isn't working for her. Depressed doesn't even begin to know how it feels to be Babs. Depressed, besides, should have got off her butt six years ago and done some Adult Retraining. She slams the machine off and goes to the phone and calls Madge.

"Yes," says Madge, "I talked to Harry. Babs can have her money the minute she goes into the clinic."

"She can't go into the clinic; she doesn't have medical insurance."

"The minute she has it she can get her share of the estate if she goes into the clinic."

"Is Harry going to buy the insurance?"

"I don't know. Maybe you could."

Blood pressure rises. Don't say anything hostile; this is mad, delicate. "I can't, sorry."

"You're so extravagant, Harriet. I don't know what's wrong with you two girls."

"It would be nice if you advanced Babs the money for the health coverage."

"She'd only spend it on drink."

"If you don't do anything, Madge, the taxpayers will wind up paying for her, and Father wouldn't like that."

"Father's dead," the sepulchral voice comes back. "Stanley's dead. The boys are dead. Your Tom is dead."

"Live for the living, Madge."

"She can have the money if she commits herself."

"I'll tell her that."

She slams down the phone and chews her fingernails. Yet another appointment with Pip the lawyer? God, the way I'm dependent on all these men. Forced into it by all these women. Why can't they let me be?

Why can't I let them be?

"Harriet," Babs calls, "I need you."

"Babs, don't drink. There's no help any more if you drink."

"Harriet, I think I'm having a heart attack."

"Babs, you must have paid your hospitalization and forgotten about it."

"But that's what I phoned you to say. I found the cancelled cheque, I really did."

"What about the heart attack, then?"

"That was a lie, Harriet. I need to be with you."

"Grab a cab and come over, then. I'll pay. I have to make dinner; I can't come to you."

"Oh, can I?" She sounds like a little girl.

Frail, sweet, she sits at the table with the others. Unsure of herself, trembling. She has spent three months in a tunnel painted white. The noise jars her–a chair scraping, a spoon that drops. The children, who have hidden the beer and the wine, watch her surreptitiously. Politely, she asks them about themselves. They might never have seen her before, so precise are their descriptions, so high and strained their voices.

After dinner, Harriet takes Babs into the living room, shoos even Mrs. Saxe away. They are silent for a moment.

"I called Madge," Harriet says.

"I know. I called her from the phone booth before I called you."

"Do you think you could manage to check yourself in somewhere and have a go at it? Just to get the money? It's wrong, but what's right these days, Babs? Sidi has to have someone to rely on."

"I've been on the waiting list at the institute now for three months."

Half a weight slides off Harriet's shoulders. It's begun, she thinks, but barely, and no one knows how it will turn out.

"It doesn't matter," Babs says suddenly, "who's responsible. Whether someone did it to me, or I did it to myself. Whether someone did it to Sidi, or she did it to herself. What matters is to decide whether to live or to die."

"Did you really have a choice?"

"I couldn't make myself die."

"So now you have to decide whether to live meanly, or to live well."

"Is there a choice there?"

"You can take Harry to court, you can take Madge to court."

"Why should they give me anything?"

"Let's say you ought to be paid for acting out their fantasies."

Suddenly there is music in the house. The stomping feet upstairs start boogeying. Babs tosses her head. "If I were drinking, I'd go up and dance with them."

"Come with me and we'll make more coffee. I want to check up on how they left the kitchen."

Down in the cellar there is a sound of clinking wrenches. Mrs. Saxe and Mick are at the bicycles again.

"Harry's a liar," Babs says. "And he always was. He knew

what was going on. I used to sneak-read his letters to Sidonia. He liked me better drunk, you know."

"It's all over now."

"Sidonia?"

"She was pretty screwed up when she came to you. Cigarette?"

"I've quit."

"My God."

Vinnie, neat-bodied, comfortably adequate, is not the kind of lover who bounces in the mind. Most of the time he can be taken for granted, which is comforting. Harriet, however, has lately found that he interferes with Depressed Housewife and gets in the way of the amateur sociology of *Maga* ("Learning Disabilities – A School-Generated Disease?" this month).

Because lately when they have been in bed they have not been alone.

First there was the hedgehog, the one Harriet turned into when she was carried, victorious, through the streets on Vinnie's elegant projection in the midst of their ecstasy. Then next week, sulkily, a porcupine lumbered across their minds and made congress impossible. Last night, *in medias res*, so to speak, the wombats invaded. "Wombats!" Vinnie cried suddenly, from under the covers at the bottom of the bed, "wombats. I'm a herd of wombats."

All she could think of was that wombats did not form herds, but prides or passles or hutches or whatever wombats form. "Wombats!" Vinnie cried again. She cast her mind back to the encyclopaedia of her school days and it returned laden with a photograph of a walking, hairy loaf of bread. "Wombats!" cried Vinnie, finishing the act and well, though her mind was far from fully appreciating it, trying to remember what kind of teeth they had and who'd done a geography project on them and why they looked like cushions badly stitched across the nose.

160

"So, okay, wombats," she said irritably. Now she wonders what it will be next, to what degree he's working up in size and tooth and claw.

Mrs. Saxe, across the table from her, snorts, "Beastly."

Harriet jumps. "What?"

"Some dreadful man's been arrested for putting corn syrup on bicycle seats. Beastly. What's the world coming to?"

What, indeed?

Harriet looks at her calendar at eight in the morning and, with every sip of coffee, becomes less enamoured of this day. It is one of the stupid ones, tricked out with errands which, whether performed by car, taxi, or subway, are meant only to exhaust the legs and the spirit. There is a form to be delivered to Sidonia's social worker in the west end (mail won't do, the form replaces a document the post office has lost); there is the bank to go to because it's Friday; there is Xeroxing to be done at the Copy Shop; and food to be bought of course, food, always food; and, more important, typewriter ribbons, envelopes, stationery to be picked up at Bloor and Yonge. However she works it out, it's a six-subway-ticket day.

"Do you feel like going downtown?" she asks.

Mrs. Saxe, as ever, is avid.

The expedition begins well enough. Wonder of wonders, it is possible to cross the road at the subway exit nearest the social worker's office, it takes only a moment to play mail-man and Harriet moves fast because she has left Mrs. Saxe in the pet shop at the corner. When they resume their progress there are enough people in the subway to keep them interested, even a pretty girl absorbed in John Aubrey's *Brief Lives*. Mrs. Saxe enjoys the stationery store, and stands transfixed by reams of paper and grosses of pencils and ballpoints while Harriet buys her requirements in hundreds and struggles against the weariness of imagining filling so many envelopes, large brown, small white, and middle-sized red,

161

white and blue. She resists dreaming of new wastepaper baskets, of thinking a better life will result from new bulletin boards. In fact, she senses, she is getting beyond buying. The family will begin to thin out soon, the requirements cease to be endless. Already most of them think she's pretty funny to go on buying them wastebaskets and ball-points and bulletin boards instead of new shoes. They have a point.

They cut through an alley and a parking lot and zip along to the Copy Shop. "It's cheaper than carbon paper, and neater," Harriet rationalizes, wondering where it will all end. The young man promises the work in an hour, and Harriet suggests lunch.

Up the street, though, there is a mob of construction workers blocking the path, and as they work their way through the hard-hats they hear a band. Suddenly they're at the corner.

"Oh, I say, a parade!" says Mrs. Saxe.

The weather is cold, for April's Canadian cruelty is to be a spring month but not spring. An open convertible passes, containing a chilly, middle-aged woman holding a bunch of daffodils in the back seat. This is followed by an open convertible, containing another chilly, middle-aged woman bearing daffodils. This time a sign with her name on it proclaims a famous actress. Then there's a man in moustaches and little round glasses, one of the school who pretend to be old farmers full of wise saws on television and radio, which amuses those who have never met old farmers. Since it is lunch hour, a fair crowd has formed at the intersection and they become aware of half a dozen school girls in kilts and blazers selling daffodils.

"It's the cancer parade," Harriet tells Mrs. Saxe.

"Curious," says Mrs. Saxe, "but what a clever clown."

Harriet watches it all solemnly, from the curb. The rest of the crowd is solemn, as well, and it is impossible to tell whether even the clown himself is smiling under his painted grin. The parade is probably halfway over, and they are between bands, because there is no sound, not even the honking of traffic. A policeman is manipulating traffic at the corner, but without a whistle. The floats and convertibles move slowly and silently down the street; a band passes bearing the flashes of the Toronto Horse Guards, but though the cymbalist looks restless, no one is playing.

"Seventy-six trombones when we hit Charles Street," an officer says to the bandleader.

"Oh, look," says someone, "there's the King of Kensington," and indeed, there he is, and all the rest of Marshallene's union, too, the ones who are seen and loved by the few who watch domestic rather than foreign television, and there are newspaper columnists, and some men in fezzes in cars marked *The Canadian Cancer Society*. A general blaze of yellow issues from a thousand daffodils held and huckstered; the blue knees of the majorettes soundlessly strut; well wrapped in fur, another set of stars, from the first Shakespeare Harriet ever saw, glides by, and behind them, three provincial policemen on motorcycles perform a strange muffled musical ride by moving down Bay Street in circles and figure eights.

You can't stand forever watching a silent parade of sad people under grey skies in a wind that chills, so she and Mrs. Saxe slip across the road and make their way past the vendors of French delicacies and eighty-cent tea bags to the new Pilot Tavern, which is now looking almost as worn, though not as interesting, as the one it replaced, and take their seats in the dark at a long table and order beer and hamburgers.

"I don't really think," says Mrs. Saxe, "that actors and actresses show to advantage in the light of the morning."

"I gave at the office, I gave at the door, I come downtown to meet you for lunch, I'm half an hour late and I spend three bucks' worth of gas in a traffic jam, I guess it's a worthy cause, to hell with them," the man next to Harriet says to the woman across from him.

"Yeah," the woman says, "they're getting to me, too.

163

There's too much of this charity stuff, and who the hell wants the whole downtown tied up with a parade?"

Harriet thinks sadly of Madge, who said, "And I even get my medicine free!" and she wants to turn and say, "It's not parades, it's this parade, because it's not about Santa, it's not King Billy on a white horse, it's fear in a handful of dust." But, being a good citizen, she says nothing, munches her hamburger and says to Mrs. Saxe, "When I envied those people their jobs and their fame, I didn't think of their having to get up and ride around in slow parades in this weather."

Mrs. Saxe makes a chilly motion. They pay and finish their rounds. On the way home the sun breaks through in the west, and Harriet thinks of the faces that were strained and eager not to show their lassitude and fear, and what the sun would have done for them if it gilds even the peeling verandahs of Gloag Street.

"I used to like daffodils," she says as she straggles in the door.

A young man in a black jacket turns up at six.

"Harriet Ross? Mrs. Harriet Ross?"

"Yes?"

"That you, Mrs. Ross?"

"Yes."

"This is for you." He thrusts a paper at her, turns, puts his hands in his pockets and dumps himself off the porch. Harriet pockets the paper and goes to find her glasses. Mrs. Saxe and Mick, she sees through the kitchen window, are working on their bikes in the back. Melanie is playing records in her room. The potatoes have come to a boil, and the paper is a subpoena.

Blood rushes to her head. I won't, I won't, she thinks. Won't live in a world like this, won't answer; haven't done anything wrong; don't do anything but work work work and now this. . . .

She is to appear with the children T. Peter and M. Patricia Littlemore to discuss the matter of the custody of the said children, and show cause why they should not be transferred into the hands of Michael and Mrs. Susan Forbush Littlemore.

She sits. She stares. The potatoes burn. She reads, as she is directed to do (because she can think now and she knows that the rule of law exists, she is the court's obedient servant, an order is Order), but she says, aloud, "The gall and the nerve," as she reads: you can give in without giving over.

She reads about herself, Harriet Ross: how she asked Michael Littlemore to leave the house in 1972, in the infancy of said children, and resisted his offers to return to the marriage, resisted counselling, and after three years divorced Michael Littlemore. How she has appeared to provide the necessities of life to the above children but has raised them in a fashion that can be referred to as disorderly and slatternly. How she has had lovers; how her income is uncertain, while the combined income of Michael and Susan Forbush Littlemore is now forty thousand dollars a year. How, in view of Mr. Littlemore's changed situation, it would be in the interests of T. Peter and M. Patricia to live with him.

"Mush!" she cries. Mick hears her through the closed window and comes shambling in. He takes the lid off the potatoes and frowns into the crusted pot. "Nother dead soldier. What's up, Mum?"

"Michael's suing me."

Mick frowns. "Again? Mrs. S. needs new bushings."

"He's never sued me before, I sued him."

"You're always after chother. Wazfur supper now?"

"Beans. You open them. The giant can, I guess. Open them, dump them in a pot. Turn the gas low this time. I've got to phone somebody."

"Don't turn 'em on til you're through: I know yah."

"It's madness."

"Wha's madness?"

165

"Michael Littlemore."

"You were crazy ta marry him." The beans fall into the pot with an obscene sucking sound. "There. If you're going to phone somebody, I'm going to Canadian Tire."

"Eat first."

"They'll be closed."

"Eat first. I don't like to break your routine."

"Whazzit matter?"

"I wouldn't be a good mum if I let you go."

"Hell, Mum, I can bike over to Summerhill and back in half an hour."

"By the time you get back it will be midnight. Eat first."

"You burned the potatoes."

"The beans will be warmed up soon and the sausages are in the oven and the salad's out. Wash up and call the others."

"Arencha gonna phone?"

"I can't, now. Four more forks on the table: come on, Mick. Just blast into the living room and tell the little ones to come. I'll call Mrs. Saxe." Which she does, rather sharply, irritated at the way life can't be put off. He and she both hate his routine but a break isn't good for him, but of course later is no good for Pip the Lawyer, he'll be gone, and she hasn't seen him for years anyway, maybe he isn't even practising.

During dinner the beans fall into their stomachs like little stones. The jello has failed to jell. They don't like the applesauce. A complaint is made that sausages are bad for adolescent complexions.

"I'll eat yours, Mel," Peter Littlemore says.

Melanie looks at him as if he's a scurvy brute. "Oh, yeah," she says, "you, the human garbage can."

"Don't run him down, don't fight," says Harriet, sharp again. The balance of power is changing in the family: Peter will tell, pretending to be mistreated.

Outside, the evening bursts into robin song. There are two of the monstrous thrushes in the maple tree, competing. She wants to wring their necks, though in other springs they have

166

reminded her of nightingales. What was it Vinnie said, anyhow, about the robins in the west? They sang sharp. It must have been the air. Oh, God, she's off the track again, it's Sue Forbush Littlemore.

Of course, if you live long enough, everything comes around twice, is bound to. My cycles are shorter, though, she thinks. Twice in thirteen years Sue Forbush has been going to take my children away. Whom can I talk to? Roger? Inaccessible. Winnie's worn him out; he lives like a woman now, does his work and goes to bed. Marsh is away.

"Sim, I know you're busy but would you look at this? It makes me so miserable."

"Sure, Mum." He is more than a son now, he's a sympathy, a collaborator.

He reads it, whistles. "That his new wife?"

"Worse than that, she's the social worker who was in the fracas with me when Tom died, remember?"

"Well, maybe you'll feel better if it's the same person twice. I mean, it's not that society's agin you, it's just one person."

"And Michael."

He stares down at the paper again, knitting his forehead, whispering the words. "They've only given you ten days to prepare a case."

"Lawyer tomorrow. And it will take a while to get a court date."

"I thought it cost a lot to go to court."

"Money they've got."

"You haven't."

"We're just breaking even."

"Did you get the lawyer guy? What does he say?"

"We could turn it to our advantage if we were smart enough."

"If they're loaded, it might be good for the Littlemores. They're funny kids, Ma. They're really into products. They get off on things in a way the rest of us never did."

"I guess they feel deprived."

"They do kind of come at the end of the line."

"That paper makes me out some kind of slut."

"I thought we were forbidden to use that word."

"I'm using it as a technical term, not the kind of abuse you lot throw at each other. What'll I do, Sim? What'll I do?"

Sim folds the paper, hands it back, and opens his textbook of calculus. Harriet realizes that he is dismissing her. She is hurt, but she knows he is right: these exams mean something to him, they are all his life.

"I'm sorry, Sim."

"Heck, Ma, it's just that I don't know what to say. What I feel like is wringing those two kids' necks, right now, but I guess they didn't put him up to it."

"No, he's gone and found himself the perfect lady to complain to."

"Well, I'm going to have to stay up all night if I even think about it. I just don't want you to brood."

"Oh, I won't," she says, knowing she will.

The matter sticks in her craw; for days she is hysterical, volatile to the point of being dangerous. When she sees a Littlemore she is unkind, and she knows she is dumping on them all her hurt pride.

"How could you?" she shrieks at them, "how could you do this to me? Dragging me through the courts."

Peter looks as if he wants to cry. "You did it to Daddy," he says. "You got the divorce."

"And for good reason, as it will soon appear. You get your room tidied up now. Sim can't think with all this stuff on the floor."

"Sim keeps me up all night. It's his calculator."

"The cat cuts off the circulation in my feet. You were wicked to tell Daddy I had lovers."

"Patsy did." Peter puts his hands in his pockets and falls over straight on the bed, like a wooden soldier.

"Mmmmm," he says. "Mmmmm. Do I really have to clean up? We're going to a movie with Dad."

"Straighten up your room, Peter Littlemore, or I really will give you over."

"They always have whipped cream. Mmmm. Gobs and gobs of it."

"Yes," she says in despair, "whipped cream and pimples and spots and expensive clothes and private schools and rooms of your own"—the sound of her bitterness like bile in her mouth—"and a good address, all those things."

"I'd miss the cat," he says, beginning reluctantly to stack his comics up. "I'd miss the cat, and Mrs. Saxe."

Who is spending Saturday afternoon in the kitchen, lovingly cleaning spokes for Mick. Humming a tuneless little tune. Looking up, smiling, at Harriet.

"They'd be better off with him," Harriet says glumly.

"Oh, dear, have you come to that?"

"He's got money; he's bought a big new house, everything. I don't know how I can fight that affidavit, Mrs. Saxe. The early part's all right. He didn't contest the divorce. I had the goods on him for forging my name on cheques. I mean, I told you he spent the baby bonus, and robbed Sim's dime bank, but he actually did forge two cheques. I could have laid charges. So we don't have to worry about that, unless we want to be kind to Sue Forbush. Though she doesn't want the scales removed from her eyes. But that bit about the way I dress them and about the diet being heavy and fat: it's true. You give kids well-cooked stodge, it's what they like; so of course they're fat, because they have his metabolism. And of course I don't buy them two-hundred-dollar cloth coats, they wear nylon and down, like all the other kids. And sometimes their things are second hand because they're too fat for hand-me-downs: can you see them in Mick's old jeans? But the

169

worst part of it is in me: I don't even like them any more. If they're going to make all this trouble through their dad, I don't want even to have them around."

Harriet plunks herself at the table, pours salt out of the shaker and makes patterns with her finger tips. Mrs. Saxe rubs slowly at spokes.

"Oh, dear," she says. "You seem to me to love them rather a lot. You indulge them, in fact."

"Do I?"

"Oh, dear, yes, the things you put up with from them all, I wonder why."

"I try to be good to them. And they're right when they say I get my living out of them. In a way."

"Surely what they bring in doesn't touch the cost."

"It's not that: in a curious way, I'm guilty about them. Because they protect me, you see."

"I'm afraid I don't."

"But what would I be if I didn't have them? I'd be an ordinary working drudge, like Mrs. Littlemore."

"Nonsense, Mrs. Ross. You'd have all your money for yourself. You could live in the south of France."

"Oh, I'd hate that. Who would there be to talk to?"

"You'd find someone. A nice little *mas* in France, in haute Provence, that would do you well, I should think. Or a hut in the south seas. If I were you, I'd buy a little hut in Tahiti. Or a little house on that island Marshallene talks about. Oh, dear, what a lovely time you could have. You will have. You don't think, do you, that they'll stay forever? There is so much time after they've gone, my dear. Years and years. Yes, Tahiti, I think. I've heard the Society Islands are very nice. I often wish Mr. Saxe had been cleverer on the stock exchange."

"It's impossible to live abroad now, Mrs. Saxe, with the dollar so far down."

"Children are lovely, Mrs. Ross, but they do grow up. I wonder if this will do." She holds up a gleaming wheel.

"Mickle's so fond of his bike."

"He seems to be doing better with it."

"Oh, he is indeed. If you'll excuse me, I'll go and put this back on."

Vinnie drifts over for another of his quiet Thursday nights, and they are sitting in the kitchen waiting for the evolution of their drifting smiles into drifting, absent-minded gestures. They are often joined in these sad, elegant moments by Mick and Melanie and Sim for a cup of tea at the end of the evening.

Tonight, it is Sim who answers the doorbell. Vinnie goes on discussing algebra with Mick and the Spanish Civil War with Melanie, who has just heard about it from The Clash. Harriet absentmindedly plunks disparate objects into the dishwasher and screws caps on bottles. There is a clanking mechanical sound that makes Vinnie prick his ears up; then a whirr: Sim has lifted Sylvia over the threshold and the mechanical chair is steaming into Harriet's kitchen at a fast pace. This is it, Harriet thinks. Lord, it is time. I wish the kids weren't here.

"Vinnie," says Sylvia, "come home."

"Well, gosh, Sylvia, I. . . . "

"Vinnie, either you live in this woman's house, or you live in my house."

The children sit transfixed. Mrs. Saxe drifts in.

"Vinnie, I know what's been going on, and I don't like it. Screwing Harriet is an act of adultery, Vinnie, and it's grounds for divorce. You're going to miss Sam and Agnes, Vinnie; you're going to miss Joey. You're going to miss them all, Vinnie, unless you come home right now!"

None of the Rosses looks at Sylvia. They sit very quietly indeed, their hands in their laps, their mouths open, their tongues forward like parrots' but not black.

"Vinnie, this has been going on far too long, and I think

171

these children and this respectable woman, Mrs. Saxe, ought to know just what Harriet has been up to with you."

"Just a minute, Syl."

"No minutes! And no excuses! Playing around with another woman's husband is adultery plain and simple, Harriet, and I thought you, with your liberated ideas about how all women should be friends, were above such things!"

"Sylvia, I'm old enough to know I'm not above anything. But I'd rather talk about it another time."

"I'm sure you would, like after the children are in bed, when you're in bed with my husband!"

"Sylvia!" Vinnie groans.

"It's time that somebody called a spade a spade on this street. You've been carrying on for months and everybody knows."

"No, they don't," says Melanie. "I've known for ages, but nobody else has said a thing. And believe me, if they knew, they would. Even Marshallene thinks they're just playing double solitaire!"

Mick stares at Melanie. "Howja know?"

"Mick, grow up. They have their little chat, and then Mum says she has to fetch something upstairs, and Vinnie trots up after her in step; he goes to the bathroom and then it's another hour before they come down."

"Well, I'm blowed," says Sim.

Sylvia glares at them all. "You see, Harriet? You see what morals you're teaching your children?"

Like trapped schoolchildren, both Vinnie and Harriet examine their fingernails at length.

"It's not that bad," Melanie says to break the silence. "You can't sleep with him, Sylvia; and it's not as if Mum's doing something awful like one-night stands. Adults are very bad-tempered when they don't get their sex."

Harriet is speechless with admiration. Mrs. Saxe begins to radiate mirth. The boys look first at Harriet, then at Vinnie, reprovingly. I'll never make it up to them, Harriet thinks.

172

They don't trust women now, and they never will: this is the wages of sin.

"Look," she says. "I'm sorry. It was a practical arrangement and we thought it wouldn't hurt anybody. But I can see we were wrong." The Old Testament sits with them at the table, a stone in its hand.

Sylvia glares. "I just thought they all ought to know what kind of woman their mother really is."

Mick turns on her suddenly. "Gerah ... geddout. Yer a mean old bitch." He shuts up as quickly as he began. Harriet, to her surprise, begins to cry. The rest are air locked together, a circle of gesticulating hands.

"Vinnie," Sylvia says, "take me out of this house."

Vinnie pushes his chair back and stands up; he turns to Harriet and cannot comfort her; he turns to the children, and opens his mouth and shuts it again. Brusquely he moves Sylvia's chair to the doorway and begins to wheel her out. Sim shunts himself over to make way.

"So kind of you to come, Mrs. Palmer," says Mrs. Saxe.

Harriet fumbles in the kitchen for a serviette to blow her nose on.

Melanie stands up. "It's my turn to make the lunches."

Sim looks half-dead, as if he wants to cry.

"I'm sorry," Harriet mutters. "I'm sorry."

The front door bangs. Harriet wonders how Vinnie is going to manage with Sylvia on the porch, how she got in in the first place.

Sim gets up and says, "I'll help them out."

"Well," says Mrs. Saxe, "beddy-byes."

Harriet is left with a Mick who is watching her warily. She tries to comfort herself by saying that the irreversible traumas are all in place by the time a child is five, but she does not say this aloud. She sits flinching under his bulldog's gaze.

Finally he says, "You got a right to some kind of life, too, Ma."

173

"Thanks, Mick."

"Only I wish I never heard about it."

"Me, too."

"Shuddup, you two," says Melanie, "and come and help me make all these sandwiches."

Madge is grey now, grey and slow. "He says I'm getting on fine," she tells Harriet, getting up out of the armchair with Father's stick. The spaniels are keeping their distance from it.

"Harry's been in town again."

"Harry?" She's really ill, Harriet thinks. She's not even angry with Harry any more. "Harry's in town?"

"I had lunch with him. We talked about Babs."

"Babs hasn't called."

"Babs's phone has been disconnected. You know she's gone to the clinic."

"Oh."

"You ought to settle the estate, Madge."

"The estate?"

"What Dad left you and Babs. Otherwise, you see, even if Babs pulls herself together she won't be able to make a home for Sidonia."

Madge's has stopped dying her hair and it is growing whiter by the day; her cheeks are sunken. Every once in a while, though, there's a touch of the old fire. "Babs should look after herself!"

"How, Madge? You and Harry have always done everything for her."

Madge closes her eyes for a long time. Clocks tick. The spaniels moan in their sleep. Far away, Sue and Beetrice clink spoons in the kitchen. This is a house of spoons, of washing them, polishing them, putting them away, getting them out again. When I'm old, I shall have only one spoon, Harriet thinks; Babs is right.

Madge opens her eyes: "Tell Harry to call me."

"I will."

Beetrice comes in with the tea tray. Harriet looks forgivingly at the thin Indian Tree cups. Time has moved so fast it has turned my whole childhood into an antique, she thinks, and these were Mother's.

"Madge, what happened to Mother, really?"

"She died when you were a baby."

"Of drink?"

"Did I tell you that?"

"Once."

"I was very jealous of you; so was Babs. You were the Poor Motherless Thing. Mrs. Deans didn't have time to do my ringlets any more."

"There was some disgrace, though."

"Oh, I think it was TB. Everything gets worse when you're pregnant, you know that. Is that all, now, Harriet?"

"I think so."

"Then you'd better go. Next time, bring that funny woman again. I like to look at her."

Marsh plunks herself down at the kitchen table and begins to leaf through the affidavit.

"Sheesh," she says. "Oh, wow. I never knew he was a novelist, Harriet."

"Novelist! He's a liar."

"No, actually, there's some sign of talent here; it's not you, exactly, is it, but it's a version of you: the worst possible you. Love affairs–that was brilliant about Vinnie, you know, none of us ever knew; most women, a man comes to the house for coffee, we think automatically, screwing, but Vinnie and you–miles of discretion; too bad Sylvia twigged anyway–but look here, it's so obviously Littlemore making up a self-righteous scenario: undesirable friends; forces them to go to the dentist alone–they *love* going to the dentist alone, they told me: you walk too fast for them–doesn't clothe

175

them adequately: same trouble you've always had, nobody realizes the price of navy blue. Honestly, he won't get away with this in court."

"I hope not."

"Don't be so pessimistic." She digs for another cigarette, scratches, twitches, works her mouth in a circle as she gets her glasses straight, takes them off and cleans them: Marshallene will tell you she's a still centre but Harriet knows she's the house's worst wiggler. "Hmmm. Maddening. Funny, though. Susan Forbush Littlemore. Must be the Mississauga Forbushes, sold their farms to the golf club and made a mint; cousins of my mother's, actually, but then everybody is, and they've all made it clear they're nothing to me. Familiar name, though. Forbush. Where've we heard it?"

Harriet whispers the tale.

"My God. Really. Crikey. I remember. Who's your lawyer? Have you still got that incredible man who looks as if he ought to have *A Gentleman* stamped on the back of his neck where the rest of us have *A Reliable Toy?*"

"Pip Sawyer, yes."

"And it's not Philip, it's Philadelphia? Marvellous. Well, surely all he has to do is point out it's all happened once before, she has it in for you, you conflict with her image of Motherhood. On the other hand . . . ." She evens her eyebrows with spit, sniffs, scratches again: "Listen, if you *don't* fight. . . . "

"I will fight. If I don't, that affidavit goes right down into the belly of some machine and there I am: discredited."

"Do you think so?"

"Well, of course, it'll be right on the record somewhere."

"Jeepers, Harriet, that's a helluvan idea for an article: I mean, we've had all the freedom of information before, but affidavits, all the stuff about our personal lives that comes up in court, all the garbage for divorces: that could be dynamite; considering how inaccurate it all is. I mean, he can't sue for custody and put you down as the Most Marvellous Mum, can he?"

"I'm not that and that's not what I want to be. I just want to make Littlemore take it back. I'm not hanging around to provide Forbush with a built-in family."

"Oh, heck, she has to sign to make it look good. But wait, Harriet, you know what would happen if you went for joint custody? Sundays and holidays and camp and clothing allowances. How much has he been paying you?"

"I haven't had a nickel for two years."

"You should have put him in jail."

"You can't get blood from a stone."

"You can get cash out of the Forbushes: Harriet, do it. I admit I'm influenced by the prospect of being able to sleep in just one morning – will you tell Patsy, Harriet, that I don't necessarily *need* to share her joys before eleven? – but really, they could go to camp and you could have a holiday."

"That's what Pip says."

"Well, don't look so miserable: do it. And ask Pip what machine all those allegations go into; if I phone him up and say I'm a writer, he'll say I'm being paranoid – it's all that business of living with plots, I figure – but it would be dynamite to find out how many scientologists have access to –"

"Coats," says Harriet dreamily. "Good navy coats with velvet on the collar. Chesterfield coats. Grey tweed coats. Little fawn duffel coats, abominable winter snowmen."

"Not all the truths about us, all the shocking truths, what our doctors think we really have, but the lies, the speculations, the slanders: the novels about our darker selves, the selves that people who want to take things away from us make up for us; where are those, Harriet? Where do they keep the allegations?"

"Sailboats and canoes and riding lessons. Skating lessons. Remember, Marsh, the outfits Sylvia made for Melanie and

Ainslie, that were like colours that had slid off each other and plunged into old bacon fat, off-puce and off-cerise, and she called them melon and plum? Elocution lessons, Norse am I and Uncle Podger but not enough to chide me for loving my old armchair; the real bourgeois vision, Marsh . . . she could buy it for them, Forbush your forebear. . . . "

"Harriet, the spy . . ." says Marshallene.

They float forward from one fiction to another.

CHAPTER EIGHT

"I think," Harriet says to the twins, "that considering what's going on – this business of your father and the courts, for instance – we'd better talk about loyalty."

"Ah, Mum," says Peter, trying to hide under his elbow, "forget it."

"I can't, Peter. It's important. How did he get all this information, anyway? Did you tell him about Vinnie?"

"You told us," says Patsy sententiously, "always to tell the truth."

"There's something known as discretion, Patsy. You don't just spill all the beans."

"You always do. I hear you telling Marshallene and Mrs. Saxe all about everything."

"Nevertheless, you'll find that some things are better left unsaid. There are things people who were once married ought not to know about each other."

"Well, she's always trying to worm things out of us," Peter defends them. "How're we supposed to know what to say and what not to say?"

"And she says she's fascinated by you, Mum; she really admires your career."

So that's how it's done. Harriet considers: how much can they understand now? How much do they know what they're doing? Do they know it was a faith they were breaking?

"We've lost something now," she says.

"What?"

"Freedom?"

"What do you mean, Mum?"

"Now it's going to be up to a judge who doesn't even know you to decide where you'll live."

They redden and shift. "Well," says Patsy, "you could just give in. Then we could go to Disneyland with them."

"Disneyland isn't a lifetime, kid."

Both of them look as if they want to cry. She doesn't know whether she's harassing them or not, where fairness is.

"What do you think, Mrs. Saxe?"

"Oh, dear," says Mrs. Saxe. "Life is complicated, isn't it? Perhaps they could learn that. Disneyland, what a temptation! Is there any of that lovely pudding left, the kind that comes in the little tins?"

The children leap up to serve her.

Mum used to be a deodorant, Harriet thinks.

She puts down the phone and staggers back into the kitchen at supper time.

"Madge is dead," she tells them.

There is a moment's silence, then the forks and spoons start to clank again. Patsy Littlemore's eyes water.

"I thought you said cancer took a long time," says Melanie.

"I thought it did. I was wrong. She went to hospital yesterday and had a heart attack this afternoon."

"Was she lucky?" Sim asks.

"The doctor told Beetrice that."

"She was young," says Mrs. Saxe suddenly. The children all stare at her. It is an exercise in imagining age for them. They nod one by one and go back to eating.

Mick, who has been trying to speak for some time, manages it with his mouth full. "Ge . . . raw! I'm rich."

They all look at him, startled. "She ssssaid she was leaving her money to me."

Sim chuckles. "Me, too, only I didn't believe her, Mick."

"And me!" Peter chimes in.

They all laugh, finally.

"You, too, Melanie? Patsy?" Harriet asks.

"She only liked boys," Melanie says gloomily.

"If I know Madge, she took it with her," Harriet says. "I have to go over to the house and see if she left any orders for funeral arrangements: Beetrice doesn't want to go through the drawers without me. Anybody want to come?"

They all have a lot of homework.

"I'll ask about the will, too," Harriet says consolingly. "You heirs ought not to be kept in suspense. I only hope she left some to Beetrice and Sue. You wouldn't mind that, Mick, would you?"

Mick munches, rolls his eyes.

"Poor Auntie Madge," Patsy says and pours another mug of milk. "Did she really have a lot of money?"

"Who knows? Maybe all she had was enough to pay the staff and the taxes and buy the dog food. Maybe she was rich as Croesus. We'll find out, but don't hope."

It occurs to her, in the taxi on the way to the house, that this is a way out for Babs, for Sidonia. She feels a little happier.

The house is already in mourning: Beetrice has lost her gloss and Sue's thinness is plain limp. The dogs snore in corners, jerking nervously. In the desk drawer Harriet finds the document she expects, the one all Mickles are trained to draw up: Instructions in the event of my death. A thousand dollars is on deposit at the usual funeral home – the one on St. Clair Avenue that all the family has been buried from; there is room in Stanley's plot. The lawyer has the will.

The nasty, realistic part of Harriet longs to rummage through Madge's house, reading letters, turning down corners of book pages, messing the whole place up to defeat the

181

terrible tyranny of Madge's Order. But she can't, not in front of Beetrice and Sue. Instead, she has to phone the hospital and the funeral home about the body, phone the lawyer, who was also her father's lawyer, at home, phone Babs.

"Jeepers," Babs says, "the old goat's gone at last. She wasn't seventy, but she lived like she was ninety-one."

"I guess she was."

"When are you having the funeral?"

"Wednesday at ten, I guess."

"Should have it in the afternoon, ten is a helluva time. The usual place?"

"The usual." A cold chill up her back, remembering pall bearers, ceremonies.

"She's made out a list of instructions for the undertaker. It's not very hard to arrange. Will you be able to come?"

"Oh, sure, for that. It's crazy, Harriet: I'm already beginning to feel liberated."

"Wait until we get into her financial things and find out if the cheese factory actually exists."

"I'm taking typing and shorthand here, just in case. Can I do anything?"

"Phone Sidonia. She should come. I'm making the children come, Babs, so they know they have a family."

"Well, gosh. I'd better talk to my shrink about this: it's already sitting on my stomach like a bottle of brandy and I don't want to bust out. Oh, poor Madge, she tried to be good, but mostly her life was a loss, wasn't it? How're Beetrice and Sue taking it?"

"With their usual dignity."

"Glad they've got some. Okay, you phone me again in case you can change the time, eh? People will hate it at 10 AM. Bye, Harriet." Off to whatever bed they have put her in, Harriet thinks, whatever life they have carved out of her nothingness.

Beetrice and Sue stand at attention at her side. "Babs says

we should have it in the afternoon."

Instead of voicing an opinion, they open the door to Mr. Bessemer, Harriet's father's lawyer. It is the first time she has seen him out of a morning coat and striped trousers but he looks the same: eighty, tall, beautiful and possessed of a beetling blue eye and a monocle.

"Ah, Mrs. Lennox, Mrs. Ford, Mrs. Ross!" As if they are appetizing.

Beetrice, who knows his ways, at once provides him with a large glass of whisky. A smaller tot to Harriet, to her relief.

"Well," he says, rubbing his open hand on his knees. "Well. A shock. An unhappy event. I thought, I will come as soon as possible to see that the good ladies are provided for. Have your wages been paid recently, Mrs. Lennox?"

"Yessir," she says, in a beaten, quiet voice. Because, Harriet thinks, she of all of us loved Madge and she knows I didn't and she is afraid. Or does she believe in spirits? How deep is my racism? My fear?

"Sir," says Sue; young, still brisk, "she paid us last week to the end of the month."

"Excellent, excellent. Marjorie was sometimes a hard woman but she believed in doing what was correct. Her death is a shock, but she foresaw it and acted appropriately. Would you be prepared to stay in the house, say, until the end of the month, or perhaps for another?"

Beetrice can only roll her eyes. Sue nods briskly.

"What about the dogs?" Harriet asks.

"Mrs. Greenpool instructed me to have them put away. Mrs. Lennox and Mrs. Ford cannot be expected to give them a home, and she felt you have enough responsibilities, Mrs. Ross."

Harriet records that she is not feeling anything but relief: so this is death.

"Good," she says.

"I will send the veterinarian around as soon as possible,"

he says. Beetrice bites her lip and looks wildly at the dogs. Who snore and twitch and waggle their bobtails in uneasy sleep, perhaps knowing.

"You will want to know how her estate was left."

"I thought that came after the funeral."

"No, Mrs. Ross, it is quite correct for me to put the family out of its misery now. I know the matter of your father's estate is contentious; I know there is need; and I know Mrs. Lennox and Mrs. Ford will have to seek other positions, the sooner the better." He reaches into his breast pocket. "In sum, it is this: the house and its contents to Mrs. Lennox and Mrs. Ford, to be sold to their benefit, except for various souvenirs Mrs. Prentice and Mrs. Ross may wish to give to their children. Each of their children is to receive a thousand dollars cash immediately. The balance of the estate is divided equally among Mrs. Prentice, Mrs. Ross, and Mr. Greenpool's nephew Ronald Oates. Mrs. Ross's previous settlement is to be deducted from her share. Without the house, the sum will still be fairly large, but it will take a year, perhaps, to realize it, depending on what securities Mrs. Greenpool had."

Beetrice and Sue are still standing. Harriet asks them to sit down. Sue refuses but Beetrice collapses suddenly and weeps into her apron.

"I'm glad," Harriet says to Sue. "I'm glad. Will you go home, Sue?"

Sue mournfully shakes her head.

"She's good to us," Beetrice gasps. "She's good to us."

"And so she should have been, for you were good to her," Harriet says, borrowing Mr. Bessemer's briskness. "Shall we have the funeral in the morning or the afternoon?"

"Morning is much more convenient," Mr. Bessemer says firmly. "Wednesday, I think, to give time for the advertisement in the *Globe and Mail*. Visiting two to four on the Tuesday, if you can manage that, Mrs. Ross. It is what is expected, and I always feel it is best to obey the forms. I will talk to the family after the funeral. Now, a final gesture on the part of Mrs. Greenpool: she has instructed me to give you these." He hands out envelopes marked with their names and Babs's in Madge's crisp, spiky prematurely elderly handwriting. Out of Harriet's fall three one-hundred-dollar bills, and a note that says, "For good shoes for my funeral."

"Crikey," says Harriet.

The old man hoists himself up and is off. One expects a hansom cab but he drives his own car still.

"I'd better go home," Harriet says. "Call me a cab, Sue?"

"Sure."

"Will you be all right, Beetrice?"

"Oh, Mrs. Ross, Mrs. Ross." Beetrice throws her hot body against Harriet's and rocks and moans. "She was so good, such a good woman."

"Listen, Sue, I'll put you in touch with my real-estate agent. Clean up the house after the dogs are gone and get it on the market right away, huh? You can probably get a couple of hundred thousand cold cash, there's still that money around. Show it with the furniture in it, and sell that the moment the place is gone."

"She said that when she died you should have the things from the French bedroom."

"Which one is that?"

In answer, Sue ushers her upstairs to a room done in grey and blue and ashes-of-roses, a room Harriet has never been able to stand because it is just like the shut-off room that was her mother's room: everything from home replicated.

"I'll think about it. Is that my cab? Take care of Beetrice, now. You can go out if you want. You're your own bosses now. But I'll be mad if you don't make a good dollar out of it: don't give it away."

At the door, Sue hisses at her, "You didn't care about her, you don't care about anyone but you."

"Madge and I had our private feelings, Sue. But I care about you, I care about you."

In the taxi she fumbles in her purse, wondering if she has four dollars for the fare or will have, idiotically, to break a hundred. Into the edges of her mind seep the grey dressing table, the grey sleigh bed, the blue and pink silk folds of bedspread and curtains, rustling. The old spaniels stagger across her private screen. Beetrice, wild-eyed, accuses her of things. Mr. Bessemer was looking at me to see if I'd sue, she thinks; I'll sue Sue if she ever talks about love again.

Back at the house, all is silent, quiet. She climbs into bed wondering whether Madge is at the hospital or at the undertaker's, and whether they were good to her or just saw her as another stiff on a slab. She tries to cry: you should, for your sister. She fails. Twenty, thirty thousand, she thinks, would be enough to put a couple of them through school. Or . . . she fantasizes extravagances, cruises, lovers, tries them on like old dresses with torn sleeves. No, they won't do. I'll buy mortgages, she decides. Who's the executor? He didn't say. Oh, hell, don't worry about that, just buy them all new shoes and get her into the ground.

"Harriet," says Marshallene, "how can you be such a masochist? You've got Vinnie manipulating away on one side and Roger on the other."

"And you in the middle, Marsh, dear."

"You let Vinnie use you, you let Roger use you."

Harriet rolls her eyes back into her head. "Vinnie used me?"

"He used you sexually – for months."

"Lord a mercy, Marsh, I thought we were having a love affair."

Marsh stares at her, doing that bulbous thing with her eyes again. "Hell, Harriet, did you really like him?"

"Marshallene, separate yourself from me: it is you who dislikes Vinnie, Roger, Mrs. Saxe, and children in general. I like Vinnie, I like Roger, I like city politics and I like children.

If I bitch about them it's because I like bitching. I am not a masochist, Marshallene."

"Stone me," says Marshallene. "That little son of a bitch, is he good at it?"

"Everyone has an innate ability and some of us bring it out in each other."

"I don't dislike children."

"Well, quit nagging me about having too many. In fact, quit nagging. You're in an empty phase, Marsh, and you're filling yourself up with me. If you suck much more up, I'm going to have to call in the fire brigade."

"You're still wrong about the Task Force."

"Marsh, old friend, I am devoted to the Task Force. It is the hand and arm of my old Methodist training, my stamp of approval, the outward and visible sign of my inward involvement with my society. I will not give it up. How's the book coming?"

"I can't get it going, I don't know what's wrong, I keep fiddling and faddling and getting nowhere, it's not clear, I can't see my way through it, it's a goddamn mess, I don't know whether I can do it any more."

"Do you want to talk about it?"

"No."

Impasse. Silence. Then Marshallene starts to laugh. A big, round, rolling laugh.

"Hell," she says, "I was talking about it. Sometimes I hate it, Harriet, hate it. You have to let it form behind you, like a ghost walking on the heels of your shoes, and you never know if it's a good ghost. I'd better go walk it off, that's what I'll do, walk miles and miles with it, walk it until it drops dead of my fatigue. Then maybe something will happen. Mind you, I'll put you and that bloody Task Force in it."

"Just so you leave us alone, Marsh. Because if I give over to you, what am I left with? Parrots?"

They have a coffee over the parrots and how they dislike parrots and how they hope Sylvia drowns in parrots, and

Marshallene goes to walk off her ghost and Harriet empties the wastebaskets and lines up the next day's interview.

It's always in the early evening that Harriet knows that she and everybody else in the world are dying, that after you're born you start the long journey, and this is it, the hurtling of the body's cycle from spring to autumn to winter. Between five and six she is wound up tight as a clock and perverse with it: she has ladled food, fulfilled demands, issued orders, made plans, packed them off in their directions. After six, she is empty; she has no morals.

And these sad, spring nights sobbing with robin song! Tonight she and Melanie went at each other when they were doing the dishes, ostensibly because Melanie said she hated vegetables, and Harriet for no reason lost her temper and reminded her that last week she was a vegetarian.

"And it's just stupid not to eat your veg. It's a waste of money, mucking them around on the plate."

"You don't care about anything but money!" Melanie rages. "Money, that's the only important thing in your life."

"Girls, girls," says Mrs. Saxe, passing through on her way to the back so she can go out bicycling with Mick. "Surely you don't mean it!"

They do and they don't. They fling each other black looks, refuse to apologize. Melanie drops the tea towel over a chair, leaving, pointedly, one spoon and a pie plate undried, and heads upstairs.

"It's about time you got the dishwasher fixed," she grumbles on her way up. Harriet dumps the dishpan and retreats to her office.

It's this point in the day that makes her wonder about the magazine world. People in magazines have cocktails and long, romantic suppers with their spouses, and put the wee children to bed in their sanitized sleepers at the proper hour.

People in real life slam doors and struggle through, adding cheque stubs as they watch the leftovers go into the garbage can. You avoid having fat kids (except for the Littlemores, who are ... Littlemores) by not making them clean up their plates, but the crunch is coming, you can't help resenting the sixty per cent of the broccoli that gets thrown out. Christ, vegetables, I always hated vegetables (though in fact she searches eagerly for restaurants that are good at vegetables), and she thinks back to the white kitchen at home, Mrs. Deans in a white apron quietly, patiently, perfectly preparing vegetables, saying, "Now, Harriet, you're old enough to put these on after school: the potatoes an hour before dinner, the carrots three-quarters, the beans in boiling salted water, fifteen minutes before. Take the roast out at six, put it on the big platter that is in the warming oven now. Put the potatoes in the roasting pan, turn them once, and wait for your father to come home." And she was reading or sulking and always turned everything on too late and her father claimed she was ruining his digestion, and Mrs. Deans had to start coming back at supper time again. Madge coming home specially to lecture her, and herself stubborn and blackhearted as Melanie: you aren't going to get me into that stuff. Well, they knew, they knew.

The sad time of day. You can get over Madge's death, or Tom's or Father's, but not broccoli. Pleasure drains out of the day like sand down an hourglass. Life is a wen.

Then, for no reason, the colour starts to flood back; for once, perhaps, there is the security of the dark. Irony reappears, broccoli is funny, death has edged back to the rim of being, where it belongs; it is no longer pervasive. The telephone rings with loud news of external events. The twins bounce downstairs full of ridiculous pieces of school information; it is safe to laugh. She is no longer skating on the crust of a sea of slime: she is lighthearted, herself again, capable, not solvent but capable, real. . . .

"This is the very best of Canadian weather," she says to Mrs. Saxe in the limousine. The twins are in the jump seats in the back. They have black and white saddle shoes. Melanie is wearing her magenta jacket and a long, flowered dress, and high-heeled sandals that are bound to sink into the new cemetery grass. Sim is gorgeously awkward in what he insists were the best bargain, well-cut safety boots. Mick has bought cowboy boots. Harriet herself, because Madge must have meant her, too, is neat-footed in black kid. If there hadn't been so much tax she'd have cut Mrs. Saxe in on the shoe business, as well.

They have sung "The Lord is My Shepherd" in the funeral home in front of a startlingly large assembly; Madge had more friends, or Stanley had more friends, than Harriet knew. They have seen people from Harriet's childhood, and cousins they have never met before. They are on the way, no, turning into, Mt. Pleasant Cemetery.

The grave is close to the road: Stanley's Greenpool plot, one of the old ones. The traffic hums by. The children cluster around Babs and Sidonia, wondering if it's right to smile. The black-suited men lay the heavy coffin – encased in squalidly shining copper – on a kind of frame. Harriet knows that Sim is figuring out the hoist mechanism that lowers it. Madge is going into the ground, she thinks, and she worries, because it doesn't bother her: a bad sign. It will hit her later, and hard. Harriet, Babs, Beetrice and Sue are handed clods of earth to scatter. Patsy throws a rose off a wreath and sucks in her breath at the indiscretion, but Harriet nods, it is all right. Around them, other graves are open, coloured canvasses covering the shovelled, ready earth, so the place looks as if it is populated by reclining giants with coloured afghans on their knees. "Ashes to ashes," the minister says. Ronald Oates stands across the grave and nods at Harriet. He is the executor. She hopes he is honest and quick. He does something on Bay Street.

The minister murmurs. Babs and Harriet, chief mourners,

are motioned to the limousines. The children follow, eager to burst into the history of their adventures, not daring. They are glad to see Sidonia again. She looks dowdy, subdued, perhaps more honest. Harriet clutches her purse.

Harriet and her tribe in one black car, Babs and Sidonia, Beetrice and Sue, Oates and Bessemer in another: what this must be costing! There are policemen stopping the traffic, little purple flags. I can't remember Tom's funeral, Harriet thinks, only the bit about the ashes. Then the crematorium flashes before her eyes and she begins to cry. So you play one death off against another to get the tears, she thinks.

At the house, which Beetrice and Sue have polished to desperation, she goes to trip over spaniels and finds none, and is flooded with loss but forced to talk to people before whom she must never swear. Whenever she goes to say, Oh, shit, she lights another cigarette. Beetrice hovers with ashtrays.

The children stand, cowed, in one corner of the grand salon, hoping to hear things, silent. Old women, the kind of old women Madge was hoping to be, inspect them critically, not quite satisfied by their shoes. Harriet thinks, this is good for the kids, I know they hate it, but this once to feel ceremony, this once to be part of the old society, where there are forms I cannot provide them with and rituals that revolt me: they will learn from this.

People begin to drift away from the Indian Tree teacups and the Royal Crown Derby bowls, though two old women Harriet recognises vaguely from the church choir thirty years ago stand transfixed before Madge's collection of Doulton figurines (they'll fetch Beetrice and Sue a pretty penny, Harriet thinks; then: I could take them for the kids as "souvenirs," but I won't), and the house is left to the heirs, the children, and Mr. Bessemer. He makes it clear he has already been long in conversation with Ronald Oates.

The house is already on the market. An auctioneer is coming to view the contents. Meanwhile, someone has suggested it be used for a film. It's a period piece to the young, Mr.

Bessemer says, though it is not clear to him what the period is, because he is a piece of it himself. Meanwhile, cash assets to a considerable value have been found. "She was a good shepherdess," he says.

Upstairs, the children wander, taking their pick under the eye of Sue, who would rather supervise them than hear what a businesswoman she has become. Melanie wants the whole of the grey-blue bedroom even if her mother doesn't. Modestly, Sim pockets a red-leather Plato. Sue urges him to the rest of the set, the bookends (colonial elephants in brass) too, but he shies away. Patsy finds a drawer she remembers that has a wax doll called Eleanor in it. Peter, whose eye is as good, claims the brass bedroom clock. Sidonia opens the closet and extracts Madge's fur coat. Eyes narrow, but she puts it on boldly and struts in mink that tries to look like muskrat and magnificently fails. Wistfully she says, "Maybe Mummy would like that," and chooses the bookends. Sue hisses, "Take the coat." Mick is in the basement, desperately looking for something masculine, like a machine.

Downstairs, Babs says to Harriet, "I don't want any of it, Harriet, do you?"

"I have covetous thoughts about the silver and china, but I never wanted that stuff before, so I won't take it now. Take the fur coat. You might take some furniture or did you put yours in storage?"

"You know me, I'm a nudist; I just walked out."

"Take it anyway. That's an order. I'm going to take the Crown Derby. I can sell it for the kids."

"You're going to take it because you want it and you don't want to have to buy it at the auction, that's what."

"Okay. You should take the silver. It was Mother's."

"I don't know: half of Jamaica may be clamouring for it."

"Sue's watching. I don't want to do them out of anything, but still. . . . "

"I'll take the little F.S. Coburn over the chair. I've always been horny for it. I don't know why Madge didn't replace it with an oilette years ago. I don't want silver. You've got a mind like a cash register, kid."

"Somebody has to. I was moved by the money for shoes."

"She was an old rascal, Madge, and a young one, too. I talk to my shrink about her all the time. She ran us, you know."

"Mrs. Deans ran me. Look, Patsy's found Eleanor. Oates is taking the so-called Chippendale desk. Shall we give Mr. Bessemer Father's photograph there? The copper kettle? What?"

Mr. Bessemer, fierce, tall, commanding, manifests himself suddenly, and says, "I collect . . . soup tureens."

"Done," says Harriet, handing him the handsome one. "Otherwise I would have had to restrain myself at Waddington's." Miles below Mr. Bessemer's watch chain, she sees Mrs. Saxe. "A tiny teaspoon?"

Sue is glaring at her. I'm not nice, Harriet thinks, but I'm here.

"Oh," says Mrs. Saxe, "I do so like the black Japanese tea caddy."

Later in the day she returns home shaking and drained. She has gone from the funeral to an interview with a beige lady in a beige marble securities office on Bay Street. Now, somehow, she has to fill in the gulf between their two lives and write about the woman. She has never been able to figure out where that degree of formidable perfection comes from, except, perhaps, French novels, which aren't big on Bay Street. She flops onto the sofa and picks the *Mystery Chef* cookbook off the shelf, hoping the old stager will whisper supper into her ear.

Mick and Melanie are in the corner, arguing. "You know it won't work, Mick; you'll only waste your money and come home and lay a trip on us as you always do when you're disappointed."

"What kind of woman are you, Mel?"

193

"You know I'm right. I mean, you're just not good enough; you always fall on your face."

Mick stammers and stutters with rage. Harriet pretends she can't hear and stares at them curiously. This, it seems to her, is an adult encounter between them.

"Lllllisten," Mick says, "you think you're so good, Miss Smart, because you get good marks in school; but let me tell you, Melanie Ross, that's no excuse for you: you're mean. I listened to you putting Pen and Elaine down when they asked you to babysit and I never heard such a load of bull in my life. You were working them over because you had that fight with them about money last year, and you were working them over about being gay. You put me down, and you put the Ps down. Ever since Ainslie left you've been mean as hell: you're the oldest girl and you're the top and you judge all of us. Now you let me tell you this: I'm going to do it, and I'm going to do it well, because I'm good at it and I'm not taking any shit from you about being Poor Mick. Maybe I can't pass French and my math's bad, but I sure as hell know bicycles, so fuck off."

Harriet goes into the kitchen, shaking her head: anger loosens his tongue, she thinks, and he's good.

Melanie comes in and stands at the counter watching her peel potatoes for good old European Students' Stew.

"Mick's growing up," she says idly.

"He's found his tongue, I can say that for him."

"He's right, too. I was mean to Pen and Elaine."

"Why?"

"I don't know. Sometimes I just feel mean. Pen's so bossy."

"No reason to throw her sex life at her."

"I almost developed one myself, last night."

"I didn't even know you were out."

"Well, I met Randy at the Burger King after school and then we went to his place and he said his parents were away. And it sort of went on and on and I thought, better get it over with."

194

"Sixteen's a bit young. And there's all this herpes around."

"Well, I don't want to get technical, but I changed my mind."

"I'm relieved."

"It was funny, really. We were sort of talking and noodling around and he said that the stupidest thing in the world was to belong to the NDP and I went to say that we had a family membership–we do, don't we?–and then I looked at him and he looked exactly like Michael Littlemore, so I picked up my coat and came home. I don't know what happened, really. It was like turning a tap off. All of a sudden I couldn't care less. He's all over me and I've had my eye on him since maybe October, and he turns into a big, fat slob." She jabs the paring knife viciously into a potato. "Do you think I'll be an old maid?"

Harriet laughs and kisses her. "You're very smart, and all the right instincts are working, and I'm proud of you, though I guess my bias is showing."

"I think I like this family better now everybody is growing up."

"So do I. Carrots, now. Do you mind if I put off the lecture on birth control? I'm terribly tired."

"Me, too. He can really talk now, can't he? The shrink must be doing him good." She's faster in the kitchen than Harriet; neat, efficient. "He might even get somewhere," she says.

"Amen," says Harriet.

Mrs. Saxe being the age she is (whatever that is), but definitely not contemporary, asks everyone about marriage, which is something she cannot imagine a woman's life without. Left alone of an afternoon with Marshallene she asks if she thinks of getting married again.

"Me," says Marshallene, "me? Married again? Sure, I

think of nothing else; every day I commit the insanity of fantasizing a new Mr. Right; every time the sun goes down I am guilty of this intemperance, this absurdity. A Mr. Right For Marshallene, I cry. I want! I want! It's my cross to bear."

Mrs. Saxe continues to smile encouragingly.

"Marriage," says Marshallene, "is a state for which I am sublimely unsuited. I dislike housework of all kinds and am well known for scorning the culinary arts. Little dinner parties make me want to get drunk and little black dresses make me want to stuff myself and burst out of them. I am capable of walking around a vacuum cleaner left prominently in the middle of the hall floor for a week. I am past child-bearing: I had that situation looked after years ago. My only child was self-supporting years ago. I am no help and no comfort to anyone. I am a writer, and writers are notoriously self-centred. I do not have to look at the outside world to find my material, nor do I need to live out someone else's life to survive; and I am probably capable of continuing to do that until I am eighty, because in addition to writing books I compile educational films and videotapes. In short, I don't need a husband.

"My experience of husbands is such that I ought to know better than to want another one. I resist all their attempts to dominate me, except in bed, and this brings on even stronger attempts to dominate me. When they fail to dominate my person they try to get into my work. My first husband told me that *All For Land* was no good—and it's still selling after twenty years. My second husband thought authors were glamorous and found he couldn't stand them. 'It's like living in a desert, when you're writing,' he used to say. 'All I want is my supper and you make me feel like an impossible dog for wanting it.' 'So make it yourself, I'm busy,' I would say. 'Busy? You're staring out the goddamned window and you haven't swept the floor for a week.' 'I'm trying to get it right in my head, you oaf,' I would say; 'go get some Kentucky Fried Chicken.' 'It's bad for my ulcers.' 'Go boil an egg, open a can of soup, do anything ... go.'

"I don't make breakfast. In the morning I dream over the paper and drink coffee until my blood is stiff with it. Then, about noon, I think about a piece of toast. Lovers are wonderful but when in the morning they have a gleam in their eye, I know it's for bacon and eggs. I burn bacon, I frizzle eggs, my 'real' coffee is always lousy. No one in the world shares my opinion that lukewarm instant is a gourmet delight. I'm unlivable with and for.

"Yet every once in a while, still, at my advanced and unmarriageable age, I dream of marriage. Marriage! Wedding bells ring. Three nieces in peach, lilac, and lime georgette sway in my head to the tune of 'The Bells of St. Mary's.' I see marines as trees walking, all burbling, 'I Wanna Buy A Paper Doll That I Can Call My Own.' I croon with Annie that you can't get a man with a gun. I start loving love again; I cast sheep's eyes at the man in the hardware store till his grim wife comes to serve me. I project sex at Tomasso the bricklayer until he runs away. I ooze at Sim, I sigh for Mick. I once made a dead set for Michael Littlemore. My hands shake when I open my son's letters, seeking always evidence that he has become my kind of man. There is that in me, Mrs. Saxe, that would lay itself gratefully at the feet of every male chauvinist pig in Canada: for a whole five minutes.

"In bed, since you like the intimacies, I have become impossible. I moan, groan, and wallow, in an undignified fashion: then I want a cigarette. People get tired of waiting for the smoke to clear. I think up new and disgusting ingenuities, but am too unathletic to subscribe to the practices of the young, who require one to be double-jointed. Straining after an orgasm makes me fart. I should go to a nunnery, take up with women, learn to be an island, entire of myself, but what do I do? I'm a grotesque old middle-aged woman, heavy and short in the leg; hairy and graceless, anything but sweet and supine: I waltz down this street, this very street, of a spring morning, as indeed, I did yesterday, whistling ('Whistling girls and crowing hens,' I hear my auntie say) 'I want some red roses for a blue lady.'

"The last person who sent me red roses wanted my son, not me. I am a blue lady because I refuse to shuck off this terrifyingly romantic and unrealistic dream of happy cohabitation. Right now I dream of a large man with a wonderful log house in the country who wants to keep me immured there forever. And when I close my eyes I see him as a kind of muscle-bound Snow White, sweeping, cooking, tidying *and* building (tote that barge, lift that bale), and driving me to all the things that delight me – high cliffs, long, low, sliding plains, and huge parties where I am the centre of attention – and, well, rocking me in the cradle of the deep. In fact, I'm forty-eight and I still want it all and I don't want to contribute a nickel's worth of work to it. I deserve to be shot. Or shafted.

"Yet I respect this dream in me. If I gave it up, was sensible, saw reality: what would I see? A line of women on welfare stretching from the cradle to the grave. Romance may be dangerous, Mrs. Saxe, but I hand it to myself for hanging on to my dream.

"The name I use is Marshallene Peacock because my father always swore I was Marshall Peacock's kid, not his. Marshall Peacock was a farmer of exquisite moral sensibility across the road and down the line who wouldn't have touched my mother with a pole. I grew up in a family that was so disorganized that it summoned all the government social services at once and proved them inadequate. One of my brothers murdered a girl, my sister Mona ran off with an Indian, my brother John is a fairly famous philosopher: we were country nobodies with an ambition to scale all heights, and absolutely no right to romanticism. What will redeem us on Judgement Day will be our terrible and perpetual need for attention – from God or man, the priest or the MP or the police, the public, the private: anybody. We have to go on proving we are human and fallible.

198

"Marriage, Mrs. Saxe? I love it, I hate it. I dream of it; once I'm in it, I feel morally obliged to stand between the pillars like Samson and push, push, push.

"I have to go now, Mrs. Saxe. I have to go to the hairdresser. And when I come back I'm going to take off my jeans and put on the old black cocktail dress and meet a tall, lean man for Black Russians on the roof of the Park Plaza. With any luck, I'm going to cut him in pieces and skewer him and grill him and eat him up. And then I'll marry him and lay a trip on him, and tell him. . . .

"Oh, hell, no: I'll go in my honest blue trouser suit and look meek and modest and. . . .

"Or shall I? Oh, Mrs. Saxe, what do you do with this big white moon-sized loneliness inside you? Tell yourself it's green cheese and eat it? Marriage? Don't make me laugh, it's unjust; don't make me cry, it isn't fair. I want to love, I want to cry, I want to eat. But I don't want to vacuum or cook. And those who want everything both ways get it no way. Two plusses make a minus. I'm therefore an island in spite of myself—as you are, Mrs. Saxe—but, by God, I'm a floating island with a fifty-horsepower motor, and pardon me while I strop my leathers and get out of here."

Sim's exams are over; he has a job in the north that doesn't begin for a week; he hangs miserably around in the morning, charging around in the vicinity of the mailbox. Harriet, waiting for her day in court, hasn't much to say to anyone. Melanie is still struggling with French and Latin; Mick is morbidly engaged with his bicycle and Mrs. Saxe; and the twins are making themselves scarce in the thick climate of anxiety. It's a waiting week.

Finally, Sim gets what he has been looking for and comes, hangdog, into Harriet's office.

"Mum?"

"Yes, Sim."

"I've been accepted at Queen's." Looking at her half-happy, half shyly sorry.

"That's terriffic, Sim."

"Do you mean you don't mind me leaving home?"

"You've got to go some time, Sim. You don't want to be mother's little helper for the rest of your life."

"I thought you'd explode."

"I've been afraid I'd have to shove you out of the nest."

"Queen's is a pretty good university, I guess."

"I guess it is. If you don't get a scholarship, do you think you can make out on a student loan?"

"I can get a job."

"Engineering's pretty heavy."

"I don't have to drink all the time with the jocks. Only thing is, Mum . . . "

She knows, she smiles, she'd give him anything, he's been the good one, the easy one, he deserves anything . . . almost.

" . . . I guess if Chris and I are going up north, we're going to have to take the car along."

"I'll cede you my share as a graduation present. How would that be?"

"Well, if you still kept it half in your name the insurance would be less, wouldn't it?"

"It would, Sim. You're off on Monday, then?"

"Sunday. We've got to get up to Chapleau by Monday night."

"You'd better get your gear together, then. Will you work right up to registration?"

"I guess so. We've got to make all the money we can."

"Don't get caught in any bush fires, then. Off with you, go sort out your clothes, write letters, fix the car. Do something!"

He goes, and leaves an already enlarging emptiness behind him.

So they have a big chicken dinner Saturday night before any of them go off on their dates – for even the Littlemores now go out on Saturday night, with their father – and Sim sits at the head of the table and makes little jokes and looks gap-toothed and comical. After the dishes are done and they are all gone, Harriet settles down in her office to read to the sound of the bicycle industry in the basement. Surprisingly, Sim returns early and knocks on her door, sticking his round, tentative head in before she answers.

"Mum?"

"Sure, come on in."

"I'm sorry I won't be with you in court."

"Oh, I don't think you could do anything but keep me company, lad."

"I feel kind of funny about leaving tomorrow."

"The house is going to be pretty empty without you."

"When I was little, I thought I'd stay with you forever and ever and help you; at least, that's how I felt when Tom died. But then last year Chris said, hell, man, Queen's is where it's at, you can't hang around home for the rest of your life."

"He's right, you know. That way you get crippled for the rest of your life. That way you're the husband and father."

He looks embarrassed.

"You were always nifty to the other kids, Sim."

"Well, I liked them."

"I hope you can bring yourself to write."

"Oh, sure, lots."

"Have you been saying goodbye to Mary Lou?"

"Naw, she's not in it any more. She wants to get married!"

"Are the girls like that now?"

"She is. It's not that I want to use anybody, Mum, but heck, I'm not going to spend the rest of my life fixing power mowers so she can have a baby."

"I should think not."

"I like kids, though."

"Good. You've been good to the twins."

"Some of the girls are pretty militant, now, about not having babies. I feel kind of bad about that."

"I'd stick to the militant ones, Sim, till you finish your

education. The life force will look after you."

"Well, I've got to get some sleep. We're leaving at five. I hope I don't make too much noise loading up the old bomber."

"All your sins are forgiven, Sim." If he ever had any. What the heck can I say to him, Harriet wonders, that will cut through? "I love you," isn't witty, it's distorted by too many movies, it's not what a mother says to a son. "Bless you"? Too biblical, and who am I, anyway, Abraham?

"There's just one more thing, Sim," she says, "if you and Chris could lug that lumber out to the front tomorrow before you go, you know, the trimmings from the old porch, the big garbage truck will take it on Wednesday and I won't have to carry it out myself."

The cloud of sentiment lifts. "Aye, aye, sir," he says. "And can you let me have a couple of bucks' worth of stamps?"

Wearily, she hunts through the drawer. Nothing is where it's supposed to be. She gives him the extra roll of Scotch tape, too, and some envelopes, and a handful of stationery.

"Don't lose your temper in court," he says. "Littlemore will hang himself if you're just silent. And you'd better wear your suit even if it's hot because that navy dress you've been wearing is pretty bad. Listen, where's the mending wool? I guess I'm going to have to do my own socks. And I think you ought to know Mick has plans to be away this summer, but nothing you have to worry about; I mean, it's not illegal and he'll tell you when he's ready, he promised me. Bye now, Mum."

He leaves her clutching a book, a stamp, and a hank of blue wool and wondering who she is.

"But of course," Babs says, "as long as they're all misbehaving I've got them on the hip, haven't I? If Harry continues to be unreasonable, and Sidonia continues to steal, I can make

202

the equation right by drinking as much as I want. Fair's fair. Even-Steven. Me the martyr. But if anybody gets better, I have to get better myself. That part I don't like."

"You could play it another way," Harriet says.

"Yes," says Mrs. Saxe, "you've every excuse, haven't you? You could drop off a balcony."

Babs shudders. "It's time I went," she says. "The Institute closes at ten. It's all very prudish ... but I'm not doing it to even it up, I'm not doing it for myself. The Road to Ruin is so lonely.... "

Harriet calls her a taxi.

Harriet sits reading; Mrs. Saxe sits reading. Mrs. Saxe is sucking her back teeth; Harriet's concentration is thus fractured, no, shattered: she feels the surface of her brain like the cracked glaze on an antique plate. She shifts, irritated; she is reading a book she has no interest in, a book that is hard for her, she has to push herself, and there is this sucking noise, this intrusion, and it is as if faces are peering around the edges of her glasses: she hates it.

She tries to be patient. I'll give her a minute more, she thinks. If I give her two minutes more I'll want to beat her up. Instead, I'll say something shaming.

So she stares at the faces at the edges of her glasses. Then, "Jeepers," she says. "I've been had."

"Heh?" asks Mrs. Saxe.

"Mrs. S., that brazen yellow-belly ... that ivory-billed bitch: it's a set-up."

Mrs. Saxe looks at her. A lightbulb appears in the cloud above her head.

Harriet says, "The business with Vinnie. Sylvia. It's a set-up. There's somebody else. I know it. Look, it's got to be her. Vinnie's a darling. Vinnie's an innocent. Vinnie is determinedly and boringly noble and innocent. Coming over here for a roll in the hay is the closest he gets to being ignoble. But

203

she: why does she have to be good because she's crippled? I always thought she was crooked as a crow's hind leg. So; he's her lawyer, he gets her a good claim, he's a bird-fancier, too, she gets involved with him, she marries him. But she doesn't like him: she likes her independence and he's her way to get it: builds ramps, he does, installs elevators, works like a slave for her. And they have the birds between them. But she: is Vinnie enough for her? There isn't a crooked bone in his body. She gathers her pleasures where she can – she has to. And to get away from Vinnie, to get out from under Vinnie, so to speak, she pins it on me."

She stops speaking and closes her eyes, letting the figures around the panes of her glasses close in on her.

"I know who she's got, too, Mrs. Saxe. Now how do I know that? Age and experience, I guess. Experience is what comes with decay, that's right. I can see it now ... black jacket, black jeans, skinny like Mick, but older; a little farouche; out for kicks. Not Vinnie, not innocent. Slouching. It's Bob Robbins's Fred she's got, Mrs. Saxe, and she's welcome to him."

She goes to jump out of her chair and phone Vinnie and tell him but she realizes he's gone and she can't. Then she spins her thumbs one over another. "He won't, though. He won't make use of it. He won't want to believe it: there's class in there, manners ... manners makyth man, all that stuff. He's a lawyer: I remember Anna Royer talking about law school, saying the law's still mediaeval: if he fights, he's done for. He'll do the gentlemanly thing: he likes his case-work, his plodding, boring accident claims. It's him, it's what gives reality to him. So even if I tell him, poor, dear, nice Vinnie – and you know, after all these years, Mrs. Saxe, a lover who is a dear, kind man is a boon, absolutely a boon. That man's only fault is his goodness.

"But do you remember what I said to Sylvia when she was here that night? Did I admit anything?"

"Oh, dear, you said she had a dirty mind."

"Mrs. Saxe, I am going to go right on saying it. And I will find out what's going on with Bob Robbins's friend Fred even if I have to ask Mick or Bob or just anybody; I will send it to Vinnie at the office anonymously: capital letters – *your wife's lover is so-and-so – A Friend*. If he won't look into it his lawyer will, because she's going to take him for a packet. And when they come to me I'll deny everything. That night she came over here we were having coffee, and that's that. I won't be a patsy for a bunch of birds. The kids are upset enough already."

She goes to the window and looks out, steadier now than she has been for a while. The air is soft and the lights of the windows gleam pleasantly through it. "Soap opera on the street. Again. Hell, Sylvia, you've had your fun. 'The Mediaeval Background of Women's Law': that would make an article. All us injured wives and scarlet women. You can't refuse to play the whore of Babylon 'cause the law says you're it. Oh, Vinnie, all your jewel-coloured birds, your Eclectuses and lories, don't give up too much for them." She lets the curtain fall. "Him and his sand-coloured hair and sand-coloured suits, he's too good to exist," she says.

Mrs. Saxe clucks and giggles. She has finished with her teeth.

CHAPTER NINE

It would take place, by Harriet's preference, in an old courthouse, say the one in Cobourg, where the lion and the unicorn have faded into grisaille and the judge would be grey, too, except for his black cap (for what failed Christian does not want to be condemned on earth to avoid the judgement of heaven?), but in fact she goes to Pip's office in a taxi and they take another taxi downtown and find themselves and the wriggling Littlemores in a modern building seated in new, limed-oak pews behind the fat neck of Michael Littlemore and the long, thin neck of Sue Forbush, himself in a brown suit (new) and herself, like Harriet, in standard, law-abiding navy blue.

It's a small courtroom, new, with white curtains at the window and two old men lounging at the front talking about the fishing season over the taped briefs.

"The judge will probably hear you in his chambers," Pip whispers. "He'll see them first, then you, and then the children and then the lot of you together, probably. He's a bit late."

Harriet waits, shushing the Littlemores and being none too friendly to them (how can I be, she thinks, now that they have made this hyphen between us?), thinking of not much, suspended, wishing she had brought a book. Michael and Sue Forbush Littlemore whisper and write notes to each other like schoolchildren. Patsy and Peter wiggle and fuss. I should have brought books for us all, Harriet thinks. I failed to imagine, I'm falling apart.

The morning is hot and drips by slowly. One old man says to the other, "Will it take long?"

"Might. This is a little one that turned into a big one."

Harriet's heart begins to seize up. I want to do the best for them, she thinks, I want them under one management or the other, shared custody is schizophrenia, I want the best for them and I want the best for me and I want Michael Littlemore to drop dead in his tracks.

He doesn't, but beads of sweat fall off his neck into his collar.

I want to be justified, Harriet thinks. I want to be Joan of Arc. She puts an arm around Patsy, who wiggles away.

"It's too hot, Mummy."

What do the twins really want, but to please? Disneyland alone?

Pip has told her the judge is a new judge, male, from Ottawa, down to help with the caseload. They can't know what to expect. "You've got to offer as much as you can. Possessiveness looks bad. I know you hate Littlemore, but you've got to try to look bland about it. You've got a good case and they don't like taking them out of the homes they are used to, but be careful."

Be careful. Out of this boredom, any statement might come. The room and its buzzing silence are like a long August heat wave. Finally, Pip comes back.

"They're first," he hisses.

Michael and Sue go into the judge's office after their lawyer, an incredibly young man with a halo of frizzy hair, like Woody Allen or a baby. They walk on eggs, they look as if they're going to sign the register after a wedding, she has her head up and a bride's small, smug smile on her face.

After another interminable wait, they file out and Pip files the twins in.

Who walk very nicely, very carefully in their new outfits, Patsy self-conscious in a dress instead of jeans, Peter proud of his new outfit, the closest imitation Harriet can afford of a suit, not what Sue would buy but never mind, she says to herself, never mind. The running shoes look grotesque, but as usual they put their feet down about leather.

They come out sober, confused, and Pip calls Harriet. There is no time to comfort them, talk to them, and the space between them is still great. Harriet unsticks herself from the pew – pews haven't changed – and walks uncertainly behind Pip. To her surprise, the Forbush-Littlemores are brought in, too. No chance to be Joan of Arc.

The judge's chambers are white and beige and the judge is almost as young looking as Michael's lawyer: not the old English actor with the death cap at all. Harriet sits nervously on the edge of a white chair, the kind of chair that makes her afraid she'll get her period suddenly and soil it, and listens to him, almost failing in her nervousness to take in anything he says. In her fantasies the other children were here to defend her, but now it's only Pip, and much as she likes him he's only a lawyer; in his private life he might think anything of her, might never think of her at all: you have this feeling, she decides, that you exist personally for your professionals, and you probably don't. To what degree do you live in the mind of your dentist? You are a piece of income, a broken tooth. What's he saying?

"I gather that Peter and Mary Patricia are fond of their father and fond of the good things of this world they think he is now in a position to provide for them.

"They are the fifth and sixth children in a large family supported by a single parent without much previous help from Mr. Littlemore. Is that right, Mr. Littlemore?"

"I've been out of work," he says.

"And you are now employed by your wife's father's company?"

"That is correct." His fat dignity exudes from the chair,

and Harriet, who is not thin herself, hates every ounce of him, or does she? She is too confused to remember. He complained about the housekeeping, he complained about the food, she says to herself, now he's complaining again.

"And you are a free-lance writer, Mrs. .... Ross?"

"Yes."

"And your income is as stated on your affidavit?"

"It was last year. It fluctuates."

"Not much to support six children on."

"One is with her grandparents in California and one will be leaving soon."

Michael looks at her involuntarily. Is he thinking about Sim?

"Still, it must take some managing."

"Yes, it does." She might go on if she didn't feel Pip silencing her at her elbow.

"Yet Mr. Littlemore feels that he would like to see more of Peter and Mary Patricia, possibly have them live with him. Don't you think that might be a help to you, since you have other problems?"

"I'd like to make sure that they're being realistic about each other. She, Mrs. Littlemore" – the title comes hard – "hasn't much experience of children. It might be hard on them."

"I see." He makes a church and steeple of his hands. "So you have at home now ... Simeon, Melanie, Sid – Sidonia. ... "

"No, she was a niece, and she's left."

"Gone home?"

"No, she's disturbed. She's with the Children's Aid now."

"I see. So: Simeon, Melanie, Mick ... le, Mary Patricia, and Peter. Some of these are adopted. I don't quite see the relationship of all these children to you, Mrs. Ross."

Sue Forbush shifts in her chair.

"Simeon, Melanie, and Ainslie, who is in California, were the wards of my first husband. Mickle is our son. I took Sido-

209

nia for a while when her parents were separated."

"So you feel you have considerable experience with children."

A courtroom is a place for reducing feeling to the minimum. "Yes."

"And you, Mrs. Susan Littlemore, feel these two children, Peter and Mary Patricia would be better with you?"

"My husband wishes to have them living with him and I am prepared to make a home for them."

"And you had some experience as a Children's Aid Society worker before you went into business?"

"Yes."

The room is fanned by cool silences. Beside this, Harriet thinks, everything is propaganda. Funny, you think in a courtroom you're finally going to be able to cry out, but it's not like that at all, it's keeping everything possible in: you leak suitable facts one by one, keeping your lips as tight as you can. Pretending there's no emotion. Pretending there's justice and calm. You could say it's hypocrisy, but what else do we have?

The judge says, "I would like to talk to Mr. Sawyer and Mr. Reasoner, and then we will recess for lunch while I make my decision."

He's about Vinnie's age, Harriet thinks, and the embodiment of sweet reason. No hostile waves, just.... It's like meeting death and finding it bland.

Out in the courtroom the old men are still talking in undertones about trout, and the children are squirming. "We'll be going for lunch soon."

"Can we go with Daddy? He said he'd take us to McDonald's."

Damn you, yes or no. "Daddy, can we go to lunch with you?"

"Sure," whispers Michael Littlemore. "Anything."

"Okay," says Harriet. Okay, you little betraying, greedy bastards. Wanting to cry with her betrayal of them.

210

"The trouble is," she says to Pip at lunch, "that any Littlemore will do anything for a hamburger."

"He probably feeds them two."

"How do you think it's going?"

"No telling. What do you think of the judge?"

"He doesn't seem to have much character, but I can't complain. What do you think is right, Pip?"

"You're angry with them, aren't you?"

"I'm pissed off. I know enough about kids to know they're like dogs, they'll go where the food is, but I still have this old thing inside me that wants it to be love. Know what I mean?"

"It's not in your hands any more, Harriet. That's what I meant about settling out of court. How's Mick?"

"Much better, now Sidi's gone: Sim was right."

"Fifteen and fourteen are hell, as I remember. Have you still got the old woman?"

"Oh, sure, she'll never go. She's another one of my orphans."

"And the Vinnie thing?"

"I haven't seen hide nor hair of him, and neither has anyone else. That night, he just left. I wish I could get a message through to him, but I don't dare phone the office."

"Is it important?"

"I think so. If you can find him...."

"He's still practising; there's no problem."

"Does he know it was a set-up? That she's been carrying on with Bob Robbins's lover for months?"

"Sylvia? Poor, martyred Sylvia?"

"All women aren't as nice as I am, Pip."

"And you're not even nice," Pip grins. "Remember that, will you?"

"Look, I don't know the ins and outs of the legalities, but if she's going to have him up for adultery and wring a judge's heart, she ought to explain what Bob's Fred has been doing there morning after morning."

"You watch the house?"

"Our bedroom windows face; we could play ball together. It's a dirty business, isn't it? Almost as primitive as Iran: you take a step out of line and off with your head."

"Vinnie might know. Haven't you heard from him at all?"

"He phoned me once and just said he thought he'd better cool it and stay away for a while, and would I look in at the birds."

Pip laughs. "There are worse custody suits about pets than children. Really, Harriet, worse. It's time to go back now; can you face it?"

Harriet looks down at her half-eaten sandwich and says she thinks she can. She feels hot and faint and old but still alive.

The room with the pews is cooler now. Perhaps the old men have opened the windows or turned on a hidden fan. They look the same: weathered, waiting. If these people could only solve their problems so we could fish, their faces say.

The judge is prompt. At half past one they all file in to his office. Patsy wiggles as a woollen sofa scratches her plump legs. Peter is tall, dignified suddenly. Pomp suits him, Harriet thinks, he's doing well.

"Well," says the judge, "I've been through the files again." Smiling at them all pleasantly, the perfect host. "And I hope I can help you come to some kind of agreement here. How would you children like to spend the summer with your father?"

Patsy sucks in her breath. "Disneyland?"

"Oh, I don't know if that is in his plans, but what I'm suggesting is this: you like your father, and he would like to spend more time with you. On the other hand, he hasn't lived with children for some time. So why don't you experiment over the summer holidays? You can still see your mother, of course, if you make proper arrangements in advance. How would that suit you, Mrs. Ross?"

Harriet grins inside herself. She'll send them to Camp Watchapoopoo, she thinks.

"That would be all right," she says in a small, cool voice. "Now, at the end of the summer, Mr. Sawyer and Mr. Reasoner will call each other up, and they'll call me up, and we'll decide what will happen for the school year. We'll talk about whether it would be bad for you to change schools, how you got on with your father and your stepmother, and how inflation is cutting into your mother's income. Do you understand, Peter? You might know how you feel a little better, after that. Do you understand, Mary Patricia?"

"Yes, sir," they nod. They really are lovely, Harriet thinks, with their beautiful red-gold hair. She'll wash it more often than I do, too.

"Now, how much of the school term is there left?"

"One more day," says Patsy in a lunge of anticipation.

"Do you have exams?"

"Not yet."

"Well, then, you've time to help your mother pack."

"They won't need anything," Sue Forbush Littlemore says in her measured voice. "Everything is prepared for them."

Pip looks startled. The judge loses his Sunday school manner and looks brisk. He stands up.

"I shall expect a call on September first," he says.

They file out silently. Exeunt with Mr. Reasoner the Forbush-Littlemores. Exeunt with Mr. Sawyer the Ross-Littlemores.

"How one longs for the absolute," Harriet says to Pip.

"Do we have to go back to school, Mum?"

"Can we go back to school and tell all, Mum?"

"Where do you want to go, Harriet? I'm off to the office. Can I drop you?"

On the steps of the building, which is like any other building, large, plain, and stone-stepped, Harriet pauses to adjust her eyes to the light. The wave of hot air catches her, and for a moment she does not know where she wants to go, what she wants to do, her personality has been wiped clean away by the tension. She no longer knows who she is, how she lives, why she wants what.

She steps down. And down. She falls.

"I don't know what happened," she says to Pip. She is lying on the sidewalk and the Forbush-Littlemores are beside her.

"Can you stand on it?" Pip asks. "Shall I get an ambulance?"

She tries and fails to stand. The guardians of the building hustle out and try to help her.

"If I can get you in my car, I'll take you to Emergency," Pip says.

"Michael," says Harriet, "I think I'm going to have to ask you to take the children home." Because she is sitting in waves of pain and foolishness, incapable of taking care of anyone, even herself.

"Is it broken, Mum?"

"I don't know. I heard something snap but maybe it was a muscle. Or whatever snaps." My mind, maybe?

"Come along, children," says Sue Forbush Littlemore. "Of course we'll take them, Harriet, if that's all right with Mr. Sawyer."

Mr. Sawyer is off getting his car. "I'll make it all right if it's all right with Mr. Reasoner."

Patsy hovers over her. "Does it hurt, Mum?"

"Only when I try to get up. What a mess I am."

"Do you want me to phone and tell Mel to make supper?"

"Would you, pet?" All tender again. For herself and for the others.

Pip stops at the curb and the Littlemores and the security guards and Mr. Reasoner manage to get her in.

"It's only a block to the hospital. I suppose I could have borrowed a wheelchair," Pip says.

"I let them go with Michael. Is that all right?"

"You are lucky he hadn't gone already. How's the pain?"

"Fierce. I suppose in the autumn they'll want to stay."

"I was hoping for something more permanent, but that's reasonable, Harriet. The kids are very mixed up. He's been dangling the goodies in their faces for a long time."

"We all find out about goodies. Ouch. I can't have broken it, can I? Look, just get me a wheelchair and I'll look after myself. I'll be hours in Emergency. I'd get you to take me to my doctor but there are steps up to his place."

So she sits and waits and is wheeled around, and calls Melanie to fetch her, hours later, and suddenly Vinnie is beside her in the bandaging room.

"Pip called me," he says. "How is it?"

"Only a sprain, but it's torn all to hell," she says, lifting an enormous, blue bare foot to him. "Elephant woman. How are you?"

"I'm okay; I'm going to pull through; I ran away for a while; I apologise. But how are you going to manage with that, Harriet?"

"The trouble with me, Vinnie, is that I could manage with six arms and no feet, it's a gift, damn it. Did you get my message? Did you know about Fred? I don't want you to get thrown out of the Law Society on a fiddle, Vinnie."

Vinnie looks down. "For a while, all I cared about were the birds. They are as beautiful as she is, Harriet. But I don't know, now. I'm beginning to feel very ... free."

An intern enters and says, "Mrs. Ross? The sprain? Ace bandage for you. You thought it was broken, didn't you? No such luck, I'm afraid. Take care of it, though: in six weeks it's going to be right as rain, but not before." He slaps and winds.

Just a sprain, she thinks. Tomorrow I'll be back out there talking the heads off distressed women, volleying with Babs, shunting Sylvia.

"I think the kids are going to go with Michael," she says to Vinnie.

"Pip thinks they'll be back with a settlement in September:

best of both worlds. You were smart to fight."

"I don't feel smart."

"There," says the intern. "Check out at the emergency window. Have you got your card? Good. Take it to your GP if it doesn't get better in six weeks, mind. Can you manage the wheelchair, Mr. Ross? Good."

Melanie is in the waiting room. "Marsh is here. She borrowed Roger's car, Mum. You are a mess. How did it go in court? Hi, Vinnie."

"Call me," Harriet says to Vinnie. "I haven't finished talking to you yet."

"I will," he promises. "Thanks for the message. I guess I knew it inside but no one had told me, yet."

"What was that about?" Melanie asks grumpily. "Can't Vinnie resist wheelchairs?"

"Pip ran into him and told him I was here."

"Well, tell us about court!" Marsh says. "Are you in? Can you manage? We'll have to lug you up to bed, poor thing. Was it too much for you? What happened? Where are the Littlemores?"

Harriet, encased in a tube of Ace bandage and pain, bats them away and puts her head in her hands and sobs.

216

CHAPTER TEN

Harriet wakes again, feeling very odd indeed. Something is wrong about the dimensions of the space around her. The room is dim and the bed is different: she isn't at home. She cranes her neck and sees that she is lying between a window and a door with a rectangular hole in it. So this is it, she thinks, I've flipped, I've finally flipped, I'm in the loony bin. Before she can register indignation, satisfaction, or despair, she is engulfed by a wave of weariness, which carries her off to sleep.

She wakes again. The door opens, and three masked men enter. She looks at them, then closes her eyes once more. There is no point in wasting energy registering emotions: this has happened and must be endured.

"Good morning," one of them says pleasantly enough.

"Gerah," says Harriet.

"Do you remember what happened? Do you remember your name?"

"Harriet Ross."

"And where do you live?"

"Ten Rathbone Place." They have rather nice dark eyes, she thinks, behind the masks. But they are human: at the address they can be seen to wince.

"Do you have children, Mrs. Ross? What are their names?"

217

She recites them, all but Sidonia.

"Good. Now, can you tell me what happened?" His voice is cool, like water. She feels weary again.

"I came out of the courthouse and slipped on the steps. They took me to the General and I had my ankle taped up. Melanie came for me. I went to bed when I got home. I woke up in the night and tried to get up to go to the bathroom. . . . I fell over."

"Did you notice anything particular about your condition when you tried to get up?"

"I was sleepy, terribly sleepy. Even the bedclothes hurt my feet. Wait: I had a fever, I was burning up, like the children when they were little. That's what must have knocked me out. What day is it?"

"Monday."

"Jeepers, four days."

They are standing at the foot of the bed, a good four feet from her. She realizes that her sinuses are full of fluid and reaches around for a Kleenex. And another, and another. They back away. They aren't notable for bedside manners, she thinks, and where's my Joe Christie, the doctor from the Pits?

"I'm Dr. Novick, and these are my assistants, Dr. Galg and Dr. Brunel. We're from the epidemiology department. We'd like to ask you some questions, Mrs. Ross."

"Proust's father was an epidemiologist," Harriet says helpfully. They are unimpressed. The buggers don't read, she thinks. Little Marcel was hooked on his mum while his dad was off inventing the *cordon sanitaire*. "He invented the *cordon sanitaire*," she says, "which is probably out of date."

"Not entirely," says Dr. Novick, backing away again as the Kleenex begins to stack up beside Harriet. "Now, all the history we have is that you are forty-six years old and live in downtown Toronto. Were you born here?"

"Born in Toronto, general health excellent, ear problems as a child, most communicable diseases, most shots, hospitalized for childbirth twice, tubal ligation once, dying for a cigarette."

No smiles behind the masks. I do like to charm people, she thinks, but these men can't be charmed. What have I got, leprosy? Thank God it's not madness.

"Now, Mrs. Ross, you appear to have picked up, from somewhere, an extremely contagious disease of a tropical variety. All the lab tests haven't come through yet; diagnosis is incomplete. We've been treating you with antibiotics and you are responding nicely – too bad about that ankle, because it keeps you from feeling well – but we'd like to know more about who you've seen lately, where you've been. Have you travelled recently?"

"In 1962 I went to Cherry Beach."

"No tropical visits then? Hawaii? Jamaica?"

She resists comment. To someone who grew up on the same fifth-grade reader she did, she could say, "The realms of gold," but these men are too young to have experienced that great Canadian traveller, the textbook sold in Eaton's catalogue.

"No."

"Have you had contact with any of the following in the past six months: desert rats, pineapple mites, exotic bats or parrots?"

"Parrots?"

"Parrots."

"Well, sort of: but nothing, well, rude."

The three masked men looked at each other and nod.

"Tell us about the parrots, Mrs. Ross."

"Lories, lorikeets, parrotlets or macaws? My neighbour across the street has an aviary."

"And do you have anything to do with the aviary? Do you enter it? Do you handle the birds?"

"She tried to hand me Joey one day and I nearly flew the coop."

"The disease we have in mind, Mrs. Ross, is called psit-

219

tacosis. It causes a virulent, pneumonia-type infection, and is highly contagious. It is contracted by immediate contact with the droppings of infected birds."

Poor Sylvia with her feathered rainbows, and where are they now?

"If you're familiar with an aviary that contains birds of the parrot family that is obviously where you've come in contact with the disease-causing elements. Can you tell me anything more about your relations with the birds or their owners?"

Harriet closes her eyes and tries to suck her body in through the openings of her soul. It doesn't work. When she opens them he's still there. Well, she thinks, it could have been VD.

"One of the aviary owners is a particular friend of mine," she says, with what dignity she can muster.

"I see. Has he had a cold lately?"

"He has a rather annoying snuffle. Could he have built up a resistance?"

"Perhaps. Parrot fever is very like a cold and attacks the weakest hardest."

"The twins have been cleaning the aviary every Saturday."

"Have they had colds?"

"I'd have noticed, wouldn't I? I mean, I'm an absent-minded mum, but when their noses run they all scream rape and accuse me of running out of wheat germ."

"And where are they now?"

"They've gone off with their father somewhere." She realizes, with panic, that she doesn't know where any of them are and tells him.

He frowns. "We may have to get in touch."

"Are you going to put a big yellow quarantine sign on the door?"

"We don't do quarantine signs any more, Mrs. Ross, but we take psittacosis very seriously indeed. Give us the name and address of the aviary owners, for a start."

"Vinnie and Sylvia Palmer, 7 Rathbone Place."

"The infected birds will have to be destroyed, and the others treated."

"I'm not really fond of birds – but the lories are beautiful." One of the downier interns perks up. "Lories?"

"They don't talk and they smell bad – but their feathers are airbrushed on and they have thick, black tongues and the colours are astonishing."

Dr. Novick forges on. "We'll have to run tests on all those who have had contact with the birds."

"Mrs. Palmer will be very, very mad."

Novick shrugs. "Mrs. Palmer ought to take better care of her birds."

"I can't pay for a single room. I've only got ward coverage."

"Isn't your husband. . . . "

"I'm a single, self-employed free-lance writer and the Lord doesn't provide."

"The hospital now has a policy of providing the facilities the patient needs regardless of coverage."

"Just so it knows." Doctors were more tolerant of conversation about money when they got only the price of two music lessons for an office visit: but more of us died.

"I'm sorry to mention it. It's the shoes and the jeans."

He smiles. "I have seven. Are you tired, now?"

"I still have to go to the bathroom. And I'm hungry."

"Good. I don't know Rathbone Place. Is it a long street?"

Forbidding herself to tell him about the Task Force, the impending destruction of the mattress factory, Bob Robbins, Pen and Elaine, Marshallene, the people from Saskatchewan, Roger and Winnie (what's going to happen to Winnie? Roger will have a fit), the New People, she says, "No."

"I think you can plan on going home tomorrow. You'll have to stay with your prescription for some time. It would be good for that ankle if you were to lie around. Since you're self-employed you can simply regard this period as your holiday."

221

"What about the kids?"

"If any of them are frail we can give them gamma globulin. Otherwise, wait and see."

They leave; she feels she has made a narrow escape. She rings for the nurse, who, also wearing a mask, helps her to the bathroom.

"I'm a pariah," she says.

"You're still hallucinating?"

They bring her a breakfast of cream of wheat and milk and juice and water flavoured with an eighth of a teaspoon of instant coffee. They take her temperature. "Good, you're down to a hundred and two." She falls asleep. Ali Baba, riding a very fat Roc, looks over his mask at her and says, "All diseases are venereal. So to speak."

She wakes, crying like a parrot, "Where's Mick? Where's Tom? Where's Pete? Where's Pat? Where's Mel? Where's Sim?" She sleeps again, in the grey and rosy world of galahs and cockatoos.

Another mask at the foot of the bed. "Well, sailor?"

"You scare the hell out of me, Marsh, in that thing."

"You'll see more of them. And will you please learn to put your own Kleenexes in your own paper bag so I don't get it, too?"

"Who's coping? How are they?"

"The twins are with Michael and Sue and they've taken off somewhere. Mel's gone to stay with Ainslie in California, where the health department, on my notification, is having, so to speak, a bird, and Ainslie's grandfather is being divested of yet another million and loving it – you're on to something, Harriet, that man loves spending money on kids – and you. Do you know what he said? 'Don't spare the expense, Mrs. Peacock, don't spare the expense. Just see that that good, good woman who raised my Ainslie has everything she needs.' Can you beat it?"

"No," says Harriet, thinking that there might even be good Frenchmen, too.

"Mick and Mrs. Saxe have disappeared but they left a note

222

to say that Sim knows about it and says it's okay."

"If she's with him I can't be that irresponsible. And school's out. I figured there was something going on."

"Good. I phoned Sim's headquarters and they say he's up alone in a fire tower but they'll keep an eye on him. They do a bear-watch every second day and they'll take his temperature or something."

"Good. What about Roger? Is he having a fit about the baby? This could knock her out."

"Roger's paediatrician – female, of course – has the situation in hand."

"Sylvia?"

"The Health Department descended on her this afternoon with a ton of tetracycline-treated seed. She fell weeping into the arms of Bob's Fred, but not before she said, 'Shit on Harriet.' "

"It must have been that new pair of lories."

"They're very beautiful but they don't do much, do they? I think you're right about the parrotlets, they have a good time all day. Oh, the city's going to hit her with about a hundred violations and she'll hate you for a while, but she'll clean up her act. Poor Vinnie."

"You aren't going out with anyone who works for the papers, are you?"

"Haven't we both learned about that?"

"Will you pick me up tomorrow?"

"About noon?"

"I'd love that. I'm down to a hundred tonight and I can go home if I am okay in the morning."

"I'll phone first."

"I keep having these wonderful dreams. The sky is all beautiful and the characters are from the Arabian Nights."

"You're falling asleep now. Good night."

"Good night."

Home. The house looks good, she thinks. Shabby, sure, but

ours. Scabbed by the right people. Chipped, worn, loved. But where . . . ?

"I figured your foot would do you no good upstairs so I got Bob and Roger to move your bed downstairs. I put the sofa in the kitchen and you're going to be right here in the living room, everything at hand and the john next door, for two whole weeks, the doctors say."

"Oh, Marsh, how good –"

"Not so fast: I, Marshallene, am deserting you: as everyone else has. The television's there, the phone's there. I went to the library and got you half a dozen thrillers. I did my duty. I'm off to a conference on the Future of Publishing, but there's a squad of masked bandits going to come and look after you, there's a sign on the door that says 'Ring and Walk In,' and I, Marshallene, I, have gone and bought an enormous and enormously expensive vacuum flask, which is by your side, full of nourishing, non-alcoholic fluids. Here, also, is my father's blackthorn stick, which he used to beat us all with: you can get to the bathroom. On the way, you ought to meditate on changes in child-rearing, and whether they were worth it. I think they were, but I'm not always sure."

Harriet basks, the perfect patient. How the children love being sick, and having their meals on a tray, and how right they are!

Harriet sleeps. Crimson and madder and pink and red creep into the edges of her dreams, like the red that creeps through the white of Rembrandt tulips. A procession of women creeps up the hill, miners' picks over their shoulders, singing "The Volga Boat Song," their jeans and jean jackets tinged with gold and a blessedly non-menstrual red.

Pen stands over her.

"Harriet?"

"Pen?"

"Drink this."

"What is it?"

224

"Liquids and pills, that's the order. Four o'clock. I came home especially."

"How's business?"

"Liquids and pills. Drink, swallow, drink. I'll be back tonight."

The reds are becoming softer, tending towards peach and saffron, as if the sun is setting. It probably is. A masked figure in the corner of the living room is hunched, drawing something, standing guard.

"Bob?"

"Still alive, Harriet?"

"Liquids and pills?"

"Liquids, not pills yet. Want to go to the can?"

"Give me an arm?"

"Sure, kid."

"Is Sylvia mad?"

"They took out a pair of those lories and killed them with a hypo and took their bodies away in a plastic bag and she screamed after them, 'Three thousand dollars,' and they gave her no change at all. She's mad. Fred's looking after her."

"I'm sorry you lost Fred."

"I'm not."

Dreams. Soaring rocs again. Ali Baba has lost weight. He looks like the Man from Montreal. "If you do insist on doing everything for yourself," he says.

Strange to be sleeping in the living room, but the space is right. It's not a hospital. In the middle of the night she gets the stick and goes to the bathroom, stump, stump, stump, by herself; feels victorious. Then goes to the refrigerator and eats and eats and eats. Handfuls of lettuce. Leftover spaghetti sauce. Anything she can find.

I'm better, she thinks.

"Morning, Harriet." Another mask.

"Roger. But Winnie?"

"I'm keeping my distance. Your pills are beside you, and I've refilled the jug."

"You're a darling, Roger."

"I try to act on my beliefs."

She has a strange sensation and thinks it is in herself, but it isn't: the house is vibrating.

"Are they pounding on the factory wall?" she asks.

"It's beginning," he says.

"Marshallene sees me as a capitalist cop-out for sitting on your committee."

"What does she see me as?"

"You know."

"But we're either inside or outside, aren't we? Just because I've chosen to be in, am I evil?"

"It was my idea for an Italian women's magazine that finished her."

"What interests me is that your idea of a women's magazine is, well, retrogressive."

"I didn't go to the L.S.E., dear."

The argument would go on, if it is an argument, and would amuse Harriet endlessly, but the telephone rings.

"Harriet?" A little, high voice, barely recognizable. Oh, Sidonia without the act.

"Sidi?"

"Harriet, Aunt Harriet, turn the TV on! Right now. Channel six!" Sidi slams the phone in Harriet's ear.

"Roger, that was Sidi, saying turn the television on. What can she mean? Has she gone into commercials?"

Roger reaches out to the old set. He's really beautiful, Harriet thinks. He's beautiful the way a woman is beautiful, and I never understood that: I was infuriated by the way men loved beautiful women, but when I see him in profile I could crawl for him. No flies on our. . . .

226

The mellifluous voice of the CBC: "We are bringing you, from the hamlet of Old Harry, in the Magdalen Islands, Province of Quebec, the beginning, ladies and gentlemen, of the very first Trans-Canada Bicycle Race. As we said before, there are forty-two entries, a good number considering the entry fee of a thousand dollars apiece, and they are now lined up on the pavement of an isolated place in this isolated part of the province, the last of the Clergy Reserves, Old Harry, Quebec. Here's Michael to tell you more. . . ."

Harriet, still confused, but dawning, stares at Roger, who is still beautiful, but impatient. Funny, she thinks, my father must have been handsome at that age, too, and I remember him only as tired and mean.

"Here in the Magdalen Islands, previously distinguished only for the seal hunt, Farley Mowat, and a wind-power project that blew over, forty-two Canadians who really believe in what the government calls Participaction . . . "

"Booo," say Harriet and Roger together.

" . . . are setting out for the prize of the century, the gold medal for crossing Canada by bicycle. Forty-two fit, beautiful. . . . " The announcer's thin hair is blowing across his face and the wind is mooing in his microphone. The camera pans seven ranks of six contestants each.

In the fourth row, white with tension, stand, beside their mechanical horses, side by side, Mick and Mrs. Saxe.

"Begorrah," says Harriet.

The announcer goes on to explain, at length and with difficulty, handicaps and routes. The contestants will not ride across the whole of Canada. They will take selected ferries, trains, and helicopters. They are not expected, for instance, to pump over the Rockies. The race is from Old Harry to Victoria via the metropolis of Grindstone, the Province of Prince Edward Island, the Marshes of Tantramar, the St. Lawrence Valley, the Holland Marsh, Riding Mountain, the Qu'Appelle Valley, Rocky Mountain House and the Doukhobor

227

country. It will end in Victoria. If anyone makes it.
Cut to: Mrs. Saxe and Mick, seraphic.
A gun shouts, a flag falls.
"Oh," says Harriet.
They are off. Down a hill by a little white leaning Protestant church. A flock of birds flies up. "Avocets," the announcer says, proclaiming his endearing bias. They whizz through a landscape of marsh, dune, and choppy sea, wind in their eyes. Mick has his hair tied back with a band, Mrs. Saxe's topknot wobbles, leg muscles flash; there are others in the contest of flashing wheels but Harriet will never notice them. Wires overhead and a long, low road, brush blowing in the wind, wheels veering towards each other, cameras on trucks following, sometimes leering out to the sea and the white beaches or the other way to a blueberry scrub, sometimes on the racers. Then another shot from in front, where they look like the camels advancing in *Lawrence of Arabia*.

"My God," says Roger, "I've got to go. Do you suppose Winnie will do something like that some day?"

"I hope so," says Harriet, half-expiring.

Bloody Madge left him a thousand dollars. Bloody Mrs. Saxe stayed all winter. Everybody dies, nobody survives, but we might have some good times . . . yet.

She opens her eyes again. Low red cliffs. A village. French. Because the houses are huddled together, not proud and alone like the Anglo-Saxons'. People waving, watching. A wheel skids. Someone who knows how to fall falls off and is sponged like Christ. Not Mick. He looked so full mouthed, Mick, he's all mouth and he can't speak, oh, poor. . . .

Oh, legs pedalling . . . oh, eyes closing.

"Ma, it's Melanie, in California. How are you?"

"Alive, love, and you?"

"We've all had tests, we're okay. Ma? There's another complication. Patsy's done a horrible thing, or they have to

228

her, but anyway, she's here, she's safe. They took them to Disneyland and she didn't get up in the morning and Sue Forbush said if she didn't get up they'd go without her and she went and locked herself in the bathroom so they did go, and she came out and called the police on them, so they sent her here."

"Oh, dear." Rigidity meeting rigidity in the night makes war.

"Well, anyway, it's going to make the papers so we figured you ought to know. The police want to charge them with abandoning her: they're sore."

"I guess they treated Peter better because he was a boy?"

"She's just frantic, Ma."

"She's been stupid, they've been stupid. You nag and con and compromise, you don't hard-line."

"We don't know whether to hug her or hit her."

"She plays on guilt. Don't be easy on her. Is Granfer upset?"

"They're playing Monopoly."

"They should be. Listen, guess what, if you can get it on American television, Mrs. Saxe and Mick are in a race."

"Are you okay, Ma?"

"Mrs. Saxe and Mick are the oldest and youngest in the Trans-Canada Bicycle Race and the CBC is making a fuss over them; try to get it. Tell Patsy . . . can I talk to her?"

"Sure."

"Patsy, you oaf."

"Mother?" In a little, lost voice.

"Patsy, you'd better apologize to them, even if you think they're in the wrong. You've made a lot of trouble."

"I hate her. She's a wicked stepmother. I like it better here."

"You made a deal, Patsy; now you have to stick to it."

"Can I come home?"

"You told the judge you wanted to go to them. So you'll have to stick the summer out."

229

"But they're awful! She doesn't let us do anything. We have to stay clean and say please and thank you and make our beds, even in hotels."

Harriet's heart fails to bleed. "You made your bed, kid. Now you have to lie on it. Listen" – can she listen behind the tears, poor wench? Will she ever listen? – "Mick and Mrs. Saxe are on TV, I've got to go, they're in a race. Let me tell Ainslie – and Patsy, you do what you're told." The bawling goes on.

Ainslie: "I wish I was with you."

Harriet: "Me, too, love."

Ainslie: "Are you all right?"

Harriet: "Right as rain, if you're dealing with Patsy."

Ainslie: "We're going to try to get the race. Maybe Mick will win. What's it like without kids?"

Harriet (thoughtfully): "Hollow, but very relaxed."

She wakes to the bustle of the car ferry *Lucy Maude Montgomery* bouncing on the waves of the Gulf of St. Lawrence. The Trans-Canada Bicyclers are taking the ferry from Grindstone, in the Magdalen Islands, P.Q., to Souris in P.E.I.

She wakes to Elaine and a plate of lasagna.

She dreams that Roger is standing over her, chastising her with an outstretched finger for owing fifteen dollars in library fines: a bad citizen.

She wakes: Mick and Mrs. Saxe are pedalling mindlessly across the Tantramar marshes. She remembers the summer the war ended and her father took them all – Babs, Harriet, Madge, Stiff Stanley – on a trip in the '38 Chrysler with the net on the inside of the roof. The tidal bore was a bore, and the reversing falls didn't look perverse at all. They drove up the eastern shore and he said, you see the poverty, you see the shacks, you see the gilded crosses on the Catholic Church roofs?

Mrs. Saxe and Mick look like terriers in the wind.

Harriet wants to phone everyone in the world, but puts her

head on the pillow instead and passes out.

Bob Robbins isn't wearing his mask any more. He hunches in the corner away from her, comfortable in her house now because she doesn't have any kids.

"Water?"

"Water. And I can go to the loo now by myself. I'm healing up."

"Harriet, you're a monster."

"And you'd love it if I came at you with Marshallene's father's blackthorn stick?"

Bob Robbins grins wide and opens his arms.

Dear God, she thinks, what have I done but somehow accidentally fathom some truth, and what good will that do me?

Mrs. Saxe and Mick are pedalling down the St. Lawrence Valley, the route of Cartier, going faster than he did, and certainly seeing less. Past the beautiful houses. Past the islands. Through St. Patrice, and its lovely summer cottages, which cause political quarrels about privilege, even as they gently fall apart.

"I wish I'd come from St. John of God," she thinks, "rather than Toronto of Toronto; or St. Rose of Ham. And what good would it have done me?"

The river lots with their narrow frontages. The scooped roofs. Our sentimentality about Quebec, and their reality. How strong you get from being put down. Patsy. Sylvia. The Québécois. The Jews.

A masked man she doesn't even know. "I'm the new owner of Number 11. Have you had your pills and your juice? I've brought you creamed salmon soup. Can you eat it?"

Oh, dear, love, it isn't a bad world after all.

"Mum?"

"Peter. Darling."

231

"Are you okay?"

"Sure. Everyone's taking care of me."

"I'm okay. We're on our way to get Patsy, now."

"That's neat. Take care of her, will you?"

"Sure."

"Have you had a good time?"

"Wonderful, Mother, wonderful." (How intelligent is he, she wonders, as opposed to how easy-going, and how can anyone understand that?)

"Can we come back in the fall? Michael and Susan are okay but I think I need the others."

"Tell the judge that, love, and tell the lawyers. But don't complain about Michael and Susan, okay? Oh, Peter–Mick and Mrs. Saxe are on the TV again. The cameras are always focusing on them because they're the oldest and youngest in the race. They're crossing the bridge to Montreal. They look very tired and very beautiful, they–"

"Mum, Susan says I've talked too much, I've got to. . . . "

"She's right, my love, they. . . . "

"Mum?"

Mick on the phone. And nobody, now, doing the juice-and-pill patrol: they know she's getting over it. Good. Enough of being a patient.

"Mick?"

"Did you see us?"

"Oh, Mick, I've been living on it."

"They phoned you were sick and they took some blood out of my arm."

"It hasn't held you up. How's Mrs. Saxe?"

"She's super–more staying power than a–a–elephant."

"I'm glad. Give her my love. Where are you now?"

"Listen, you aren't mad I finked out on you?"

"I finked out on you. No, I'm thrilled with you. Where are you now?"

"Gananoque. We're crossing Toronto day after tomorrow."

"Mick, I don't think I can come."

"We'd feel better if you stayed home. I mean, we want to streak and not talk to you."

"Good. Sim's got the car, see, and I'd have to rent one to get there."

"Bye, Mum, hope you don't mind paying for it."

I'm still sick, she thinks, if it took this long for it to sink in that it was a collect call.

Hunched like an old owl, refusing to be masked, brilliantly expressionless, Babs sits in the corner talking.

"I feel terrible about Madge," she says. "I'm just beginning to realize how bad we were to her. Our own sister."

"Could you just put the television on so I could see Mrs. Saxe and Mick? They must be in Manitoba by now."

"Madge was basically all I had. My own flesh and blood. And I neglected her in her hour of need."

"She wasn't too good to you in yours."

"My own sister, and I didn't even go to see her when she was dying."

"We didn't know she was dying."

"I accused her of lying to me about money."

"She lied about money all the time."

"I could have helped and I didn't."

"You couldn't have helped because you didn't know how ill she was. None of us did, except Beetrice and Sue, and they weren't telling."

"I let her die all alone."

"She had Beetrice and Sue and the dogs and you were ill."

"My alcoholism is not an illness; it's a perversity."

233

Harriet struggles out of bed, paying for her impatience with pain from an ankle that is healing very slowly indeed. She hobbles to the television set and switches it on, thinking, me and my easy solutions; I think: if I could just get a couple of days in bed, if Babs could just haul herself to the Institute, if Mick could just find something to do . . . and it happens and, of course, it doesn't quite happen. . . .

"Harriet, I just can't get over the fact that that poor, lonely woman is in her grave!"

"Do you feel she can feel it or something? Why does it horrify you?"

"I feel she's cold and alone and shivering."

"Babs, she's just dead. And before that she'd been dead to us for a long time. She hadn't been herself since Stan and the boys died, you know that. She was nutty as a fruitcake. Taking you money in the tea caddy!"

"But that was generous of her!"

"She'd owed you money for twenty years. She waited until you were down so she could appear to be handing out charity."

"Harriet, you're so mean!"

"Shh. You're giving me a thirst. Look, here they are. Do you know, I can do the CBC announcer's spiel off by heart now?"

"Harriet, it just isn't important."

"Babs, nothing is important except what one chooses to make important, and death. Come and look at Mick and Mrs. Saxe."

The other riders have chosen the anonymity of racing costume. They are muscled and flashing in vests and shorts. But Mick and Mrs. Saxe, in their queer wrappings and head rags, bent over their handlebars, pump rhythmically across the landscape as if they were bicycling through Harriet's office, relentlessly and evenly pushing forward through the books into, Harriet thinks, the future, rather than away from the past: out into the something more, and good for them.

234

"I should have ... " Babs says.

"Do you do a lot of therapy there?"

"Group."

"You don't feel so alone?"

"Oh, I never felt alone!"

"Has Harry settled?"

"Well, now that Madge has left me money, I don't feel I. . . ."

"Babs, Sidonia's problems are not solved. She's just on hold, so to speak. There's a long trip ahead."

"That woman she's with is just wonderful."

"And just hired, Babs. You're going to have to make a home."

"I never appreciated Madge. To me she wasn't herself, she was just a domineering sister-figure."

"Look, they're holding their own very nicely, aren't they?"

"You said they were winning; they're only in the middle."

"That's how you win: slow and steady; anyway, they're ahead on the handicap system."

"Harriet, has it ever struck you how much you're like Father?"

Harriet, suddenly weary, turns her face to the wall.

"I have to go. It's going to be time for Modern Business Practices when I got back. Did I tell you Harry asked me out for lunch and I said no?"

"Yes." Wondering if he meant to fill her up with martinis.

"He seemed very disappointed. I think he's a bit tired of the gay life in the Bahamas, really. He said he missed snow."

Life is as long and flat as the prairies, Harriet thinks, and your knees become extensions of bicycles and you're a machine by the time you get across.

"You don't seem to be listening."

"I'm still a bit feverish; I'm sorry. Look, Babs, don't grieve over the past. Beetrice called and said they'd got a handsome price for the house and Sue, who'd said she wouldn't speak to me again – or implied that, if I'm not making things up – came on the line and said she was thrilled with Mick. They're going to be all right. It was brilliant of Madge to leave them the house."

"I made Sidonia put the coat in storage."

Babs is rising uncertainly. Harriet rummages wearily in her bag of nostrums, unable to find a new one.

"Everything's going to be all right, dear," she says.

Babs looks at her steadily and sharply. "Harriet, how you came to be such a softy I'll never know. Everything is *not* going to be all right, and you know it."

"Have it your own way, Babs. Me, every morning, I say, 'Every day, in every way . . . ' because it's all I can think of. It's better than worrying, and better than dying."

Babs still stands uncertainly in the doorway. "What happened to that boy friend you had?" she asks.

"The one from Montreal?" Feebly, not knowing what to say.

"You've had a lot of them, haven't you? I was faithful to Harry."

"I never doubted that you were."

"I don't know what to do about it now. A couple of times I've dragged men home from bars."

"You really know how to do it to yourself, don't you?"

"Well, after all these years I don't know what, really."

"Don't ask me, Babs. If I knew I wouldn't be in this fix now."

"You're not much help, Harriet."

"I guess not. Run along, now, or you'll be late for your lesson."

Lovely sleep, she thinks. I knew a man once who read rune stones, I knew one who collected beer mats, who collected birds, who. . . .

She wakes, groggy: Bob is hunched in the corner, sucking on a beer bottle like a baby.

He grins: "Figure if I haven't got it yet, I don't need my mask. Don't throw your Kleenexes at me, huh? Seen Sylvia?"

"Not yet."

"Some hot, that one. The Ministry of Health has been by again."

"Heard that."

"She's got Fred in there vacuuming the place out, and Vinnie giving them all their little pills."

"So what else is new?"

"I just look out the window every once in a while to see who's winning, Vinnie or Fred."

Out on the street there's a buzz, a whirr.

"There she is, going by, fierce as a ton of birdseed. Sheesh, will you look at that Mick, and the little old lady! I shouldn't ought to have been so hard on her, she's something."

"Are you on nursing detail today, Bob?"

Bashfully: "I guess so."

"Go heat us up a can of soup, will you? I feel kind of dizzy. My sister was here for a long time."

She digs her head into her pillow, trying to get back to the little feverish technicolour dreams. She doesn't remember them when they're over, but they loom somewhere back in her consciousness like sweet acid drops and she wants to taste them again, though he's worse than the kids and can't find the pot, the soup, the can opener, the spoons. She manages it, finally, and wakes, later, beside a bowl of congealing chicken soup. Roger is lounging in the doorway again.

"Congratulations. Your infectious period is now over."

The sound of falling brick shatters the silence again.

"Bob's out there watching," Roger says. "They give the wall a shove with the machines, and then a little kind of moving tractor like something out of *Star Wars* puts out a mechanical claw and wriggles and wriggles the bricks free. That way, they don't fall on your house or Vinnie's. I've never seen him so happy. As a matter of fact, the rest of us have been watching, too. Even Winnie is fascinated. I've got the minutes of the Task Force for you to sign."

"You mean I have to get up and be businesslike again?"

"This, too, shall pass."

Harriet sits up in bed with the bills and the bank statement in her lap. If she cranes her neck to the right she can just make out the little *Star Wars* figure pushing the loosened brick of the factory wall away from Vinnie and Sylvia's house. He's been shortened as the wall has been shortened, but he's still a handsome vision: the first of the robots. What's it going to be like when that wall is a street? she wonders. When we're connected to the rest of the city? She has seen the plans for the development many times, but this is the first day they've been real to her. They're going to let in the world, she thinks, and I may not like it.

She glances down at the sheaf of papers again. She doesn't like this, either. So much for fancy Gothic porches. The trouble with me, she thinks, is that I never take into account the fact that it costs to feed people. If I have a bed, I put an extra head in it. And the taxes and the car insurance are going up. And we shouldn't have all eaten out on Chargex that night, except that we enjoyed ourselves so much. And the calls to California!

And *Household Words* has decided, at long last, to dispense with Depressed Housewife.

They're right, and I've wanted to get rid of her for years, Harriet thinks. She's past her time, and she's boring me, she makes me feel like a women's liberation sellout, she's. . . .

Supported us.

The Lord loveth a cheerful giver, but what happens to people who don't count before they give?

238

Then a thought occurs to her. "Marshallene!" she roars. "Marshallene!" No answer. She's still at the conference on publishing. What the heck did she put in that last column she rewrote when I was at the hospital?

It's only ten in the morning. Harriet's head is clear. She sits quietly, smoking, thinking, adding and subtracting again and again. She remembers asking Pip the lawyer, whose bill is included in the stack, whether she won or lost the court case, just before she fell. Well, did she win or did she lose? A summer away from those cavernous appetites is clearly a financial win, she thinks. But what will I do with myself without Depressed and the income? When the children go, what's going to keep me from floating straight up into the sky like an unleashed balloon?

Money. Always money. People say I care too much about it. If I don't think about it all the time, I slide into debt. There's no margin. Madge could leave me a million, it still wouldn't be enough. But I had my desserts from that estate years ago.

It's all this ... hope, she thinks, that ruins us. Like the hope of heaven that keeps us from living really well because we can't imagine that life will simply stop. All this business of dreaming about making a great city or a great family and carrying on, pushing at the kids to do their homework to prepare themselves for a world that doesn't exist, and working away at print for a world that doesn't want it any more. Darn it, we're living as if we're trying to finish a nineteenth-century novel when it's been over for nearly eighty years. Madge and her leather shoes and what proportion of the world wears them? Us and our "nice" public housing, when half of Cambodia lies in filthy camps. Me, slugging away like a nitwit to support a passel of ungrateful kids where welfare and the Children's Aid would have taken better care of them – that's the future.

The bunch of us on the street trying to create a little middle-class enclave, hoping hundreds of others would troop

239

after us into the neighbourhood, and relieve it of the ugly reality of sagging porches and falling-down shades, and push values up so that we're somebody. I'm as out of time as my father, who lived in a rich neighbourhood and didn't know how to live like a rich man because he didn't believe in rich men. I hope he saved his soul.

Hope! She switches on the television. There they are again, pedalling towards the horizon.

Haring towards the prize. Her heart swells for them, she knows whom they are imitating. Hope's corruption, she tries to say to them, just look at this bank statement, hope is dumb. She doesn't have the heart.

"All these years I've worked and toiled," a little martyred voice inside her says, "and what's it been worth?" When she pays the bills she won't have a hundred dollars left.

And how many times has she hypocritically said to the children, "Money doesn't matter"?

But there they are and the announcer is going over the ratings and handicaps and Mickle Ross and Adeline Saxe are third and fourth. And the numbers have thinned. There are mountains in the background; they're already in B.C.; half the competition is gone.

Close-up of Mick's face: it seems to be clearing. Every day another worry line goes, there's just the wide, striving mouth, the goofy, turned-up nose, the bulging eyes. The old man's face he wore this winter is gone. Mrs. Saxe looks more than a little fagged out, but she pedals bravely on.

And I haven't worried for days, Harriet thinks, about where they eat and sleep. I'm growing up.

Hope. There was some old Christian poem we had to learn in school, about a kind of Pandora's box. Was it hope or grace, the last virtue in the chest that connected us to God?

But what about reality? What about this? (Shaking the sheaf of bills at the *Star Wars* man, whose patience is as inhuman as his automotive trolley body), what about buy and

240

sell, pay your own way, and where is the fancy man who'll get me out of this?

Remembering the day, when she was a teenager, when she came to the conclusion that all married women were tarts. Which was before she knew that they were cleaning women.

Hope. You could do a good article on hope, but would anyone buy it? Is that what the new young are into, as they say? Do they even know the word?

But who are the new young but Mick and Melanie, Ainslie and Sim and the Ps? They know about hope. Ainslie would come home to us if she didn't; Melanie would stay all summer with her instead of going to wait on tables in Banff; Sim would loll instead of fire-watching. And even foolish Patsy, trying to manipulate Sue Forbush, is indulging in hope: I will get what I want without having to pay for it. Perhaps it's innate.

Of course you've spent too much, you dope, she says to herself. It's July, and you always spend too much to outfit them for the summer and give them their exam treats, and the taxes and insurance come in then; you're always broke in July. And look, ordinary lawyers charge at least five hundred to take you to court, and seventy dollars an hour in the office and you, who talk too much and are always in trouble, Pip charges much, much less. It's still a fortune: but you do have to pay for mistakes like Michael Littlemore. And you're not where Babs is.

I thought life was going to be all Dover Beach and sighing, "Ah, love, let us be true to one another," but Tom died on me. If I suffer from Hope, I should think of him! He might have had a *crise de feminisme* and stopped me working for *Maga* and *Household Words*, he might have found another of his fertile, dark ladies, he might have gone to an analyst and turned into a stockbroker. He died and left his goodness etched on our windowpanes. It's not that the good die young, it's that dying young enables us to pronounce them good.

241

Hope. The television switches to a soap opera. Harriet feels she should watch it in case she has to write one, but she knows she won't and can't. Leave that to Marshallene.

Hope. She falls asleep again.

Towards nightfall, Marshallene comes back. She sits on the foot of the bed and gives Harriet a viewy-hole account of the state of the publishing business.

"Will books survive?" she asks. "Is the Gutenberg era over?"

"Probably," Harriet says, not thinking very hard. "If McLuhan—"

"A guy got up, a little curly-haired guy—actually, I don't know if he was little or not, I just associate those kind of curls with littleness—"

"You talk a lot about moving to chastity, Marsh, but I've never heard you describe a man without his body."

"He got up and read a statement of pure rage, one of the best statements I've ever heard about Canadian publishers, and he said afterwards it was what the Guild of Illuminators had said about Gutenberg."

"They were right."

"It scares me."

"Marshallene, I have this awful feeling that you and I will go on and on."

Marshallene pauses, almost tenderly. "Harriet, when you were ill and raving I finally realized that we were going to die. Not now: some day. It was the first time I had taken it in."

Hope.

Schmope.

Another day, but not, as the vulgarism has it, another dollar. Marshallene comes in, brisk in blue denim, with food, for which Harriet is grateful, because it still hurts her to stand at the stove, although she is otherwise almost recovered.

"I ought to move upstairs again. How on earth did they get the bed down?"

"Notice the hall walls?"

"I thought so."

They sit at the window drinking coffee, and watch the *Star Wars* man, still neatly and efficiently tipping bricks one by one into the next-door yard.

"That time I was in Europe," Harriet says, "I stood for an hour and watched workmen repairing a piece of pavement in London. They were scraping the old tar out and neatly reboiling it and laying it again: nothing got wasted and it took infinite care. That was twenty years ago, but I was impressed. Even then, none of us here indulged in that level of craftsmanship." They both stare at the machine.

"Funny: it does."

"If it just slugged the wall over it would ruin our properties."

"Our? They're both yours, Harriet."

"You owe me two months' rent, kid."

"I know. When I get the Film Board cheque."

"You were smart to go into film."

"I can't do journalism. Not like you."

"I can't do it either: I just do. They've cancelled Depressed."

"Hurrah. You've spent fifteen years, Harriet, looking for depressing things to write about."

"I'm depressed trying to figure out how to live without Depressed."

"I've got a thing about Pen, now."

"So's Elaine."

"Shit, you're right; I'd better turn my head around. How's Sylvia?"

"The wheelchair sounds like a wasp when it comes down the street. I put my head under the covers."

"Vinnie?"

"Guilty. Limp. I guess she's Mummy. Maybe they can work it out."

"If Fred goes back to Bob."

"Bob doesn't want him."

"A little bird told me Roger is house-shopping down on the waterfront."

"Winnie's teaching him he's middle class.

"Tell me more about publishing."

So she does.

In the evening Sim, who has been relieved, to prevent cabin fever, phones from Sioux Lookout. He's in a tavern, watching a rerun of Mick and Mrs. Saxe on television.

"I said he'd be okay," he says.

"He is, Sim, he is."

"How's everybody else? Babs? Sid? Melanie? Peter and Pat?"

How that man can love, she thinks. Hope isn't a bad thing.

The next day, she and Marshallene totter out for the groceries. The air feels strange on her shrivelled skin. Marshallene is tanned, but Harriet feels white as an old, old bone. She buys a loaf of bread, a package of sliced ham, and one tomato. Marshallene makes her buy half a dozen yogurts and some orange juice, and she is grateful.

"You forget," she says.

Marshallene steers her home to bed. It isn't quite over.

When she gets in, she feels light as a cloud, and thinks of Renaissance paintings of the Ascension: bodies spiralling up. Better than pedalling horizontally. Alas, impossible.

Now it's the last day of the race, and though she's put off thinking of it, she's twittering like a bird with nervousness.

244

And though Marsh has said something about inviting people, she hasn't got any food in, she can't, she doesn't feel well enough, she is fragile as an old piece of wedding silk, shaky in the kitchen and docile, even, on the telephone. The editor has phoned her anxiously about whether she's hurt by the cancellation of Depressed and she hasn't been able to do anything but assure the editor she's absolutely right; which isn't assertiveness. In addition, she is shaken by the discovery that she loathes canned soup, which she has fed to the children for fifteen years because when she made the real thing they fished through it for bay leaf and celery and parsley as if it were the bottom of Lake Scugog, which made her want to vomit. But she does not know what there is left to eat except club sandwiches, and you have to buy them in a restaurant.

She feels weak and trembling as she turns the television set on. The race isn't on yet but she doesn't quite have the courage to turn the set off. Instead, she stares out the window and sees Roger and Bob coming down the street carrying paper bags: hope, she thinks.

"Come in if you're fat, stay out if you're lean."

And then Pen and Elaine, and a subdued Vinnie, wearing the colours of a mouse who is very nice indeed, and they perch everywhere, anywhere, trying not to exercise their various quarrels. Suddenly, too, the new couple, whom she always hoped would develop, Marnie and Archie, they are called, and they aren't interior decorators at all, but a planner and a social worker. So the street isn't going to hell.

"The kids are alone," Pen says, "so I'll sit by the door and keep an eye out." Elaine looks grateful.

Just as wheels start to flash across the screen, wheels being wheeled off a ferry at Sidney, B.C., the announcer says ("Oh," says Elaine, wincing for home, "the Sidney Bakery!"), wheels flashing onto the road and Mick being Machievellian about getting a place for Mrs. Saxe, the buzz of an irritated wheelchair erupts on the street. Vinnie, cross-legged on the floor, draws his heels up to his balls. The buzzing stops, and Bob's Fred deposits Sylvia in a lump on the bed beside Harriet, and sits down beside Pen. Nobody speaks.

This is the last stretch. They've done every piece of Scenic Canada the Mint has thought of putting on paper money except the Arctic, and certainly better pieces than the Government Advertising Agency (Adscam?) ever thought of putting in *The New Yorker*. They've pedalled through Farley Mowat, L.M. Montgomery, Bliss Carman, Hugh Mac-Lennan, Ralph Connor, Margaret Laurence, Sinclair Ross, W.O. Mitchell, and Ethel Wilson-land. Now they're starting down the home stretch.

The land on either side of the road looks Californian but damper. There are drive-ins and low villas. Most of what Harriet can see is Bob's right ear and a bunch of angry motorists being held up by a Mountie while the racers go by. Mick and Mrs. Saxe are not in the front rank, but they are there, determined and faithful. Mick has a bandage around his right (left?) knee, and Mrs. Saxe has a Don Quixote look about her now; she is smaller and even shabbier, and the rags her clothes have turned into are streaming in the wind. But she pedals, she pedals. Past ponds that have been groomed into parks, and ranch houses rhododendroned into mansions. Crass plazas and Olde Englishe beer halls, then monumental rock clefts (Rock of Ages, Harriet thinks, the Canadian engineer's all-too-often fulfilled dream), sad, solitary groupings of ancestral firs, the suburbs of Victoria, the. . . .

There are only eighteen of them left, one couple having disappeared into the enthusiastic low maw of Vancouver, another having collapsed on the *Queen of Sidney*. Eighteen of the forty-two (Bob passing out another round of frosty gin) including Mick and Mrs. Saxe are still in, and you were so excited, she reminds herself, when he got through his grade six because they all beat him up every day for his speech defect and Sim wasn't there any more. And. . . .

"Jeesus, looka that," says Bob. Because someone has tried to cut in on Mick. "What's the prize?"

"Five thousand and a medal."

"No wonder."

The announcers are filling in time, mumbling into their microphones: how far everyone has come, how lovely it was, all kinds of winds and landscapes and weathers, this great Canada of ours. ("Fuck it," says Sylvia on the bed, and she knows. Harriet, to her amazement, moves closer to her.) The stories of the other racers: a storekeeper from St. John's, not St. John's actually, St. Shott's (and which saint was Shott?), an Alberta electrician and his wife, a B.C. fisherman; representatives, in fact, from all regions, though most of Manitoba has dropped out, which is out of character, though the human body is, too. According to the handicap readouts, Mick and Mrs. Saxe are now in the lead.

They are getting closer. The buildings are thick on the road, and more and more of them are stores. Mick has to pause as one old woman works herself painfully across a pedestrian crossing, waving her stick. Victoria the geriatric, and is anyone holding the stopwatch, taking into account the fact that he did not run her down? He starts on her heel and just misses her.

"Help," says Marshallene.

The phone rings and is hand-over-handed to Harriet whose eyes, like tapioca, are still glued to the screen: it is Dr. Munster, who wonders how Mick got the money.

"My sister left it to him. Won't it do him good even if he doesn't win?" Roars from the crowd. Mick and Mrs. Saxe are really in the lead. "Oh, Dr. Munster!" Click. Thus he maintains his superiority.

Harriet has to go to the bathroom. Bob is still handing around gin. There's less and less lime and water in it. They will be in dangerous condition by the. . . .

"The kids are on the street, I'd better go home," Pen says.

Bob is watching Mick and ignoring Fred. Dear God, Harriet thinks, whatever happens, the drama will go on.

Bob's Fred, Sylvia's Fred, he's the uncomfortable one. He

shifts from haunch to haunch. Marsh puts a soothing hand on his shoulder. He wrenches away. Roger leans on the door frame. He palms Harriet a note: *Would you sit on a Task Force that pays?* She nods and swells.

"*Mon dieu*, they are almost there," Sylvia breathes.

There's a huge commotion at the front door. Roger lets in a little black-eyed woman, a human battering ram.

"I'm looking for Mrs. Harriet Ross," she screams.

"Shsssh!" they all hiss, as eighteen rear ends rise out of their saddles for the home stretch.

"What have you done with my mother, Mrs. Adeline Saxe? I've been looking for her for a year. You've kidnapped her!"

Bob leaps up, puts his hand over her mouth, and wrestles her into a sitting position on the bed beside Sylvia. With two hands he wrenches her face towards the television screen. It stays there.

"This is the home stretch," the announcer says, and begins to talk about them all as if they are race horses, and Harriet giggles to remember the idiotic excesses of Beetlebaum, which were the Newfie jokes of her day, and bites her tongue as she sees Mick and Mrs. Saxe are not in the lead but pedalling like monstrous automata, third and fourth again. But then, suddenly passing some department store, some Brighton Pier excrescence, some Hotel Negresco in Victoria, Vancouver Island, British Columbia, Canada, North America, the World, the Universe, somebody stumbles, something happens, nobody's fault that Harriet can see, and Mick takes his feet off the pedals and puts them on the handlebars, puts his fingers in his ears, sticks out a long, all-too-red tongue and coasts past the Empress Hotel in full view of all the cameras. And crosses the finish line. First.

And there's a banner on the Empress Hotel that says, *Welcome, Police Association of Canada.*

Harriet laughs, and Harriet cries, and Mrs. Saxe pedals right up in there behind Mick and comes second. And the

248

announcer says, "It's sunset in Victoria, British Columbia." And the person whose job it is to begin to lower the flag begins to lower the flag; the cameras cut to the other contestants and then to the line of totem poles by the provincial museum, and then back to Mrs. Saxe and Mick and the bicycles piling themselves on the legislature lawns one by one, and the piper strikes up, strutting, "The Road To The Isles." And the sun goes down over the Empire. And Mick and Mrs. Saxe have won a gold medal, two tickets to Hawaii and five thousand dollars apiece, and Bob Robbins brings on even more gin.

Mick and Mrs. Saxe stand entwined by the fists like boxers grinning at the television cameras. The piper continues to strut. Jesus, she thinks, in a minute he'll play "Amazing Grace"; and he does. The totem poles appear to sway.

Melanie on the phone.

"Are you in Banff? How do you like it?"

"Oh, Mummy, I'm so thrilled, he's done it at last."

"What?"

"He's finished something! And I love it here."

Babs: "Well, ain't you proud."

Harriet, trying not to hiccup, assures her she's proud of her, too.

"Oh, Marsh. Oh, Roger, I wouldn't have got through the winter without you."

The CBC on the line, wanting to know what she thinks of her son. "Oh, marvellous, wonderful, that kid. It was a secret and he kept it, and he won, I'm so proud." If she hadn't been drunk she'd have said something respectable, like, "Mickles always win, eat Mickle cheese," but it's all right now. She collapses onto Sylvia, hands the phone to Henrietta Saxe, whose voice is the voice of a chicken complaining about the feed. Out of the corner of her eye, she sees Vinnie wanting very much to run away and Roger returning to relieve the babysitter. And she looks back to the screen and they are still standing there, frozen, knocked dead by the camera, Mick and Mrs. Saxe. And she realizes that Mick has done all the talking and thanked all of them, her and Melanie and Sim and Babs and the Ps and even his Aunt Madge, who left him the entrance fee. She beams and claps Henrietta Saxe on the shoulder. Henrietta Saxe winces and moves away.

"Do you really want your mother back?" she asks.

"Really, Mrs. Ross, you are the most disreputable person I have ever met."

"Get out," Harriet says, certain, suddenly strong, for the sun is still setting behind the legislature and the piper is still playing, somebody's pibroch she is glad she can't recognise. "Get out. Your mother's a jolly old turd and I am a person, too, and I am not putting up with you. You want to be responsible: fine. You want to oppress me for being good to your mum: get out."

Henrietta stays put. Harriet doesn't know how to end it all, but she knows it isn't an *auto-da-fé*. Bob takes the woman by the arm.

"Get out," he says. "Get out."

Fred winces.

Sylvia huddles up to Harriet.

"I'm not a bird," Harriet says.

Vinnie's eyes pop.

Bob escorts Henrietta Saxe off the premises and down the street. While the announcer is still mumbling about the trip for two to Hawaii Mick and Mrs. Saxe have won, Bob returns with a long board under his arm and begins to make a speech.

"On the eve of Rathbone Place–I mean the end of–I mean the wall's down and who will we be any more–I mean–hell–" and he turns his board around to reveal, in beautiful Roman lettering, the words *Lunatic Villas*. "I am now going to install this sign on Harriet's house."

It's a put-up job, because Vinnie has a ladder ready, and holes have already been drilled in the brick.

"How are the birds?" Harriet asks Sylvia, and she receives a report on Sam, Agnes, Joey–all much better now.

250

"I'm glad it wasn't Sam and Agnes."

"Are you?" Sylvia's white, hostile face turns on her stately, stiff neck. So that isn't over.

A man comes to the door with a load of Chinese food. Vinnie pays. They eat. Gross mess is left. Bob and Marshallene clean it up. Harriet lies in the middle of her bed, alone, raving.

"I wanted to come to some great philosophical conclusion," she says. "I wanted to win through to a slogan. But I haven't, I haven't."

"Mick and Mrs. Saxe won the race," they say. "You've had too much to drink. Go to sleep. Mick and Mrs. Saxe won the race."

Like a doll or a baby she rolls over on herself and falls fast asleep. In the middle of the night the cat wakes her up because nobody has fed him and, instead of being angry at him, she strokes him, limps into the kitchen and tries four can openers before she finds a fifth that will work; then she watches him nose the bits of meat off the edge of the plate so he can't find them.

"If you were a kid I'd take you to a doctor," she says.

The night is smooth and July. Mick and Mrs. Saxe won the race. Mrs. Saxe's daughter Henrietta makes running worthwhile. When will Melanie take a lover and rub my face in my affairs? The Ps will/will not come back. I am not Depressed Housewife any more. What was that about hope?

She limps along the bookcases, pulling out one book after another. Finds, finally, the old *College Survey*. Then the poem. Of course. George Herbert. Naturally, George Herbert. "Hope in the bottom lay" isn't there.

Because it's *rest*, not *hope*, Harriet, you noodle. Rest is the pulley that hauls us up to God. You were always bad at memory work.

In the moonlight, Bob's gilt *Lunatic Villas* glimmers over the Gothic porch. Harriet goes back to bed and lies in the dark, listening for nightingales.